MW01610762

THUNDER MOON

Thunder Moon

by

Larry V. Franklin

Appaloosa
Press

Imprint of Sovereign Publications
Lexington, Kentucky - USA

AN APPALOOSA PRESS BOOK
Imprint of
Sovereign Publications
Dorothy Deering, Publisher
128 E. Reynolds Rd, Suite 2
Lexington, Kentucky, 40517

Phone: (606) 971-0080
Fax: (606) 971-9190
E-mail: sovpublish@aol.com

07 06 05 04 03 02 01 00 99 98   5 4 3 2 1

ISBN 1-889501-20-4 (pbk.)

Library of Congress Catalog Card Number 97-67790

This one is for my mother, Millie Lorena Franklin, still a true cowgirl in her own way. Thanks for always being there for me.

ACKNOWLEDGMENTS

Thanks to all those who made this book possible, including my wife, Carolyn, who stood by me throughout the writing process. Her advice, editing, and support along with that of my daughter, Amy, was invaluable. Thanks also to Cheryl Watson for her input and also to my agent, Dottie, who has stood behind me and supported me all the way.

ONE

A DARK CLOUD, heavy with rain, passed across the full moon, blocking out the dim light it cast over the campfire that lay hidden in the red rocks. The Indian watched closely, searching for an answer to his dreams. The cloud continued on, allowing the light to return as the man squatted beside the small fire, staring into it, pondering. A raindrop fell into the fire causing a hiss and steam to rise quickly into the cool night sky.

The warrior glanced up, and another raindrop landed on his upturned, weathered face. His left hand reached up to wipe away the wetness, but he allowed it to linger there, stroking the deep scar that ran from the corner of his lip to the left side of his eye. He finally wiped away the dampness on his face and turned to watch the lightning flash in the western sky.

The horizon lit up across southern Utah as another flash streaked past the moon, causing the Indian to stand as more raindrops fell in a steady rhythm now. Once again a lightning flash lit up the sky, causing the man to stagger back from the fire, his eyes wide in amazement as he came to realize that the thunder and lightning were speaking to him.

"The Thunder Moon speaks...and Patches listens," he whispered, still watching the lightning and hearing the thunder in the distance. "I will obey the Sky Spirits. Red Rock Pass will be cleansed of the one who desecrates holy ground."

Jake Whitmore rolled off his bed hitting the floor hard. He lay there for a few moments moaning in pain and then pulled his drunken body back to the bed while reaching for the almost empty whiskey bottle on the dresser. It took several efforts to remove the cork from the bottle neck as he fell on the bed, spilling most of the remaining liquor.

"Darn it!" he shouted, picking up the bottle.

He took a deep drink from the container and climbed off the bed, staggering to the door, the whiskey bottle still in his hands. He stopped at the doorway to steady himself as he finished off the liquor, then managed to make it to the fireplace in the next room before he stumbled and fell.

He lay there moaning and finally rolled over, reaching for the whiskey bottle beside him. He managed to grip it with his callused hands and brought the bottle to his lips. Disappointment showed on his worried face as he tipped the bottle and discovered that it was empty.

"It's empty, Rachel," he said, anger mingling with his disappointment.

He tossed the bottle into the fireplace, hearing with satisfaction the sound of the glass bottle hitting others that had been thrown there previously. He pulled himself up with the aid of a rocking chair nearby, then stood staring at the chair, a tear beginning to form in his eye.

"Rachel...Rachel, why did you leave me?" he asked aloud as the tears began to trickle down his dirty unshaven cheeks.

He staggered from the room and into the kitchen, steadying himself at the iron stove and knocking a heavy skillet to the floor in the process. In his sorrow and anger, he lashed out with his hands, scattering unwashed dishes from the stove; many fell to crash onto the floor. He backed away, staring at what he had done.

He found the full bottle of whiskey in the table drawer and eagerly ripped off the cork to take a long, deep drink. He swayed and staggered back, losing his balance and spilling whiskey from the bottle onto the floor. He steadied himself, wiped his mouth with the back of his dirty hand, and staggered back into the room.

The lightning flash caused him to glance toward the opened front door, and the following thunder crash caused him to jump. Unsteady on his feet, he fell into the rocking chair, but managed to break the fall. Whiskey splashed again on him, and he wiped what he could from his clothing and face with the sleeve of his shirt. He tipped the bottle again to drink deeply from the bottle, then staggered to the open door.

Another lightning flash lit up the front of the house and revealed a recently dug grave near the big cottonwood tree. He made it to the steps of the porch and tripped on them as he tried to descend to the ground. He fell hard to the dirt and spilled whiskey from the bottle, but quickly stood to continue toward the grave.

Another flash lit the way for him, and he staggered forward, only to fall again halfway to his goal. He sat up, took a drink from the bottle, then tried to stand. His legs refused to obey the signals sent by his brain. Disgusted, he finished off what whiskey remained in the bottle and threw it into the night.

A dark cloud passed before the full moon, blocking out most of the night light as he stared at the grave. He waited for the moonlight to return, then slowly began to crawl toward his goal. "Rachel, my love, where are you?" he asked, shouting toward the grave, almost crying. "Why did you have to die? I can't go on alone."

A raindrop fell upon his bare head, then another. He glanced upward into the dark sky as more drops descended. He lay in the dirt, too exhausted to continue, and began to cry softly until the steady rhythm of the rain cleared his head somewhat.

He rolled over, stared at the grave again, and came to his hands and knees. Exhausted and drunk, he almost made it, but his arms and legs refused to cooperate any longer. Finally, in agony and sorrow, he lay in the dirt as the rain came down steadily, soaking the ground, the grave, and the drunken man.

One final effort brought his six foot frame to the grave, where he reached out with his hand to sift the wet dirt with his fingers. Tears mingled with the rain and the mud, but he didn't care. He had reached his goal, and now lay face down in the mud near the cottonwood tree. He raised his head once to glance around when a loud clash of thunder echoed through Red Rock Pass.

"Rachel...my dear wife. I loved you so," he managed to whisper before he passed out, his fingers sifting for one last time the dirt and mud on the grave.

Kennon Matthews looked up at the full moon as a cloud, heavy with the rain that was soon to come, passed across it. He cracked the long, snakelike whip over the rumps of the two lead horses to the Concord stage and glanced at his partner, Vern Perkins; he noticed that the shotgun guard cradled the big ten-gauge scatter gun in the crook of his left arm as he pulled at his rain slicker to close it around his thin neck.

"Gonna get rained on before we get to Newton's Station," said Matthews, spitting a stream of tobacco juice over the side of the stage, then wiping his bearded chin with the back of his shirt sleeve.

"Yeah...might ought to tell the little lady inside so she'll be prepared fer it," replied Perkins, finally struggling into the raincoat. "I'll take the team so you can git into your rain gear."

"Might ought to stop for a minute and give the team a breather," said Matthews, pulling on the reins to bring the coach to a halt. "I'll slip into my gear and you can roll down the canvas on the windows for the lady."

The six horses came to a stop as Matthews applied the brakes to the coach and then reached into the stage boot for his yellow slicker. He watched Perkins haul his bony body down from the coach and open the door to the vehicle.

"Gonna git some rain afore we git to Newton's Station, Miss Thurston," he said, looking inside. "I'm a gonna roll down the canvas fer now for ye."

"Thank you, Mister Perkins," she replied, a half smile on her face.

Perkins noticed the long blonde hair under the yellow bonnet that matched her dress and the smooth face of the young lady in the moonlight. Her smile showed even white teeth, and having seen her slim figure earlier at Green River where she had gotten on the stage from Salt Lake City, he knew she was a beautiful woman. "Gonna git uncomfortable for awhile, but it can't be helped. We'll be into Newton's Station in a couple of hours."

The guard climbed back to his seat beside Matthews and nodded. The driver spit another stream of tobacco juice over the side of the stage and cracked the long black whip again over the rumps of the lead horses. "Git up there, Jack and Bill. We got a long way to go," said Matthews, frowning as he readjusted the cumbersome raincoat about his neck. "We gonna get wet. This is gonna be a hard storm."

"And a bad night, too," replied Perkins, pointing to the full moon as another dark cloud crossed its face. "It's a bad omen according to the Indians. A thunder moon, they call it."

"You believe in them superstitions from the Indians?" asked Matthews, glancing at his partner.

"Must be something to it, cause them heathen Utes sure live by the signs," said Perkins, frowning. "Makes me nervous just thinking about them red devils."

"Ain't got no cause to worry none about the Utes. They been pretty peaceful the past few years under old Ouray. He keeps them young bucks in line," said Matthews trying to reassure the older man. "Besides, there is some talk about them Utes going to a reservation up in Colorado since silver was discovered over in southern Colorado."

"I ain't worried about old Ouray and his bunch. It's that wild one, Patches, that scares me. I heard talk that he's upset about all these new settlers moving into southern Utah," said Perkins, worried. "He's been talking about cleansing the land of the whites."

"It's all talk, Vern," replied Matthews, not really believing it. "He's always got along with the Mormons down here."

"Sure, they love them red devils like they were the lost children of Israel or something like that," answered Perkins, a little disgusted. "These new settlers ain't all Mormons. That's what worries me."

"You got a point there, partner," replied Matthews, beginning to worry now. "These new settlers are pushing hard to have all the Indians removed to reservations by the army. Already, minor clashes have occurred, but thanks to old Ouray, peace has been maintained."

"For now, but that thunder moon up yonder tells me things are a gonna change," he finally said, glancing at Matthews. "Ouray ain't got a lot of control over Patches."

"We got more problems to worry about than Utes. With them silver mines opening up in Colorado, we got all kinds of trash drifting in here," said Matthews, changing the subject. "The stage out of Cortez was robbed and the guard killed two weeks ago, and I heard another stage got hit right out of that new town, Silverton. We ain't that far from them places."

"We ain't carrying any money this trip. All we got is Miss Sarah Thurston from Salt Lake City coming to visit her brother at Brewster's Crossing," said Perkins, looking back at the moon again. "Ain't no outlaws gonna waste the time to rob us this trip."

"Maybe...just the same, you stay alert."

The five riders halted their horses at the rim of the canyon in the driving rain. The leader, a hard-looking man in his late twenties, eased back in his saddle and rubbed his three-day growth of beard, then glanced at the others, his dark eyes filled with hate and anger.

"Buck, you and Rusty ride down to the house and watch it closely while the rest of us ride to the barn," the leader said, pulling his rain slicker tighter around his neck to keep out the water. It didn't help much and only added to his discomfort and anger.

He watched the two younger men gradually work their mounts down the slope of the mountain to the floor of the canyon, then nodded to the other two men to follow him. He kicked his horse hard with his spurs and forced the horse to take the decline quickly in the darkness of the night. Only once did he glance back to see if the men followed, then turned his attention to the barn and the dim light in the house beside the big cottonwood tree nearby.

Reaching the barn, he only nodded to his followers as his right hand gripped the butt of the heavy Colt .45 pistol at his side. It was the newer single-action army model that he had traded a young army recruit for in

Colorado. He rode toward the barn corral and noticed three horses under the shed. He turned and signaled for his men to dismount.

One opened the barn door and allowed the big man to enter. He led his black horse inside, his hand still on the butt of the pistol. Satisfied that no danger lingered inside, he unbuttoned his slicker and turned to the other two men who had followed him inside. "Check the barn out and see if you can find a lantern. It's too dark to see anything in here."

"Sure, Joe," said one of the men, fumbling around searching for a lantern.

"Charlie, check on Rusty and Buck," said Joe, frowning. His hard stare wasn't seen by Charlie, but the older man knew from the tone of voice that Joe was angry, so he quickly complied, re-buttoning his slicker and stepping outside the barn and into the rain.

"Found one," said the other man, lighting the lantern. "You sure you want a light? The man in the house may see it."

"Let him. There's five of us and only one of him," replied Joe, coldly. "I ain't a gonna spend the night in the dark and out in the cold rain."

"You see them three horses in the corral?" asked the other man, carrying the lantern to Joe.

"Yeah, I seen them. We'll take them with us when we ride out in the morning," replied Joe, taking his slicker off and shaking the wetness from it. "See what's keeping the others, Bob."

Bob walked to the barn door and looked outside. He turned to grin at the big man with the dark, black hair that fell down below his ears. "They're coming and they got the man with them."

Joe laid his slicker across the saddle on his horse and waited. He watched Bob open the doors wide and smiled when the others pushed a half-dressed man into the barn. He saw the fear on the man's face as he wiped the wetness of the rain from his blonde hair. Charlie pushed the man, who fell to the floor of the barn and slowly raised his head to glare at them.

"What's your name?" asked Joe, walking to the man.

"Thurston. Karl Thurston," he replied, his young face still showing fear. "You didn't have to do this to me. I'd have let you use the barn to get out of this storm."

"You a Mormon?" asked Joe, frowning, his hand near his pistol as he stopped in front of the young rancher.

"Yeah...I'm a Mormon," replied the youth, watching the gun hand of Joe. "I got a very sick wife in the house. Take what you want, but leave her be."

"We'll take what we want, that's for sure, Mormon," answered Joe, a wicked grin on his face. "You Mormons are suppose to turn the other cheek and treat us Gentiles real nice, I hear. I'm from Missouri myself. My old man helped run you and Joe Smith out of Missouri years ago, so what you got to say about that...Mormon?"

Karl Thurston didn't answer. He looked at Joe, then to the others, a pleading look on his face. He got no help from any of them. Joe walked around the man, the wicked smile still on his face, his hand now holding the pistol.

"You gonna kill him, Joe?" asked Charlie, grinning.

"I ought to finish what my old man started in Missouri, but then I never did like my paw. He was a mean old fool, so I guess I could let this fellow live," said Joe, looking at Charlie, then to the frightened man on the ground. "What do you think, Bob?"

"Don't need to kill him. He said he's got a sick wife," said Bob, frowning. "Let's go to the house and find some grub to eat and just take the horses in the morning."

"Well...Karl Thurston. Bob Hanley says we ought to let you live because of your wife. Old Bob is just a fat old fool, so I'll ask Charlie Barker here what he thinks," said Joe, laughing. "What do you say, Charlie?"

"Kill the bastard and we'll take good care of the widow for him," said Charlie, smiling.

"No! Leave Elizabeth alone. We ain't done nothing to any of you," said the young man, trying to stand.

Joe kicked the man in the side, and he went down, rolled over and glared up at the man, defiance showing on his face, but also a mixture of fear and anger appearing also. That provoked Joe into action. Another swift kick brought the youth to the ground again, and the big outlaw moved in closer, landing several more well aimed kicks to the downed man's body and head. He finally backed away, satisfied as he saw the blood coming from the man's mouth.

"Back away from him," shouted the young, dark-haired woman who had entered the barn with a shotgun in her hands. The barrel pointed at the midsection of Joe, who backed away from the fallen man, a surprised look on his face.

"Buck, you were suppose to be watching the house," said Joe angrily as he glanced at Buck then back to the woman who was wet from the rain.

She leaned against the barn door, the shotgun still covering all the men. The wet shawl draped over her nightgown hung past her arms, and she moved to push it up. Joe saw his chance, leveled the pistol still in his hand, and fired twice, the two heavy .45 caliber slugs hitting the woman in the chest and knocking her back against the barn doors. The force of the impact drove her out into the rain and she fell hard, dropping the shotgun into the mud.

Nobody moved. A pale look came to the young man's face as he realized what had happened. He reacted first, driving his body hard into Joe and knocking him down. He struggled with the man for the gun, but Charlie and Buck entered the struggle and pulled the man off their boss.

"You bastard, you killed her," shouted Thurston, trying to break free to attack Joe again.

Joe stood and leveled the .45 again and before anyone could react, he hammered two slugs into the body of the young man, driving him back along with Buck and Charlie. His dead body slumped to the ground as the two men released him.

"Dang, Joe, we didn't need to kill them," said Bob Hanley, frowning. "We don't need a murder rap hanging over our heads here in Utah."

"Ain't the first murder we committed and ain't a gonna be the last," said Joe, holstering the pistol. "That crazy woman would have shot me if I hadn't shot first, Bob."

"What's done is done," said Rusty, frowning. "Let's see if there's any grub in the house, then let's clear out of here for Colorado."

"Rusty's right, Joe," said Charlie, looking at the dead man on the floor of the barn. "Let's take what we want and get out of Utah."

"You afraid of the law around here, Charlie?" asked Joe, trying to smile. "Paul Neel ain't much of a lawman anymore."

"Just because he's the sheriff in Brewster's Crossing doesn't mean he don't know how to use that .44 of his, Joe," said Charlie, seriously. "You ain't seen him use that gun lately. I have."

"That was five years ago in Platteville," said Joe, frowning. "He's gotten soft out here in Utah."

"Maybe...but I ain't wanting to find out," replied Charlie, walking to the barn door to pick up the shotgun that the woman had dropped. "Let's eat, then take the horses and get to Colorado as fast as we can."

"There's another ranch over in Red Rock Pass. I hear the man has some fine horses," said Joe, walking to his horse and taking the slicker from the saddle. "We ought to ride over that way in the morning and check out his stock."

"You know the man?" asked Bob, frowning.

"No, does it make any difference?" asked Joe, looking at the serious expression on the face of the older heavyset man with graying hair.

"Ever hear of Jake Whitmore?" asked Bob, looking hard at the young outlaw. "The Jake Whitmore from Platteville, Colorado, that killed Pete Henderson and his brother Marvin."

"Yeah...I heard, but I thought he went back to working for the railroad," said Joe, soberness coming to him.

"He did, but quit and moved out here to Brewster's Crossing on the Colorado River. The bartender at Green River said he had a ranch at Red Rock Pass. I think we ought to pass up on him and take these horses to Colorado."

"Joe, I've heard of this Jake Whitmore fella. He's a gunfighter," said Charlie, glancing at Bob Hanley for support. "I'd rather avoid trouble with him, if possible."

Joe Blackburn looked at Bob Hanley, then to Charlie Barker and finally to the two younger outlaws, Rusty Mullens and Buck Rawlins. He saw that none of them had any desire to tangle with Jake Whitmore. "All right then, if you bunch of squaws are afraid of a has-been gunfighter, we'll ride for Colorado in the morning when this storm passes."

The loud thunder clap woke Paul Neel. He lay on the bed beside his wife, trying to return to sleep, but it did not come. He finally sat on the side of the bed, glancing out the window and into the dark, rainy night. Another lightning flash followed by thunder brought him to his feet. He walked to the window to stare outside, parting the curtains for a clear view of the rainy night.

Something troubled him deeply, but he couldn't figure it out. He glanced back to the bed and saw his wife, Emma, still asleep, her graying blonde hair covering most of her face of thirty plus years. Another lightning flash brought his attention back to the window and scene outside.

The light of the flash revealed the small town on the Colorado River. He saw from his window the dim lights of the Golden Horn Saloon, but knew few customers, if any, remained in the business in this kind of weather, and this late at night. Probably only old Lenny Norris, the swamper, cleaning out the place. Doss Cockrell, the owner, was most likely in bed by now with one of his working girls.

He returned to the bed and lay down, pulling the quilted blanket over his body. His wife stirred and moved closer to him, but did not wake. He closed his eyes and tried to relax, but the sleep he desired failed to return. He adjusted the pillow, then turned over to stare at the window and the rain outside. The storm had lasted longer than most that had came through southern Utah in the three years that he had been sheriff of the county.

Another lightning flash and thunderclap brought him out of bed again, kicking the blanket from him as he sat on the side. Emma woke then, reaching with a soft hand to rub his back. "Something bothering you, dear," she whispered quietly.

"Don't know," he replied, turning to pat her hand. "I can't place it, but something isn't right."

"Nothing could be happening in this weather. Nobody in his right mind would be out tonight."

The rain slackened and he finally stood and returned to the window to look outside, parting the curtains again for a better view. He saw a quick glimpse of the full moon before another dark cloud passed in front of the celestial body to darken the night sky, troubling him. "You ever hear of the thundering moon, dear?" he asked, returning to the bed.

"No, dear. What's a thunder moon?" she asked, moving over for him to lie beside her before coming into his arms.

"The Indians believe in signs and such. A thunder moon is a bad omen for the Indian. An omen of something bad to happen, either to them or someone else," he said, adjusting the pillow under his head. "Nothing good comes from a thundering moon sign."

"Is that what's bothering you?" she asked, a little frightened, knowing from past experience that her husband rarely spoke of such things unless he was really worried.

"Don't know, Emma dear, but I just saw a thundering moon sign in the night. If those Indian superstitions are right, we're going to witness some bad things happening around here."

TWO

Jake Whitmore rolled over onto his back and glanced up at the morning sun that crept above the rim of the canyon. He tried to sit up, but his head pounded from the hangover and he lay back on the ground. He looked to his left, his mind focusing on his surroundings. The empty whiskey bottle caught his attention and stirred a strong desire for the liquor. He struggled to stand and glanced at the house before trying for the bottle.

The front door of the house stood open, and his yellow dog, Buster, lay quietly on the porch in front of it, apparently asleep. He glanced down at his clothing as he reached for the bottle and noticed his shirt and trousers were caked with red mud.

Wiping his face with the back of his dirty hand, he realized that he too was covered in the red dirt of Red Rock Pass. "Darn it," he whispered out loud, picking up the bottle.

Disappointment came to him as he saw the bottle contained none of the pain-relieving liquor. Jake turned toward the house, remembering full bottles of the booze remained inside, but tripped over the grave of his wife and fell hard, face first into the dirt.

He rolled away from the mound of red clay and stared at the final resting place of his woman. The pain of her loss returned and so did the desire for the whiskey. He pulled himself to his knees and finally stood to head for the house.

Before he reached the porch, the yellow dog woke, recognized his master, and wagged his tail, making a swishing noise on the pinewood porch. The man stopped and looked at the empty bottle, then threw it away; he watched it tumble through the air to land near the rocks thirty yards away.

The shattering glass of the bottle caused him to stare hard at what he had done. He wiped his face again, smeared the dirt and mud on his hand and face, then cleaned the hand on his pants. The smell of fresh water drew him toward the rocks and the cool spring he knew lay a few yards beyond. He kicked the broken glass off the well-worn trail as he passed and turned away from the dog trotting to him, his tail still wagging.

Jake approached the spring with caution, and seeing no snakes, he squatted beside the pool. Buster lay beside him as he began to wash his hands and face. He finally stood and removed his boots, then stripped off his dirty shirt and pants to stand in his yellowed long johns and socks.

"Buster, I gotta quit this drinking," he said, patting the dog on the head as he squatted again beside the water. "It ain't a gonna bring Rachel back. We're gonna have to learn to live without her."

The dog only licked at his hands and continued to wag his tail. The man stripped from the long johns and finished his washing, then stood and gathered up his boots and clothing to leave the pool. He walked carefully out of the rocks on his bare feet with only the socks to guard against the stones along the path to the house.

Reaching the house, he dumped the dirty clothing on the porch and stood naked, gazing toward the meadow farther down the pass. Several head of cattle grazed there, and he looked at the dog, frowning. "We gotta get back to work. It's been well over two weeks since Rachel got sick. Them cows need to be looked after with spring coming on."

Something caused him to turn his attention back to the springs. He froze as he saw the Indian mounted on a pinto pony near the rocks he had just left. He knew the Indian to be a Ute. This one was larger than most, standing close to six foot. He wasn't young, but not old either, and he sat straight on the horse.

Jake backed away, reaching for the opened doorway with his hand as he held his stare at the warrior who hadn't moved. He found the doorway with his hand, but didn't enter as the Indian kicked his horse and rode slowly forward, a Springfield .45 caliber, single-action carbine in his right hand. The weapon rested across the saddle of the pony and posed no threat at the moment, but Jake wasn't taking any chances.

His hand found the butt of his .44 Smith and Wesson pistol in the holster that hung on a peg just inside the door. He gripped the weapon and pulled it from the holster to let it land loosely at his naked side. He realized then that he was completely naked, but as the Ute approached, his attention was on the face of the man. He noticed the deep scar that ran from the Indian's lip to the left side of his eye.

The warrior wasn't painted for the warpath, though the Utes had been known from time to time to raid an isolated ranch or attempt to right some wrong done to them by whites. This one had a serious look on his scarred face as he pulled the horse to a halt near the porch. He glared at the growling yellow dog who stood his ground beside his master.

"White man, you go from this place. You no belong here," the Ute said, anger in his voice as he waved his hand toward the west.

Jake really wasn't surprised that the man had spoken English, as he had heard many of the Utes spoke good English and Spanish. "This is my ranch. I've been here three years and this is the first time anyone has told me to leave. This place special to you?" responded Jake, still watching the Indian closely. It wasn't the first time he had Indians visit his place. All the other times had been friendly encounters as long as he had rewarded them with tobacco or food. "You want tobacco...or food?"

"White man pollute holy springs. No right to be here. Go, Patches commands you," said the warrior, seriously.

"You called Patches?" asked Jake, not moving. "I've heard of you. You're suppose to be some medicine man for your people."

"I be called Patches by the whites, but my true name is He-Who-Talks-With-The-Wind. You not worthy to live at holy springs. You stupid drunk man on firewater. Go, before I have to make you go," said Patches, turning his paint horse around and riding off.

Jake stood in amazement as he watched the Ute ride down the canyon of Red Rock Pass and scatter his cattle as he passed. He continued to watch until the Indian disappeared. "Well...what do you make of that, Buster?" asked Jake, glancing at the dog. "You think that crazy Indian is serious about us moving? First I heard this place was special to the Utes."

He gathered up his dirty clothes and entered the house. A bottle of unopened whiskey sat on the table, and he walked to it. Jake picked up the bottle, glanced at the dog standing in the doorway, and returned the bottle to the table. "If that Indian is serious, Buster, I'm gonna have to stay off this stuff. We ain't a leaving Red Rock Pass."

Kennon Matthews leaned back on his chair to watch Mrs. Newton clear the breakfast dishes. He glanced at the others seated at the table. His shotgun guard, Vernon Perkins, sat to his right and finished the last of his gravy with a hot biscuit.

The pretty Sarah Thurston sat to his left and handed her empty plate to the woman as she passed. He wondered about her traveling alone in southern Utah. It wasn't Salt Lake City or the other safer places found in northern Utah. He knew very well the dangers that lay in this rugged area with outlaws and Indians still around.

She glanced at him, a warm smile upon her young face. She had taken his stage at Green River and said that she was to meet her older brother at Brewster's Crossing. She had said something about her sister-in-law being sick or something like that. He returned the smile and glanced at Harvey Newton, the station manager.

"Harvey, what do you hear about the government moving the Utes to reservations?" asked Matthews, frowning.

"Not much," replied Newton, sipping coffee from his cup. "They're all suppose to be on reservations now, but nobody forces them to stay. They roam from those two reservations in eastern Utah to the White River Reservation in Colorado to this one down near Cortez. Army ought to make them stay put."

"Army is too involved in Montana and Wyoming right now with the Sioux and Cheyenne. You heard about Custer and his command last summer, didn't you?"

"Yeah, shame General Custer is gone. He had the right policy for these stinking Indians. Kill'm all," said Newton, glancing up at Matthews.

"I hear the one called Patches has been trying to stir up the young bucks of the Utes," said Perkins, joining the conversation. "Old Ouray keeps them pretty much in line though."

"Patches has been hanging around Grand Valley and down around the lower Colorado, I hear," said Newton, frowning. "Hasn't caused any trouble, but he scares a lot of people."

"Are the Indians dangerous?" asked Sarah Thurston, glancing at Newton.

"Could be if someone stirs them up. Every so often they raid a ranch or cause trouble, usually to get back at us whites for some wrong done to them. Don't make much difference which white man or woman, just so the person is white," answered Newton, looking at her. "Last real trouble around here was about six or seven years ago up along the Green River. Jake Whitmore lost his parents to the Utes. He's got a ranch across the river near your brother's place just outside Brewster's Crossing at Red Rock Pass."

"No need to worry, Miss Thurston," said Matthews, glancing hard at Newton, showing his displeasure at alarming the young lady. "Vern has that ten-gauge scatter gun with him. Ain't no Ute...or outlaw a gonna get close to our stage."

"When will we make Brewster's Crossing?" she asked, still concerned about Indians.

"Should make it by tomorrow morning," replied Matthews, standing. "We ought to get started. The storm has passed and we got some miles to make up today."

Perkins finished his third biscuit and stood to follow Matthews from the station, his shotgun cradled in his arm. He opened the door to the coach for Sarah to enter, then glanced back at Mrs. Newton, who came to stand beside her husband in the doorway of the building. She dried her hands on the end of her apron and smiled.

"Thanks for a good breakfast, Mrs. Newton," said Perkins, smiling as he climbed up the stage to sit beside Matthews.

Harvey Newton walked forward and handed up the mailbag to Perkins while his two sons steadied the team of six horses. "See you two next trip," said Newton as he stepped back for the stage to leave.

Newton's wife came to stand beside him as Matthews cracked the long, black whip over the rumps of the two lead horses. The coach leaped forward as the horses pulled the stage out of the front yard of Newton's Station and headed south toward the Colorado River and Brewster's Crossing.

"Boys, gather up all the horses from the pasture and pen them up in the corral beside the barn," said Newton as he turned to face his two teenage sons. "I'm a little worried about some Utes sneaking down here at night and stealing the horses."

The man turned once more to glance toward the stage, now only a small speck in a cloud of red dust. Even the recent rain hadn't made much difference with the red soil of Utah. He watched for awhile until the coach disappeared, then turned to see that his sons had already begun to gather in the animals. Kennon Matthews had him worried now after talking about Patches. The Ute had been known to steal a horse or two from the stage-line stations. He wished the army would force all the Indians back to the reservations. Maybe this time they would.

Patches lay still in the sagebrush near the house. He watched the white man he knew as Whitmore walk from the cabin toward his barn. The man wore his gun belt, a large revolver butt showing plainly from the holster. Patches knew little of this man, but enough to be cautious with him. He remembered Ouray's warnings about this white man who had dared build his home on the sacred springs at Red Rock Pass.

Ouray, one who preached peace with the white man, was an old fool. So the white man Whitmore had fought as a pony soldier in the white man's great war back east. It was nothing to a Ute warrior to worry about if he was prepared for battle. That, Patches thought, was the problem with the Ute Nations, and why they bowed to the pressures of the white man's demands for more Ute lands to settle and to dig for the yellow stones called "gold" and for the ones called "silver." He knew all too well about the white man's greed. Even the Utes sacred valley of the aspens was gone now, and his people had gone like the Navajo's sheep to the reservations in Utah and on the White River in Colorado.

Patches knew his own tribe of Uncompaghre Utes were weak because they failed to practice the old ways that had once made them a united Ute Nation, the masters of the high mountains where no one dared challenge. Only a return to those old ways would prevent the white man from taking all the Ute lands as they had already done to other tribes.

Patches' anger continued to build as he thought upon all the wrongs the whites had done to his people. Nine years ago war had broken out when the white soldiers came to force them to reservations, but the Ute wasn't spiritually prepared and lost that encounter. Even Ouray had acted like an old dog, and with his tail between his legs, had called for peace.

He saw that the white man had reached his barn, and now Patches watched closely as the man caught his bay horse with the two stocking feet. *So, the young one had stopped his drinking of the firewater. What could he be up to?*

Patches didn't know, but he edged closer, parting the sagebrush to get a better view. The man hadn't taken his warnings to leave. Patches really didn't believe he would. Only a war lance in his white heart would settle the issue, and Patches knew that wasn't going to be easy. He should have shot him earlier this morning when the fool was drunk, but the spirits had whispered to him that he should give this man a warning first. He had, and now he waited to see if the man would leave. In a few days, if the white man still hadn't left, Patches knew that he would have to return and cleanse this sacred ground. He would need others, and he knew that wasn't going to be easy. Wild Horse would probably ride with him, but the others were like dogs, only wanting to lie around camp to eat and sleep.

Patches saw the white man saddle his bay horse and lead him to the house. He watched as the man entered the house, then returned with a rifle and bedroll to stand on the porch, first to look toward the springs, then the rims of the canyon, and finally down the valley in his direction.

The man mounted his horse and rode out toward him, his yellow dog following. Patches crawled away, knowing if the dog got a scent of him, he would alert the white man of his presence. The dog would have to die soon.

He was too good a watchdog, and Patches knew that Whitmore relied on this animal to alert him to danger.

The Indian reached the rocks and crawled behind one to watch the man pass. The dog stopped to sniff the ground where he had lain, barked once, and followed his trail toward the rocks. The Sky Gods were against him he thought as he leveled the Springfield carbine across the rock at the approaching dog. He would have to kill this pesky animal if he got much closer. He waited and worried about an unwanted encounter with Whitmore.

The warrior sighed in relief as the white man, who had stopped to watch his dog, whistled for the animal to return. The hound obeyed, but not before staring in his direction for a few moments, then turning to rejoin his master.

Patches watched the white man ride on, the yellow dog following. He stood to watch a few moments longer, then returned to his paint horse hidden in the rocks. He guided the mount back up the winding, faint trail to the rim of the canyon, then caught a glimpse of Whitmore and his dog heading north along another trail on the north side of the pass.

The Indian wondered where he was going. The white man's town on the Colorado River lay to the west. Only a few scattered ranches lay to the north along the river. He kicked his horse hard and headed along the rim to another trail that led north and toward the big river.

Patches stopped before taking the trail down toward the river. He watched as the white man disappeared along the northern trail he had taken. He knew well where the trail came out. It was near the ranch where the young Mormon couple lived. They had been friendly to his people and more than likely were friends with this white man, too. He didn't know, but he would be there to see. If Whitmore didn't appear there, then the only other route he could take was to the northeast or to the river to the north. Whatever trail Whitmore took, Patches knew he wouldn't be hard to find.

He turned his paint horse to guide him down the faint trail. Patches believed that the white men knew nothing of this old Indian trail that in ancient times had been a regular path from the big river to the holy springs where Ute shamans had practiced the old spiritual ceremonies of the warrior that had given his people the strength and courage to keep this land from all intruders. He would watch this man Whitmore for a few more days, and if he failed to leave the sacred springs, then he would consult the Sky Spirits again as to how to rid the springs of the pollution brought to it by Whitmore.

Joe Blackburn rolled over and pulled his blanket back over his body, then smelled the coffee and slowly opened his eyes to look at the men gathered around the morning fire. Bob Hanley squatted near the coffee pot, a cup in his hand. He laughed at some crude joke from Buck Rawlins, who lay against his saddle beside the fire. Rusty Mullens sat on a log nearby making biscuits and laughed also.

Joe glanced at Charlie Barker, who still slept on the other side of the campfire. He was supposed to be on guard duty, but Joe knew Charlie was one to be slack in his commitments. Hell, they all were slackers, he laughed to himself. That was why they were outlaws in the first place. Joe kicked the blanket from him and sat up to reach for his boots. He moved his .45 caliber Colt pistol that lay close beside him and pulled on the big boots.

"About time, boss," said Hanley, grinning. "Thought you was a gonna sleep the whole morning away. Must have been dreaming of Maybelle over in Jacktown."

"Naw, just tired from riding late into the night," replied Joe, standing and reaching for his gun belt. That was never far from him. "What's fer breakfast?"

"Coffee, fried biscuits, and some bacon we got from that ranch we robbed yesterday evening before we crossed the river," replied Hanley, reaching for the coffee pot. "We gonna ride into Colorado or hang around here some more?"

"Ain't much here, except Whitmore's ranch, if anyone is interested on recrossing the river to steal some of his fine horses," answered Joe, walking to the fire.

Hanley handed him the hot cup of coffee and reached for another cup. "Ain't much interested in facing Whitmore."

"Ya scared of him?" asked Joe, sipping the hot brew.

"Naw, just got respect fer him, that's all," replied Hanley, pouring himself a cup of coffee.

"I don't want to recross the river if we don't have to," said Rawlins, frowning. "I ain't a good swimmer, you know."

"You could use a bath more often," said Mullens, his youthful face cracking a grin.

"Gonna take one when we get to Jacktown," replied Rawlins, grinning. "Ruby Parker is a waiting for her lover to return."

"Yeah, sure, and half of Colorado, too," answered Mullens, laughing.

"So...I'm still the best she has ever had," said Rawlins, laughing also.

"I say we hit the Green River stage, then hightail it to Colorado and sell these stolen horses, lay low for a few weeks, then drift down south," said Hanley, looking at Joe seriously. "I hear there might be some good pickings around those silver mines."

"Every Tom, Jack, and his dog is down south trying to steal what they can, Bob," replied Joe, frowning. "We'd have to stand in line to rob some shipment, but I like the idea of knocking over the Green River stage. Might be a few passengers with a little gold."

"Ain't worth the trouble," replied Mullens, frowning.

"They'll have a team of six horses," said Rawlins, looking at Mullens, then glancing toward Blackburn. "We can sell the horses over in Jacktown."

"We'll get six horses out of the robbery at least," said Joe, glancing at Hanley for support. "What do ya say, Bob?"

"All right with me. The money will keep us in booze and women for a week. Why not?" replied Hanley, grinning. "How we gonna pull this off?"

"Near Muleshoe Pass is a good place. The stage will have to slow the horses to a walk on that upgrade before reaching the summit," said Joe liking the idea. "Just before they start the downgrade run, we hit them hard and fast. We can be done in a couple of minutes and then head out for Colorado."

"Still say it's more trouble than it's worth," said Mullens, placing a large iron skillet on the fire and dropping bacon in to fry. "I say we look for something easier to grab. The stage will have a shotgun guard for sure."

"So?" asked Joe, frowning. "We can get the drop on him when they reach the summit. Be no trouble. Might not be much in the way of gold, but six extra horses to sell in Colorado is better than nothing. We ain't got much to show for this trip."

"I agree," said Rawlins, looking at his young partner. "Be easy as stealing candy from a baby, Rusty."

"Well...all right," replied Mullens, taking a fried strip of bacon from the skillet. "I'm still uneasy about facing a shotgun, especially after that woman pointed that scatter gun at my gut last night."

"Forget last night, Rusty. The less we talk about that killing, the better off we are," said Joe, worried. "Didn't want to kill that gal, but she gave me no choice, besides she was a Mormon."

"Being a Mormon ain't no reason to go killing them, Joe," said Hanley, worried also. "Makes little difference what religion she was. Just killing a woman is enough to stir up the whole area."

"Then let's pull this stage job quickly and get out of Utah," said Mullens, dropping the biscuits into the hot bacon grease. "We sure the stage will be there?"

"Yeah, it'll be there. Comes once a week from Green River," said Joe, frowning. "Let's eat breakfast and get set up for the stage. Someone wake

Charlie. I'm going to saddle up before I eat."

"Hey Charlie, wake up," said Hanley, shouting at the sleeping man. "We gonna rob the Green River stage."

Charlie Barker slowly woke, sat up and rubbed his eyes, then glanced at Hanley, and finally the others. "Rob a stage?" he asked, still half asleep.

"Yeah, sleepy head. Joe has decided to knock over the stage today, then head for Colorado," replied Hanley, handing the older man a cup of hot coffee.

"Waste of time," said Barker, taking the cup. "The Green River stage ain't got no gold."

"They got six good horses we can sell in Colorado," replied Hanley, reaching for one of Mullens' hot fried biscuits and a strip of bacon. "It's better than nothing."

"Guess you're right, Bob," said Barker, frowning. "We ain't got much to show for our efforts. I'm all for returning to Colorado with something, even if it's just horses."

THREE

Jake Whitmore pulled his horse to a stop at the base of the trail and scanned the rims of the rocks above for the Indian. It had been more than an hour since he had caught a glimpse of the Ute who had confronted him at his ranch in Red Rock Pass. He didn't see him, but he was sure the redskin still followed.

Jake worried about what the Indian had said. Something about the springs at Red Rock Pass being sacred or holy. It was the first time he had heard that since moving to the pass. Old Cody Wedgeworth never said anything about the springs being sacred ground to the Utes when he had sold the homestead to him three years ago, and Cody would have known, too.

Wedgeworth had been around these parts for some time, having trapped and lived with the Utes since coming to Utah right after Brigham Young led the first wagon train of his people to Salt Lake Valley in 1847. Some said old Cody was as old as the mountains he roamed in and around southern Utah and western Colorado. He would have to look up the old man and see what he knew the next time he went to Brewster's Crossing.

Jake glanced at the dog, who lay in the shade waiting patiently for his master to continue. "Won't be long, dog," he said, scanning the rims of the mountains one last time before continuing along the trail. "Karl and Elizabeth's place is at the end of this decline, so you'll get to rest some. Been a few weeks since I visited the Thurstons. Eliz was down sick with what Rachel had, you know."

The thought of his dear wife brought back the physical hurt inside. He missed her, and he now realized that his three days of hard drinking hadn't washed away that hurt, but only delayed it. Rachel had been a good woman, a loving wife. Although he wasn't a Mormon, she had been faithful to her religion to the end, saying it was God's will that she be taken.

He didn't have the faith that she had nor her strength to endure. Even after losing their two children at birth, she had kept her faith, never blaming God, but still clinging to the hope of bearing children. When he had lost what little faith he had and turned to whiskey, she hadn't given up on children or him.

That faith had caused him to throw away the bottles of remaining whiskey and continue on, but when she died, he had lost it again. He had returned to the liquor for comfort, finding little in the whiskey that only delayed the pain. Now he had to go it alone with only their shattered dream of a ranch to force him on. He would build this ranch and make it a place of beauty for her.

Jake guided his horse toward the Thurston ranch. Young Karl Thurston had been of help and was a good neighbor. Even when his own wife came down with the same sickness that took his Rachel, the man came to him, offering comfort, help, and his Mormon prayers.

He caught sight of the barn first, then the house as he rode down the trail to the ranch. He didn't see Thurston's horses in the corral near the barn where the man usually had at least a saddle horse. Maybe they had already to Brewster's Crossing for Thurston's sister, who was coming to help with Elizabeth.

Elizabeth would be in the house. He headed for the hitching rail in front of the structure only to pull up short when he saw the barn door open and the woman lying on her back, her shawl over her face. He saw the bloody chest and the shotgun leaning against the barn door. Buster backed away, smelling death and wanting no part of it.

Jake dismounted and glanced around to look for signs, puzzled as to what had taken place. She appeared dead as he walked toward her still glancing around for signs. He saw none. He knew the ground would be washed clean of any signs because of the rains last night, but still hoped for something to tell him what had happened. He squatted beside her to notice that she was indeed dead, and he looked into the barn to see Karl Thurston on his side, apparently dead also.

Jake stood and glanced at his dog which remained with the horse, not yet ready to approach the barn where death still lingered. Inside the barn, Jake squatted again and scanned the interior for signs. There were plenty there, at least five to seven horse tracks and several different boot marks in the dirt inside the barn. He searched the barn, finding nothing else of importance except that all of Thurston's horses were gone.

Jake wondered who could have committed the killings. It could have been the Ute after the horses, or he had gone crazy like he did this morning.

The Ute didn't attack him, and these murders appeared to have occurred last night. He walked past Elizabeth Thurston and headed for the house. He glanced along the rims of the mountains that surrounded the ranch, but saw nothing. He still felt the Ute was near.

Entering the house, Jake stopped just inside the doorway to survey the interior. The place was wrecked as if someone was looking for something. Outlaws, thought Jake as he continued inside the house to search it for evidence relating to the murders. If Karl had any gold or money, it was gone now. He returned to the front yard and stood staring at the barn wondering what had taken place. Probably a gang of outlaws rode into the place last night, and Karl had confronted them, only to die for his efforts. It appeared that Elizabeth had come to help and died too.

He returned to the barn and found a shovel, then walked to the big tree beside the house and began to dig the graves. Buster joined him there and lay in the shade to watch. Jake stopped several times to glance around and scan the rims of the mountains for the Ute but didn't see him. When the two graves were finished, he returned to the house for blankets and then went to the barn to wrap the two bodies for burial. He knew what to do as he realized that he had just done this for his own wife several days before.

After covering the graves he stood staring at the two mounds of dirt, his anger building for the loss of these two friends and especially for his Rachel. Someone had murdered these people, and he was going to do his best to find them and see that justice was done. He left the shovel in the dirt beside the graves and returned to his horse to mount.

"Come on, Buster," he said, glancing at the dog. "We got work to do."

Jake Whitmore rode out of the ranch heading for the river and a crossing he knew, believing that the killers would have taken that route. He would soon know when he reached the river, but if the murderers had gone northeast on this side of the Colorado, it would require little effort to return and pick up their trail. His place would have to wait for the work needed there with his stock. He had a burning desire inside to take out his frustrations and anger on the killers of his friends.

Jake scanned the rock rims one last time before turning his attention to the ground and the trail that he hoped would soon reveal signs of the route the killers had taken. He failed to notice the Ute who lay on a hilltop watching, his keen eyes taking in all that had happened. The Indian watched until the man had disappeared down the trail, then stood and returned to his horse to follow.

Joe Blackburn waited impatiently for the stage to slowly make its way up the grade toward the summit of Muleshoe Pass. His eyes locked upon the shotgun guard and the big ten-gauge scatter gun he carried. Joe glanced at his partner, Buck Rawlins, and watched as the youth placed his red bandanna over his face. It was almost time, and he followed Buck by placing his own bandanna over his bearded face; he then cocked the .45 pistol that was in his hand.

He knew that Bob Hanley and Rusty Mullens would ride out from the rocks behind the stage to help get the drop on the two men on the stage, but the success of the robbery depended on Charlie Barker, who waited behind the huge boulder across the narrow road with the Winchester. He would have to stop the stage and cover the guard. If the driver refused to stop, then he knew Charlie would shoot. That was why he had placed the older man in the most important position for this holdup.

He and Buck would rush the stage from this side to cover the passengers inside. They had robbed a few stages before, so he felt sure everyone knew what to do. He hoped there would be no gunplay. Killing that Mormon rancher and his wife was enough to really stir up this area for awhile. They would have to stay in Colorado for some time until things cooled down on this end of the Colorado River.

His body tensed as he saw the stage make its way past Bob and Rusty's position. There was no turning back now, he knew, and he gripped his pistol tighter and adjusted his mask on his face, ready for Charlie to start the robbery in a few moments.

He was coiled like a deadly rattlesnake ready to strike, only there would be no warning rattle when the attack came. He glanced once more at Buck to be sure the kid was ready, then turned to watch the boulder where Charlie lay hidden. It seemed to him that a minute passed, instead of the few seconds it took for the stage to reach the boulder and the summit. The stage stopped then, and Joe knew the driver would allow the horses to catch their second wind before starting down toward the river eight miles away; he also knew that it wouldn't make it this trip as he heard Charlie step from the rocks shouting.

"Keep your hands free. This is a holdup," said Charlie Barker harshly, the Winchester model 73 leveled at the chest of the guard with the shotgun.

Joe and Buck moved then, running toward the stage to assist. "Don't move," shouted Joe nervously as he saw the hesitation in the eyes of the driver.

"Throw the scatter gun away," said Charlie shouting as he continued to walk toward the stage.

Too many commands from the outlaws confused Vern Perkins, and he cocked the hammers back on the ten-gauge. The loud noise was enough to cause Charlie Barker to fire. The heavy slug caught Perkins high in the chest, knocking him backward and causing him to drop the shotgun over the side of the stage. When it hit the rocky ground, both hammers slammed into the rocks, causing the big gun to discharge both barrels at once.

The .36 caliber pellets scattered rocks, dirt, and fear. The six horses pulling the Concord coach tried to bolt away, but Kennon Matthews pulled hard on the reins and pushed in the brakes to the coach to hold the horses and stage in place.

"Don't shoot," said Matthews shouting as he continued to hold the horses and steady the wounded Vern Perkins, who lay back on the seat moaning in pain. "We ain't got no gold."

"We'll see, old man," said Joe, pointing his pistol at the man. "Climb down from there. We're taking the horses."

"My partner is hit hard, you can't leave us here without horses," said Matthews, protesting. "He'll die."

"His problem," said Charlie, his rifle held steadily at Matthews. "He shouldn't have tried to use that shotgun."

Joe Blackburn climbed to the top of the stage to make sure no strongbox lay hidden there, then pointed his pistol at the driver. "I said climb down."

Matthews complied and walked to stand beside Sarah Thurston, who had been ordered from the stage by Buck Rawlins. Matthews glanced at the two riders who led horses from the rocks behind the stage, then whispered to Sarah. "Do what they say. They're a hard bunch."

Joe Blackburn searched the pockets of Vern Perkins, taking what little money he had, then climbed down to face Matthews and the young woman. Buck Rawlins kept his pistol pointed at them as the two riders dismounted and started to unhitch the six horses from the stage.

"Well, well, what do we have here?" asked Joe, walking to Sarah Thurston. "This the only passenger?"

"Yeah," replied Buck, nervously, glancing at the big man. "She ain't got much in this here purse."

Joe took the cloth purse, pulled the few greenbacks from inside, rambled through it some, and then threw it on the ground and looked at Matthews. "You got any money?"

"A few dollars in my left vest pocket," replied Matthews frowning. "Leave us at least one horse. Vern will die out here."

"Naw, we need the horses," said Joe, looking back at the woman. "Charlie, you want to take this woman with us?"

Barker walked to Sarah and grinned, then turned to Blackburn. "She's too skinny and probably don't know nothing."

"Probably one of them Mormons," said Joe, frowning. "I heard some of them Mormon women are really good. You a Mormon, woman?"

Sarah looked at him defiantly and glanced away, not answering, her anger building inside. Blackburn laughed, then turned to Barker. "You're probably right. She don't know nothing."

"We're ready," said Bob Hanley mounting his horse. "Let's go."

"Gather up their guns. We'll take them with us. Might get a few dollars for them," said Joe, walking to his horse.

Sarah watched the five men ride off, leading the stage horses and several others they had hidden in the rocks. Her anger turned to tears, but she quickly wiped them away when Matthews climbed the stage. "Need some help with Vern, Miss Thurston. Gotta get him down and in the shade, then I'll head out for Brewster's Crossing for help."

"Is he gonna die?" she asked, worried as she helped the wounded man down.

"We gotta stop the bleeding first, then I'll know," said Matthews, climbing down from the coach. "Let's lay him inside and see what we can do for him."

Sarah watched Matthews work on his friend, then stand to glance at her and shake his head. "Is he going to make it?" she asked, looking at Perkins who lay on the floor of the coach, moaning in pain.

"He'll die before I can walk to Brewster's Crossing and get help back" said Matthews dejected. "They could have left us a horse. They're a cold, hard bunch."

"You should try, Mister Matthews. I'll stay with Mister Perkins," she said, touching the shoulder of the older man. "I'll be all right."

"You sure?"

"Yes, go while there is still daylight."

Jake studied the rocky ground at the river's edge and finally stood to gaze across the river, then turn to his dog. "They crossed here, Buster. At least three to five men and about ten horses. You ready for a swim?"

The dog naturally didn't answer, but sensed a change in his master and followed him to the horse. Jake mounted and guided his horse into the water, quickly finding himself hanging onto the saddle as the horse swam the river, coming out downstream at a well-worn path.

Jake slipped from the back of the bay to sit on a rock and watch the yellow dog wade ashore, shake the water from himself, and trot to lie beside him as he removed his boots to pour water from them. He withdrew the pistol from the holster to wipe it dry with his bandanna that hadn't got wet.

He stood to holster the pistol, a .44 Smith and Wesson double-action revolver, then pulled the carbine from the saddle boot, a Winchester model 73, to dry it also. Finished, he returned the weapon to the saddle scabbard and mounted. He glanced back across the river, scanning the rocks and ridges for the Indian. Nothing. He hadn't seen the Ute for several hours now, but something, some sixth sense, told him the warrior was nearby.

Jake turned the bay and headed up the faint trail, trying to put the Indian from his mind. The stalking Ute wouldn't leave his mind, and he finally stopped his horse and led him into the rocks beside the trail to wait. He knew his position was well-hidden, and he called his dog to him to have the animal lie close to him.

The wait wasn't long. He first caught a glimpse of the paint horse, then the rider. The Ute was a good six feet in height with a muscular build and appeared to be in his late twenties or early thirties. Jake watched him pull the paint to a stop at the water's edge, then dismount to study the ground.

The Indian wasn't taking any chances, but mounted and rode the horse into the river. Just what he wanted Jake couldn't guess, except the man had a lot of time on his hands or was a little crazy. His words of warning still lingered, and Jake shuddered at the thought of an Indian attack on his ranch. That brought up old memories of six years ago on the Green River at his parents' homestead. He had waked to a screaming Indian attack in the early morning hours. The raid had left him with an arrowhead embedded in his left shoulder; part of it still remained. The raid also had left his father and mother dead and a younger brother and sister frightened.

That's when he had taken his little sister and brother to Utah Valley and met Rachel Watkins from Spanish Fork. Thinking of Rachel brought back the old hurt and the murder scene at the Thurston Ranch. He stood and glanced once more at the Indian who had now crossed the river to disappear into the rocks below the trail. He mounted the bay and continued up the path, his mind returning to his current mission, but the thought of the Ute not totally disregarded.

He came upon the outlaws' night camp suddenly, and he realized that he had been thinking more about the Ute than the trail and why he was following it. He dismounted and walked to where the fire had been. "Stay, dog," he said, glancing at the hound.

Jake squatted to study the camp as he reached out to place his hand on the fresh dirt placed over the campfire. It was still warm, and he knew he was but a few hours behind the killers. He would have to put the Indian out of his mind now.

His keen eyes scanned the area, taking in all the details. First, he determined there had been five men camped here. He stood to study the area where the horses had been picketed, counting ten separate horse-dropping piles. That told him the outlaws must have taken five horses from the Thurston Ranch. He walked to the droppings to see that five had a fine mixture to them, telling him these five animals had been fed grain recently. The other five piles had a coarse mixture which told him that those horses were on a lot of grass with little or no grain. These were probably the ones the outlaws had before stealing the ones from Karl Thurston.

There wasn't much else of importance. Jake saw the coffee grounds beside the campfire, the bacon rinds, and the few scraps of biscuits and dried grease. They were living the hard life, and Jake stored that information away in his mind as he returned to the horse and dog.

"Five of them killers, Buster," he said, glancing at the dog as he mounted the bay. "Looks like they are heading for the main road from Brewster's Crossing to Green River. Must be wanting to bypass Brewster's Crossing for good reason. Paul Neel is well known around here."

Jake rode on, scanning the trail often for signs of the outlaws. They weren't trying to hide that trail, thought Jake, frowning. He glanced back once more along the trail for the Indian, but saw nothing.

As he rode over a rise in the trail, he saw the abandoned stage and knew then what his five killers had been up to. He sat there for some time surveying the area, seeing nothing until he saw the woman step from the stage. Her long blonde hair fell past her shoulders, and from that distance he saw the bright red of blood on her yellow dress. He kicked the bay hard with the spurs and rode quickly to the road below.

As he approached, he noticed that the young woman had been crying, but quickly wiped away what tears there may have been. He saw concern on her face as he stopped short of the coach to dismount.

Buster ran to the woman, wagging his tail for the woman to pet him, which she did, but her stare remained locked on him. Jake frowned at the dog, but guessed Buster had been missing Rachel and took to the first woman he saw.

"I'm Jake Whitmore. You all right?" he asked, glancing around to see if anyone else was there. "Where are the horses and the driver?"

"Five men stole the horses and shot the guard. The driver, Mister Matthews, went for help on foot," she said, avoiding his eyes. "The guard started bleeding again. I couldn't stop it and he just died."

Jake walked to the coach to peek inside and saw the dead man. "Vern Perkins," he said, turning back to the woman. "When did Kennon leave?"

"A few hours ago. The robbers rode off toward the northeast," she said, looking up. "Did you know Mister Perkins?"

"Yeah, some," said Jake, frowning. "I'll take you to Brewster's Crossing. We'll pick up Kennon on the way. You get a good look at the outlaws?"

"Some. They all wore masks, but two were young and the one who shot Mister Perkins was older and was called Charlie."

"Well...Miss...?" asked Jake, looking at her.

"Thurston. Sarah Thurston from Salt Lake City," she said with a half-hearted smile. "I'm to meet my brother at Brewster's Crossing."

"Karl Thurston?" asked Jake, glancing away as he led the bay forward for her to mount.

"Yes...do you know him?"

"I did. Buried him and Elizabeth this morning," replied Jake a little too harshly as he tried to break the bad news of the murder to her gently, but failed miserably. "I'm sorry, Miss Thurston."

She stared at him in disbelief, then collapsed into the red dirt beside the stage. Jake went quickly to her to gather her up in his arms and lay her in the shade of the coach. He returned to his horse for the canteen of water and then went back to her to wash her face with the cool liquid.

She had a beautiful face, full of life, and her long blonde hair fell across it to give her a youthful look. She stirred and opened her blue eyes, concern and shock showing on the face as she pushed back the hair. "Karl and Elizabeth dead?" she asked in a whisper, her face pleading for the answer no.

Jake could only shake his head as he held her in his arms, feeling her shudder and watching the tears that formed in her eyes begin to make their way down her cheeks. Jake's anger returned as he watched her suffer because of five men who had little regard for human life. To kill for the sake of eleven horses was hard to believe, but three people lay dead...all for eleven lousy horses. It just wasn't worth it.

Patches stood in front of the group of Indians, a frown upon his scarred face. His anger with his own band of warriors continued to build. He glanced at Buffalo Hump, his most outspoken foe, then to One Bear who had been leaning his way thus far in the council.

Smoke continued to make its way upward to the opening in the tepee. The small fire gave off little warmth in the early morning hours before dawn, and Patches pulled the army-issue blanket tighter around his shoulders. He looked out at the assembled Indians to try once more to convince them to join him in his quest.

"Brothers, I have seen the Thunder Moon and He has whispered to me. We must return to the old ways. It's the only way for us," he said, waving an arm in the air to add to the drama of his plea. "Who will ride with me to cleanse the springs at Red Rock Pass of the white man, Whitmore?"

Wild Horse stood from the back of the group. "I will go, my brother. The Sky People have spoken."

"Horse dung," said Buffalo Hump, glancing back at the youthful Wild Horse. "A storm passed last night. No Sky Spirits spoke. We all saw the full moon, too. Besides, the white man Whitmore has been good to the Utes, even after a few fools killed his parents on the Green River a few years ago." He looked hard and accusingly at Patches.

"Am I not the medicine man of this band?" asked Patches, his anger showing now. "I know what I saw and what I heard. We have become weak as dogs, licking at the few handouts given us by the whites. So Whitmore gave us a few cows last winter to eat. He still pollutes the holy springs."

"The springs at Red Rock Pass aren't holy to everyone anymore, my brother," replied Walking Snake who sat beside Buffalo Hump, an old buffalo robe draped about his shoulders. "There is no need to fight with the white man; besides, there are too many and we will lose."

"Not if we return to the old ways," said Patches pleading. "The Thunder Moon has shown me the way. I will go to the cave of the old ones and pray to the Sky People for guidance. It is the Ute way. If they say to leave the springs in the hands of the white man, I will obey...but if the Sky Spirits say to cleanse the springs, will you help me?"

Walking Snake hung his head and avoided the eyes of the man standing before him, then glanced to Buffalo Hump for support. The old warrior stood.

"Brothers of the Uncompahgre Ute. Patches is our young shaman now. I listen to him with my ears, seeking understanding to his words, but my heart tells me that we must follow the words of our chief, Ouray. We must not fight the white man. They will destroy the Ute off the face of this land if we do. Even now, the mighty Sioux who defeated the pony soldiers last summer have grown weak and are going to the white man's reservation. We too will soon be confined to the reservations assigned us. Because we have lived at peace to some degree with the whites, we still enjoy the rights to travel our old lands and visit our brothers, the Uintah Utes, to the north, but if we raid the white man, then they will force us to stay on the stinking reservations."

Buffalo Hump sat, smiling to himself for what he believed to be a good speech. Patches' scarred face turned red with anger. "We see, my brothers, that Buffalo Hump is still long-winded as ever to babble his words of peace at any price with the whites. I say we must purify ourselves before the Sky Spirits and obey the sign given by the Thunder Moon."

"Does the white man Whitmore know you were part of those who killed his parents on the Green River?" asked One Bear, looking at Patches.

"I...don't know. He didn't recognize me when I confronted him at his ranch," replied Patches, a little concerned now. "It really makes no difference."

"It does to most of us," said Buffalo Hump, frowning as he found controlling his own anger hard to do. "What you do affects the rest of us. Is this quest of yours really to get to the white man, Whitmore, or do you really speak for the Thunder Moon?"

"And if I did speak for the Thunder Moon, would the great Buffalo Hump and his cousin Walking Snake ride with Patches on the warpath? I think not," replied Patches, angrily. "The Thunder Moon has spoken, and I will do what has been commanded of me by the Sky Spirits...with or without your approval."

The young warrior turned and left the tepee before his anger exploded into violence. He had worked hard to keep it within. Wild Horse followed as silence fell over the group. Lame Deer finally stood and spoke, breaking the long silence.

"If Patches really does speak for the Thunder Moon, then we must follow," he said, making his way out of the tepee.

Running Horse and Two Ponies quickly stood, and without speaking, followed Lame Deer. One Bear finally stood, glanced at Buffalo Hump, and left the council in silence.

FOUR

Jake looked up at the full moon again, well aware of the woman who rode behind him with her arms wrapped tightly around his waist and her head resting on the back of his shoulder. He thought that she was asleep, but when he relaxed his muscles, she stirred.

"Are we there?" she asked, still sleepy.

"Almost," he responded. "I can see the ferry from here and the lights of the town, but it'll be another hour before we can make the river."

"Will Mister Matthews be all right?" she asked, concerned.

"Sure. Kennon just wanted to go back to the stage and be with Vern. They were friends, you know."

"I don't understand why they had to kill him," she said, shuddering. "You think they are the ones who murdered Karl and Elizabeth?"

"They're a mean bunch," he replied, guiding the bay carefully through the rocks on the trail. "The trail of the killers I followed led to the stage. They have to be the ones."

"Where do you think they're going?"

"Probably Colorado to sell the stolen horses, or they might ride north up along the Green River and drift over into Wyoming," he answered, not really sure. "When we get to town, Sheriff Neel will head up a posse to pick up their trail. If they stop to steal some more, we might catch them."

"Then what will happen to them?"

"We'll kill them if they don't give up, then hang the rest."

"I still can't believe Karl and Elizabeth are dead," she said, her voice almost failing her.

"They were good neighbors. Elizabeth was down sick with what killed my wife last week, but she was doing much better," he said, his Rachel returning to haunt his mind. The young woman's arms tightened around him as she lay her head back on his shoulders.

They rode in silence to the ferry on the north side of the river. Amos Dryden pulled up his suspenders over his dirty shirt and reached for his old army coat as he walked from his small fire beside the river to greet the rider and the woman.

"Oh, it's you, Whitmore," he said, recognizing the man. "Been waiting fer the stage. She's late. You seen her?"

"Yeah," said Jake, dismounting to help Sarah down. "Outlaws jumped the stage at Muleshoe Summit and killed Vern Perkins, then stole all the horses. Miss Thurston here was the only passenger."

"Vern dead?" asked Dryden looking at Sarah with interest as he rubbed his three-day growth of gray beard on his wrinkled face. "How did it happen?"

"They jumped them when the stage stopped at the summit to give the horses a breather. They didn't give Vern much of a chance according to Kennon," said Jake, leading the bay onto the ferry. "Is Sheriff Neel in town?"

"I suppose. Probably at home, though," responded Dryden as he followed Sarah onto the ferry to begin the crossing. "I'll go get him when we cross."

"Tell him the same bunch that robbed the stage also murdered Karl and Elizabeth Thurston out at their ranch last night," said Jake, whistling for his dog to come to the ferry. "I was trailing the killers when I came upon the stage. There was five of them."

"The Thurstons murdered?" asked Dryden, glancing at Sarah, who avoided his stare. "Any idea who they are?"

"No," replied Jake, taking the hand of the woman when he noticed that she began to shake. "Tell Wallace Granger that Kennon will need at least four horses to get the stage into town."

"I'll sure do that, Mister Whitmore. You gonna ride with the sheriff after these killers?" he asked, starting to pull on the ropes that would take the ferry to the south side of the Colorado River.

"Yeah, I'll ride with the sheriff. Tell him we'll be at the livery stable."

"Sure thing, Mister Whitmore," said Dryden, tying off the ropes that would secure the ferry.

"You seen Cody Wedgeworth around?" asked Jake, remembering the Ute again.

"He was drunk earlier over at the Red Dog Saloon. Probably still there," answered Dryden as he finished with the ferry.

"Want to ride?" asked Jake, turning to Sarah beside him as he watched Amos Dryden hurrying into town in the direction of the Red Dog Saloon to announce the stage robbery and the murders.

"No, I'll walk," she responded, glancing at him. "Thank you for bringing me to town. I'd like to visit the ranch...see the graves, and straighten up the place some. I think I should stay a few weeks and see what I can do to close out Karl's business. Dad may want to come down to sell the ranch and cattle."

"Karl ain't got many cows. Maybe seventy to eighty head at most. They run with mine right now," said Jake, frowning. "They should be all right for awhile. I'll look after them till your family decides what they want to do with them."

"Thank you, Mister Whitmore," she replied, smiling. "Would you be able to take me out to the ranch in a few days?"

"Call me Jake, Miss Thurston. I'll be glad to take you out to the place when I get back from helping Sheriff Neel," he said, smiling. "Ain't much to do out there, though. The place is in good shape."

"Jake...will the murderers of my brother be caught?" she asked, stopping and waiting for an answer.

"They got a good day head start on us," he answered, avoiding her eyes in the dim light of the night. "They keep riding northeast, they'll beat us to Colorado, but they can't stay there forever. That bunch will be back this way and I'll be waiting for them. Karl was my friend."

Joe Blackburn stood, reached for his saddle on the ground beside the fire, and walked to the picket line to saddle his horse. He glanced back at the other four men who were cleaning up the campsite and breakfast dishes. Bob Hanley grabbed his saddle and bedroll and walked to the horse line to stand beside Blackburn.

"Joe, you really think a posse is on our trail?" asked Hanley, a little worried.

"Yeah, Paul Neel ain't a gonna let us just ride scot-free to Colorado after killing them Mormon ranchers and sticking up the stage," replied Blackburn, glancing at Hanley as he saddled his horse. "Neel is a Mormon too, I hear."

"You really got it in for Mormons. What did they ever do to you?" asked Hanley, a little afraid of Joe Blackburn's mean streak.

"Nothing done to me, but my old man helped run them out of Missouri when he was a kid. Said they weren't nothing but trouble," replied Blackburn, reaching for the saddle girth under the horse's belly. "Besides, they got things going their way here in Utah. Ain't right they run everything."

"Sure, they run Utah with Brigham Young in charge, but I hear the old

Prophet is sick down in St. George. He ain't a gonna be around long to run things," said Hanley, throwing his saddle on the back of his sorrel horse. "Besides, the Mormons got all the good horses and cattle we steal."

"We ought to get moving. No need to hang around here tempting fate," said Blackburn taking the girth to loop the saddle's leather strap through the brass ring several times, then pull it tight. "You can bet that posse got an early start this morning. If we ride all day and cross the river to the southeast side near Doan's Ferry at noon, we can outrun any posse into Colorado."

"Everyone is about ready now," said Hanley, glancing back at the others. Charlie Barker had his saddle in hand and walked to the picket line.

"We gonna lay low in Jacktown for long?" he asked, grinning. "I ain't been with the women for awhile."

"None of us have been with the women, Charlie," said Hanley, frowning. "If we don't get a move on it, that posse might catch up with us and there won't be no being with the women."

"You really think Neel will bust his britches to catch us?" asked Charlie, looking at Hanley, then Blackburn.

"Yeah, he'll bust his britches. We killed them Mormons, and Neel is a Mormon," said Blackburn, tying his bedroll onto the back of his saddle. "Charlie, line out those extra horses, and let's get moving. I got a feeling Neel ain't far away."

"You scared of him?" asked Charlie, seriously.

"Some," replied Blackburn, glancing up. "He's still good with the gun, but is old and worn-out."

"I say we ride back into these parts in a couple of weeks and grab what cattle we can get, then head on down to Granite and those silver mines," said Hanley looking at Blackburn. "We can sell the cattle, then hang around for some easy silver shipment and knock it over."

"Sounds good, but like I said before, there's too many others down in southern Colorado trying to steal what they can," said Joe Blackburn, stepping into the stirrups of his saddle to mount. "The cattle job sounds good. We'll see about that later, but right now, I want to get into Colorado, fast."

Buck and Rusty joined them to watch Blackburn ride out of the camp. "What's eating at Joe?" asked Rawlins, concerned. "He's taking all this Sheriff Neel talk too seriously."

"Maybe," replied Hanley, climbing into his saddle. "You're still wet behind the ears, son, and you don't remember a few years back when Paul Neel gunned down Joe's partner, Sammy Poole, in Platteville?"

"No. Who was Sammy Poole? Never heard of him," said Rawlins, surprised.

"Poole was one of the fastest men around Colorado a few years back. Neel was a deputy marshall in Platteville, Colorado, just north of Denver. Neel beat Poole to the draw and killed him along with Eli Pickett. Both were Joe's riding partners."

"What about Joe? He there?" asked Rawlins, glancing at Blackburn, who continued to ride out of the camp.

"Yeah, Joe was there. So was Charlie," replied Hanley, turning his horse to leave. "Ask Charlie what happened."

Rawlins watched Hanley follow Blackburn down the trail that led to the Colorado River, then turned to Charlie Barker, who mounted his horse. "Well...Charlie, what happened?"

"Me and Joe were lucky to get out of that one alive. Paul Neel ain't no man to cross lightly. You can bet he's on our trail and if he catches us before we get to Colorado, he'll hang us on the spot," said Barker, frowning. "Joe's paw was with us in Platteville that day. Me and Joe got away after Neel killed Poole and Pickett, but old Nathan Blackburn got arrested for murder."

"Well?" asked Rawlins after Barker didn't continue. "What happened to Joe's paw?"

"Paul Neel pulled the lever to the gallows that hung Nathan Blackburn."

Sheriff Paul Neel pulled his gray horse to a stop at the edge of the campsite and turned to Jake Whitmore. "Check it out, Jake."

Jake dismounted and walked into the recent campsite of Joe Blackburn's gang. He squatted by the dead fire and placed his hands on the coals. They were still warm. He stood and walked around the site, counting five areas where men had slept, then studied the horse picket line.

"Well?" asked Neel impatiently as Jake returned to his horse.

"Same bunch I followed yesterday," he said, looking at the sheriff. "Five of them with sixteen horses. Looks like they left camp in a hurry this morning."

"How far we behind?" asked the sheriff, stroking his long gray mustache as he looked steadily at the young man.

"Three hours at most, Sheriff," replied Jake, mounting his bay.

"We'll never catch them at this rate. Should have left earlier this morning," said the sheriff, angrily. "Where do you think they're heading for?"

"My guess is up the Grand Valley and into Colorado, Sheriff," answered Jake, frowning. "If they ride hard today they'll beat us to the border."

"They gotta cross the river somewhere, Paul," said Baker Stevenson, adjusting his large-framed body on his saddle as he cradled his big Sharps .50 caliber rifle.

"Doan's Ferry would be my guess" said Jake, looking at the sheriff. "If we leave the main trail and ride across those boulder fields to the south, we might beat them."

"That's hard riding, Paul," said Wallace Granger, protesting. "Some of us ain't in great enough shape to take on that kind of riding."

"All right then," said the sheriff, disgusted as he turned to face Granger. "Wallace, you take what men don't want to take the short cut and follow the trail to the river. I'm going with Whitmore across the boulder fields. I'd like at least a crack at these killers."

"Ain't that we don't want to catch these murderers, Sheriff, but some of us just can't take that hard riding," said Granger in his own defense.

"It's all right, Wallace. I need someone to follow the trail to make sure they're heading for the river," replied the sheriff, turning his horse off the trail. "Anyone who wants to follow me and Whitmore to beat these killers to the river, follow me."

Neel rode off the trail with Jake following. Baker Stevenson, old Cody Wedgeworth, and two other men followed. Wallace Granger watched as the sheriff worked his gray horse carefully through the rocks, then glanced at the remaining nine men. "Let's go."

Jake watched the back of the sheriff as the man hurried his horse along as fast as he could. He knew Neel wanted these men. Karl and Elizabeth Thurston had been a popular young couple around Brewster's Crossing; their having been members of the same church as Neel also added to his haste. Vern Perkins' murder wasn't overlooked either, Jake knew. Neel had known the stage guard since coming to southern Utah.

Jake glanced back at Cody Wedgeworth, who followed Baker Stevenson. He pulled his horse to the side to allow Stevenson to pass, then dropped beside the old man. "Cody, I've been meaning to talk with you since last night."

"I wasn't much for talk last night, Jake," said Cody, grinning. "Lucky to just be riding this morning after that drunk I pulled yesterday. Sorry about Rachel."

"Yeah, thanks," replied Jake, glancing away. "Rachel said it's the will of God, but I have my doubts."

"Ought to talk with the sheriff about that, Jake. He's an Elder in the Church, you know."

"Maybe. It's been hard for me to accept Rachel's death. Ain't even written her folks in Spanish Fork yet," said Jake, glancing back at the older man. "Been needing to talk to you about the ranch."

"Now son, no need for you to pull out, just because Rachel is gone. She'd want you to stay and make her dreams come true," said Cody, looking hard at Jake. "I'll ride over this week and stay awhile with you."

"I'd appreciate that, but I ain't a gonna pull out," replied Jake, seriously. "Need to talk with you about the springs at Red Rock Pass."

"Something wrong?" asked Cody, concerned.

"Maybe. A Ute named Patches rode into the place yesterday morning and told me I was on holy ground and to leave," he said, glancing again at Cody to see a look of surprise on his old face. "Sounded serious about it. He followed me all day, then disappeared after crossing the river. Thought you might know something about Red Rock Pass being sacred ground to the Utes."

"Patches, you say?" asked Cody, suspiciously. "He back around here?"

"Yeah, it was him. Big scar on his left side running from the lip up past the eye brow," said Jake, wondering if Cody was trying to avoid a direct answer. "Is the springs sacred ground?"

"Well...don't rightly know if it is or not," he finally said, watching Sheriff Neel glance back at the two, then continue on. "I came to this part of the country about 1850 from Illinois. Did some trapping up in the Uintah Mountains and over in the Tetons in Wyoming, but heard only old tales about the Pass being an old Ute holy springs. None ever claimed it while I was among them for the past twenty-seven years, though."

"What about the Ute called Patches? He some holy man with them?" asked Jake, guiding the bay carefully along the path Neel had taken.

"He's a young shaman of sorts. Not many pay him much attention, but he could be dangerous. I first met him in the Walker War in '54. He was a young buck then, full of fight and hotheaded. Then in '68 he was in on the fight when the government ordered them to the reservations, and I heard it said he was part of that bunch that went on the warpath six years ago up on the Green River."

Jake looked up at the mention of Green River. He slowly turned to face Wedgeworth. "Was he in on the killing of my parents?"

"Hard to say. Nobody ever knew who all was in on those raids. Stalking Horse was hung by the army over in Colorado for leading the Utes, but that's all I ever heard identified as in on it."

"What about the springs, Cody. They sacred ground to the Utes or not?"

"Like I said, Jake. They could be from way back, but nobody is claiming it now. Never had no trouble out there when I was a living at the Pass," said Cody, a little worried. "I think I'll ride over to your place a little early and stay with you for a few weeks. Patches ain't one to take lightly."

Patches untied the paint horse in front of his tepee and turned to face his wife, Morning Star. Anger showed on his face as he turned back to lead his horse to the center of the camp. Lame Deer and Wild Horse waited for him there. Patches scanned the village for any others who might be committed to ride with him. He saw none. "Is this all?"

"One Bear and the others wait for us outside the camp. They don't want the mocking that is sure to come from Buffalo Hump," said Wild Horse, disgusted. "He has already talked several out of going with us."

"The old fool is scared of the white man. It's the reason the Ute is a weak nation now. Few will answer the call of the Sky People to act," said Patches angrily as he mounted his horse. "They will soon see that the Thunder Moon has spoken to me, and our first act must be to cleanse the springs at Red Rock Pass of the white man, Whitmore."

"Here comes the loudmouth, Buffalo Hump, now," said Lame Deer, disrespectfully. "He will have to have the last word, as usual."

"Let him. It won't change what we have to do," said Patches, frowning as he watched the old warrior stop in front of him.

"The council decided last night that you should wait until we hear from Ouray," said Buffalo Hump, looking around for the others. "What you do affects the rest of us."

"Would you have me disregard the Thunder Moon?" asked Patches, trying to be careful with his words. He realized that Buffalo Hump, though long-winded and full of horse dung, still carried a lot of influence with this band and others of importance in the Ute Nations.

"No...if the Thunder Moon really spoke, but that is still the question, isn't it?" answered the old warrior, realizing that he was dealing with a young hotheaded man. "Let Ouray decide. If he says the Thunder Moon spoke, then I will ride with Patches against the white man."

"I will not wait. The Thunder Moon spoke and I will obey. Each day we delay, the Sky Spirits grow more angry with us for not acting," replied Patches, a little anger creeping into his voice.

"You must not do this to our band, my brother," said Buffalo Hump, pleading. "If you go, we'll have to move. The anger of the white man will be against all Utes."

"The spring grass grows green. We should have moved into the high mountains already," said Patches harshly. "We have remained in our winter camp too long."

"My brother, do not do this to us," said Little Crow, who stood beside the old warrior.

Patches looked harshly at Little Crow, then at Buffalo Hump, his anger getting the best of him. "You are all old women and cowards. You refuse to believe me and act like whipped dogs before the white man. You will see that I am right. Stay here and let the women protect you and lap up the firewater from the white man or go to the great Ouray like the dogs you are and live with him on the stinking white man's reservations."

Buffalo Hump's anger boiled over, his face turning a deep red to blend into his dark brown skin, but Patches saw the anger and waited for the outburst that he knew the old warrior would give. It came slowly, but the harshness was still there.

"You would call me coward?" he asked, his efforts to control himself gone now. "When you were born on the White River, that same summer I led a raiding party against the Arapaho across the mountains and got this." He opened his buckskin shirt to expose a large scar across his bronze chest and frowned.

Patches wasn't impressed. All in the camp had heard of the war party that Buffalo Hump had led against their enemies, the Arapaho, but Patches regretted now that he had called the old warrior a woman and a coward. Now, they would have to endure another long-winded speech from him.

"This, young wolf cub, I received from an Arapaho war lance while saving your father, and this, twenty summers ago from the white man's gun in mountains to the south, when I led a horse stealing raid," said Buffalo Hump, exposing a scar where a musket ball had ripped into his left shoulder. "The coward is you who refuses to listen to wisdom. All you will do is wake a sleeping bear when you try to kill the white man Whitmore. In the end, he will kill you."

Patches' anger exploded even though he knew he must control it. Being called a coward was too much for his young pride. He couldn't respond with words, but his actions struck deeper than any words he could hurl at the old warrior. Kicking his paint horse hard, he rode over the man with the shouting protests from the assembled men who came to watch the confrontation between the old one and the young shaman. No greater insult could have been given, and Patches knew as he continued to gallop out of the camp that Buffalo Hump would now be a sworn enemy and slow to forgive.

Little Crow helped the old warrior to stand. He rubbed his shoulder where the paint horse had stepped on him. They watched Wild Horse and Lame Deer ride after Patches. "We must leave this place quickly. The young fool will cause a war here, and we'll all be blamed for it."

Buffalo Hump nodded his head and continued to rub his injured shoulder, his embarrassment showing. "Send someone to follow them and see where they go first, then send another to tell Ouray what the young fool is up to."

Patches glanced back at the group of men with Buffalo Hump, his anger still not under control as Wild Horse and Lame Deer caught up with him at the edge of the camp. "Buffalo Hump will be long to forgive that insult, my brother," said Lame Deer, frowning.

"I don't care. The Sky People are stronger than Buffalo Hump or Ouray," he responded, determined. "Where are the others who ride with us?"

"There," said Wild Horse, smiling as he pointed to One Bear and the others who rode toward them.

Patches anger faded as he counted over two dozen men riding with One Bear, far more than he expected. "Ho, my brothers," he shouted, happily.

"We see that old Buffalo Hump tried to stop you. Let the fools stay in camp with the women and dogs," said One Bear, frowning. "It's where old men and dogs belong."

"Then we ride to obey the Thunder Moon," said Patches, turning his horse to ride on. He glanced back at the village once more before leading his cheering and shouting men toward the west.

"Where to, my brother?" asked One Bear, riding to his side.

"To Red Rock Pass and the sacred springs. We drink only holy water from now on, then we ride to the caves of the old ones to purify ourselves and pray for guidance."

FIVE

Jake eased closer to Sheriff Neel, his Winchester model 73 in his hand. He lay quietly to watch the approaching outlaws. Neel turned to the young man and grinned. "We got here in the nick of time, Jake. You think these are the same ones who robbed the stage and committed the murders?"

"Appear to be. Six of them horses look like the stage horses, and the other five appear to be Karl's," replied Jake, straining to see as the five men approached Doan's Ferry. "Too bad we couldn't have gotten here a few minutes earlier and set up for them."

"Think we ought to charge down there and shoot it out with them? They're gonna cross the ferry before we can stop them," replied the sheriff, concerned. "Don't want them to get away."

"Best we let them cross, then follow. We can ride hard and jump them before sundown," said Jake, frowning.

"You're probably right," replied Neel, glancing at the others to signal them to remain hidden.

Neel crawled back to the waiting men to inform them of the plans. Jake watched closely from the ridge, trying to remember the faces of these killers. He was sure they would catch up with them soon after crossing the ferry, but would just six men be enough to take these hardened outlaws? He didn't know, but he knew Neel would try, regardless.

"Soon as the ferry returns, we ride," said Neel, a stern look on his face. "We'll get a piece of these murdering dogs yet."

Jake saw that the ferry had discharged the five men and their horses and was making its way back to the shack of Leonard Doan; Doan managed a living from the ferry that was too far off the traveled trails of importance to keep a man very busy. Jake suspected the outlaws were headed for the Grand Valley and then into Colorado and Jacktown, just outside Utah.

He returned to his bay hidden in the rocks to join the other five men and mount. He saw the determined looks on the faces of the sheriff, Cody Wedgeworth, and Baker Stevenson. Ben Westman and Henley Ferguson showed no expressions, but Jake knew both had served in the war and were men who had little fear of the coming fight.

The six men reached the ferry as Doan pulled it ashore. "Howdy, Sheriff," said the old man, spitting a stream of tobacco juice into the water as he glanced at the other men to see the hard looks they cast across the river. "You after them men I just pulled across the river to the south side?"

"Yeah, Leonard," replied the sheriff, dismounting. "They robbed the Green River stage and killed Vern Perkins. Them horses are stolen and they murdered a couple on a ranch the other day, too."

"Hell's fire, Sheriff, if I had a known that, I'd a delayed pulling them across," said Doan, working fast to get the posse on board the ferry.

"Leonard, Wallace Granger, and nine other men are following. Tell them to hurry up when they get here," said Neel, watching the south side of the river with interest. "They're about an hour behind."

"Sure thing, Sheriff. Them five fellows are a hard bunch," said Doan, excited. "Known they were wanted men the minute I laid my eyes on them."

Jake drew his Winchester from the saddle boot as he mounted his horse and saw that Neel had done the same thing. The ferry landed, and the sheriff jumped his horse off the barge to be followed by Jake and Henley Ferguson. Jake pulled his bay to the side to allow Ferguson to pass and glanced at Cody Wedgeworth and Baker Stevenson, who led their mounts ashore to prepare to mount. Westman was already mounted, but still on the ferry, when the first volley rang out, the loud gunshots echoing across the river to bounce back and forth down the river canyon.

Jake turned to see Ferguson topple from the saddle and Sheriff Neel and his horse go down with the second volley that came from the ridge up the trail. The bay went down then, screaming in pain as Jake jumped clear of the horse, only to lose his Winchester. He rolled away from the kicking animal and saw the carbine and went to it as several rounds kicked up red dust and rocks around him.

With the Winchester in hand, he crawled to a large boulder and fired off a shot in the direction of the ridge, then lay back to glance at the ferry. He saw Westman and his horse go into the river; the horse had been hit, but the man appeared to have jumped clear of the animal. Leonard Doan was down, but struggling to seek cover at the ferry. Baker Stevenson popped his bald head up from behind a rock and fired off a round from the big .50 caliber Sharps, the loud boom echoing down the river.

Cody Wedgeworth crawled to him, his Henry carbine at his side. "They must have seen us when we started down to the ferry. They got us pinned down good and all our horses dead or ran off."

"You see the sheriff?" asked Jake, concerned.

Cody peeked over the rim of the boulder, drawing a volley of fire that kicked chips of rock from the boulder where they lay. "He ain't moving. His horse is on top of him, and Henley ain't moving. Your bay ain't a moving neither."

Stevenson fired off his Sharps again, and the outlaws on the ridge answered with several volleys. "They got us afoot and without horses. We ain't going nowhere," said Jake, disgusted.

"Ain't no way we gonna get to them now," said Cody, firing off a round then ducking down as return fire slammed into the boulder. "We might try flanking them."

"Granger and the others will be here within the hour. All we can do is wait," said Jake, glancing over the rim of the big rock to look at the sheriff. A round landed close to him, sending a sharp piece of rock into his cheek, drawing blood. Jake jumped back to cry out in pain as he put his hand to his cheek.

"Better keep down, son," said Cody, grinning. "We can't do no damage to them from here."

Baker Stevenson let off another round from the big gun, then ducked back behind his rock to reload. "Baker, save your rounds. They got us pinned down. We'll have to wait till Wallace gets here," said Cody, shouting toward the man.

The firing died down and finally ceased. "What do you think they're up to, Cody?" asked Jake, glancing over the rim. "They gonna leave or try and rush us?"

"Probably leaving. They know all our horses are down or gone," said Cody, disgusted.

"They're pulling out," said Baker Stevenson, shouting as he walked forward, pointing to the ridge.

Jake stood, then went to the sheriff, who stirred. "Sheriff, where are you hit?" he asked, squatting beside him.

"Got it in the shoulder, and the blamed horse fell on my leg. I think it's broken," said Neel in a lot of pain. "Get this dead horse off me. I had to play dead out in the open like this."

"Ferguson is dead," said Cody, joining the men to help pull the dead horse from the leg of the sheriff.

Ben Westman joined them, soaking wet from his swim in the river. "Lost my horse," he said, frowning. "Old man Doan ain't a gonna make it. Took two in the chest."

Jake stood to watch the five riders on the rim of the canyon slowly make their way to the east. "Baker, you think you could pop one of them from here with that old buffalo gun of yours?"

"It's too far for me, Jake. My eyes ain't what they use to be when I was younger," responded the bald-headed man, glancing toward the rim. "Shame them killers are gonna get away with committing two more murders."

"Jake, take a crack at them with Baker's long gun. I'll help steady it for you," said Cody, turning to the young man.

"Give'm a parting shot, Jake," said Neel, angrily.

Jake took the big Sharps from Stevenson, checked the rolling block chamber to be sure a round was inserted with the heavy .50 caliber slug, then raised the rear sights for long-range shooting and glanced at the five riders. He guessed the range was well over seven hundred yards, maybe closer to eight. With a scope, the weapon was deadly at over one thousand yards. His shot would be a lucky one at most.

He laid the long barrel over the shoulder of Cody Wedgeworth and brought the alignment of the sights upon the last man in the group. Jake held his breath, then let it out slowly as he tightened up on the trigger to take out the slack. He noticed that Cody had done the same thing and let out his air slowly, too. He released the remaining air in his lungs, then squeezed off the shot.

The barrel of the gun bounced on the shoulder of the older man, the echo of the shot bounding across the river to bounce back and forth down the river's canyon. Jake watched in amazement as the last rider seemed to stop, stand up in the stirrups of his saddle, and finally topple from it.

"Damn," said Cody Wedgeworth, surprised. "That's one hell of a shot."

Joe Blackburn pulled his black horse to a stop outside the town and waited for Bob Hanley to ride to his side. "You think Charlie is dead?" asked Hanley, pulling his sorrel beside Joe's mount.

"Don't know. He wasn't moving when we hightailed it off that rim," said Joe, glancing at Hanley. "I wasn't going to hang around for another lucky shot from Whitmore."

"Damndest shot I ever seen," said Hanley, angrily. "I say we ride back to Utah in a couple of weeks and kill him."

"Was thinking that same thing. Charlie rode with me a long time. Shame to see him get killed that way," said Joe, bitterly. "Old Neel got it though. Seen him and his horse go down."

"Yeah, and one other for sure. Don't know about that one on the ferry," replied Hanley. "Good that you saw the posse coming. They wasn't expecting an ambush. We got them good."

"Whitmore is a gonna pay for killing Charlie, Bob," said Joe, seriously. "I ain't a gonna let this just slide by."

"I'm with you, but first let's get these horses sold and go get drunk in Charlie's memory," said Hanley, watching Buck and Rusty lead the stolen horses toward Cal Burrell's stables in the dim light of the lantern that hung over the barn doors. "You think Buck and Rusty will stay with us?"

"Don't know. That lucky shot from Whitmore spooked them some," said Joe, turning the big black to follow the stolen stock to the livery stable. "If Gus Deason and his boys are in town, we might talk them into riding with us back to Utah. I know Gus wouldn't pass up a chance to steal a herd of cattle to sell down in Granite."

"Hadn't thought of Gus and his bunch," replied Hanley, frowning. "Can we trust Deason and his gang?"

"Trust Gus Deason?" responded Joe, grinning. "About as far as I can throw his fat hide."

"Bull Deason must be a good three hundred pounds...and just as mean. We'll have to watch him close to make sure he don't steal us blind," said Hanley, grinning too, liking the idea of riding with Bull and his boys again.

"Think he'll ride with us if he knows we're going up against Whitmore?" asked Joe, turning to watch the face of Hanley closely in the dim light.

"We won't tell him until it's too late," said Hanley, grinning again. "If Bull smells money, he'll charge right on in there to take it."

"Howdy, boys," said old Cal Burrell, rubbing his rear end with his hand as he walked from the barn. "Kinda late ain't it?"

"Yeah, Cal. We been riding hard the past couple of days. We got twelve fine horses, one with a saddle. Can you take them off our hands?" asked Joe, glancing around to make sure they were the only ones on the street this full moon lit night. "We have kept you in cheap horses for some time, so don't try to give me any bull on the prices this time."

"I know, Joe, and I ain't asked about where they come from neither, have I? Jest like right now, I ain't a asking about them Green River Stage brands on six of them horses or that Utah brand on the others. I gotta move them Green River horses to Denver or up to Wyoming before I can get a profit on them. Gonna cost me to move them, Joe, so I can't be a spending a lot of money on them, but I'll give you a fair price on the Utah horses," replied Burrell, protesting.

Joe knew Cal's fair price was well below the right price for these animals, but didn't want to waste time tonight on horse trading. "All right Cal, whatever you can give."

"Saddle included on this one?" asked Burrell, looking closely at the horse and saddle. "Ain't this the gelding I sold Charlie Barker a couple of months ago?"

"Yeah, the same. Charlie ain't a riding with us anymore, Cal, so we want a fair price for the saddle," said Joe, a little disgusted with the old horse thief.

"Something happen to Charlie?" asked Cal, looking around at the other men.

"You ask too many questions, Cal. Just pay up. We been riding all day and half the night," said Joe, ready to end this horse trading, angry at himself for letting the old man beat him again at horse swapping.

"Can't pay top dollar for them Green River nags, Joe," said the old man, dropping gold coins into the outstretched hands of the outlaw.

Joe eagerly counted out the gold pieces as Burrell finished dropping them into his big hands. He turned to Bob Hanley as the last gold dollar fell into the others, making that clicking sound that was like music to his ears. "Come on boys. The drinks and women are waiting for us."

Joe walked out of the stables to hand each man his fair share of gold. "I'm riding back to Utah to even up the score with Whitmore. You fellows going back with me?"

"You know I will, Joe," said Hanley counting his share of the money.

"We gonna take all his horses?" asked Rawlins, grinning and glancing at Mullens for his approval.

"Yeah, all his horses and cattle too. Maybe round up the stock of that rancher we killed the other day and drive them all down to Granite and sell them to the silver mines," said Joe, liking the idea more as he thought and talked about it.

"I'll go...if we can get some more help. Whitmore is good with that rifle, and I hear he's good with that .44 he carries," said Mullens, a little hesitant with his reply.

"Thought we'd look up Bull Deason and his boys for a little cattle-stealing trip. Might try to knock over a silver shipment while we're down south if the deal is right," said Joe, knowing the mention of silver might farther influence the two young outlaws to stay with him.

"I'd be interested in the cattle and silver jobs, but I'd rather stay away from Whitmore and his horses," said Mullens, remembering the long shot that killed Charlie Barker. Charlie hadn't been more that a few yards behind him. That shot could have been for him.

"Whitmore and his horses are part of the deal," said Joe, harshly. "Charlie was my friend. Whitmore is a gonna pay like old Paul Neel did today for hanging my paw."

"We ain't sure Neel is dead. He could have been playing Indian on us and just faked it," said Rawlins, worried now. "If he ain't dead, then it ain't safe to return to Utah so soon. Let's wait awhile before deciding what to do, Joe."

Joe was hesitant, but Hanley broke the tension. "To hell with Neel and Whitmore. Let's go get rip-roaring drunk and find some women, then worry about Utah when we sober up."

Patches watched the others drink from the sacred springs as he stood guard on the rock overlooking the house at Red Rock Pass. The white man wasn't there, but a search of the house and barn revealed that Whitmore wasn't planning on leaving. Patches shaded his eyes to block out the bright noonday sun and gazed down the small valley to the west. Wild Horse had suggested that the man had left, but Patches knew he was still around, probably in the white man's town with the yellow-haired woman he took from the stage. It was strange what white men would do to their own kind: dig the yellow and silver rocks, then kill each other just to possess them.

He saw that his men had finished at the springs, water bags filled that would keep them in sacred water for several days. Wild Horse came to him, grinning. "The white man has run away, my brother. We should burn his house and barn before we leave."

"Not yet. The spirits have only said that he must leave. That is all for now. We'll not anger them by doing something they do not wish for us to do."

"Then we ride to the sacred cave of the old ones?" asked Wild Horse, glancing at the house, still desirous to burn it.

"Yes, but we leave a warning war lance in the front of the white man's house. He must understand that he must go...or die," replied Patches, seeing that the others had mounted their horses to leave.

Patches followed his men from the springs, taking the old trail that led up from the water hole to the canyon rim above. Not far from the trail would be a faint path that led to the cave of the old shamans of the Utes. He knew it had been a holy place for the Ute medicine men at one time. He had visited it recently and saw the drawings and markings on the wall. They were of the very old ones who lived here long before the Ute came. He would study the drawings closely to learn what the cave spirits wanted of him.

Lame Deer dropped back to ride beside him. "Running Horse follows us to spy for Buffalo Hump. What should we do?"

"Running Horse follows?" asked Patches, surprised. "I should have known Buffalo Hump would send out spies. He must not know where we go. Stop him and send him back."

"I will see to it," said Lame Deer, frowning as he signaled several warriors to hide.

Patches passed three men who had slipped from the backs of their horses to lay hidden in the rocks and brush along the old trail. Patches smiled at the trick. Running Horse would be surprised when he rode into the trap.

Minutes passed as Patches rode slowly behind the others, waiting for the cry that would signal him that Running Horse had indeed ridden into the ambush. His wait seemed an hour, but in fact only a few minutes had passed when the victory war-cry came.

Patches turned the horse quickly around and rode back to the ambush site to see Running Horse lying on the ground holding his head. He glanced up defiantly. "What is this, Patches? An attack upon a brother?"

"You claim to be a brother and you do this for Buffalo Hump?" asked Patches, angrily. "Go back to him and tell him I will kill the next spy he sends."

Running Horse stood quickly, his defiance fading as he realized Patches' threat was real and that he was lucky to be alive. "You will regret this," he said, mounting his horse.

"I already regret that I have let you live. Go back to the women. That's where your kind belongs, not among warriors," said Patches, pointing the single-shot Springfield carbine at the belly of Running Horse. The frightened Indian quickly turned his horse and left.

"I will follow him to make sure he doesn't return to spy on us," said Lame Deer, frowning.

"If he tries to follow again, do what has to be done. The Sky Spirits will justify it," said Patches, watching Running Horse glance back once more before disappearing down the old trail. Satisfied that the Indian was indeed leaving, Patches turned his horse again to the trail and headed for the cave. "Leave another to watch the trail. Old Buffalo Hump may have sent more than one to spy on us."

Patches rode on to the cave along the faint path that had seldom been used for several hundred years. He forgot about Running Horse and Buffalo Hump, even Morning Star, his wife, as he approached the cave. This was a special place, and somewhere within the cave he believed he would find the answers from the Thunder Moon and the Sky Spirits. The cave could very well be the home of the Thunder Moon Spirit. The markings and drawings had suggested that, but he wasn't sure yet. The one thing he was sure of was that the Thunder Moon had spoken to him, and he knew it was a direct command to him through the Thunder Moon from the Sky People. Clearly, the Thunder Moon had said the first step was to cleanse the sacred springs, but how to do so had not been said. He would fast and pray for that answer tonight. He knew the most simple way would be to ride into the ranch and kill the white man, but what appeared to be the simple way wasn't always the desire of the spirits. Whatever they wanted, Patches knew he must obey...even if it cost him his life.

Several days after the shoot-out at Doan's Ferry, Jake led the posse into town from the east. Two dead men lay draped over their saddles, covered with rain slickers and tied down to keep them in place. Cody Wedgeworth followed, leading a horse that pulled a travois with the injured Sheriff Neel strapped to it. Baker Stevenson followed the sheriff, his big Sharps rifle resting across the front of his saddle. Wallace Granger brought up the rest of the tired men, leading the two horses that carried the dead.

Jake glanced back at the sheriff. Neel had suffered with the busted leg and the fever that came with the bullet still in his shoulder. Jake saw Granger lead the two horses carrying the dead toward the stables. Ferguson had no family and few would mourn his passing, but the outlaw whom Neel had identified as Charlie Barker, a longtime outlaw from Colorado, was going to have nobody to mourn his death in Brewster's Crossing.

Jake noticed that the few people who were in town began to gather in the street to watch the riders pass or greet the ones they knew with questions. Jake headed for the house of Sheriff Neel. He knew Herman Hielmann would be needed with his doctoring. Hielmann wasn't a real doctor, but Jake knew the man was good with wounds, having served in a field hospital in the war.

Kennon Matthews stepped from the swinging doors of the Red Dog Saloon to join the people in the street. He saw Jake and headed quickly to him. "What happened, Jake? You catch up with them killers?" he asked, glancing at Neel.

"We got ambushed by them at Doan's Ferry. Henley is dead and old man Doan, too. We buried Leonard at his place," replied Jake, stopping the horse to dismount. "We killed one the sheriff identified as Charlie Barker. I think he's the one who killed Vern."

"We buried Vern yesterday," said Matthews sadly. "Gonna miss him. We been together seven or eight years."

Several men helped Neel into his house as Hielmann arrived to follow them inside. Jake waited for a few moments then turned to leave. "Cody, let's go get a cold beer and clean up some. You joining us, Kennon?"

"Ain't drinking no more for awhile," answered Cody, avoiding the stare from the young man and Matthews.

"Something wrong? You sick, Cody?" asked Kennon shocked.

"Naw, just got to keep a clear head for awhile," said Cody, seriously. "Jake had a run in with a Ute named Patches. The Indian told him to leave. Said the springs out at Red Rock Pass was sacred ground. I'm gonna stay with him a few weeks."

"Patches?" responded Kennon, serious. "I heard of him. He's a bad one."

"Jake, I'd advise you to lay off the booze, too. This Indian problem could get real serious. You'll need a clear head to face it," said Cody, looking straight at the young man. "I'll be ready to ride in a hour. Want to lock up my stuff at the shack."

"You seen Sarah Thurston?" asked Jake, glancing at Matthews as Wedgeworth walked away.

"Took her out to the Thurston Ranch day before yesterday," replied Kennon, frowning. "I tried to talk her out of it, but she said she couldn't wait and would go alone, so I took her."

"She still there?" asked Jake, worried.

"Yeah, fer as I know. She's a determined woman. Got her mind made up to clean up the place. Don't need it as far as I could see."

"Didn't you tell her how dangerous it was staying out there alone with outlaws and Indians running loose?" asked Jake, a little angry with Matthews.

"Didn't know about Patches making threats, and besides, them outlaws was a hightailing it to Colorado," replied Kennon, protesting his innocence. "Jake, she ain't your responsibility. She looks like she can take care of herself. I'm a gonna ride out there tomorrow and check on her before I make the run to Green River. Gonna try to get her to head back to Salt Lake. Ain't much she can do here."

"We know that, but will she?" asked Jake, turning as Martha Neel came to the porch of the house.

"Jake, Paul wants to see you before you leave town," she said, worried.

"Me and Cody will check on her this evening, but you make sure she's with you tomorrow, Kennon," said Jake, turning to head for the house. "That Ute ain't nobody to fool around with."

"All right, Jake. I'll do what I can, but remember, she's got a mind of her own," said Kennon, not really believing he could get Sarah Thurston on that stage to Green River.

Jake entered the house with Kennon close behind. Paul Neel lay on his sofa, his broken leg propped up with pillows and a wet towel on his forehead.

"Jake, glad you came," said Neel, weak from two days on the trail with his wounds. "Doc says I have a fever and this lead in me has got to come out. Said I'd be laid up for months."

"True, Jake," replied Hielmann, laying out his tools for removing the bullet in the man's shoulder. "The sheriff would be dead if you hadn't taken your time moving him here. The bullet has caused his body to get poisoned."

"What he's trying to say is that I ain't a gonna be fit to sheriff around here for a few months," said Neel, staring at him. "I need you as my deputy...to look after things. Them outlaws might ride back this way knowing I'm laid up."

"I...don't know, Paul. Gotta look after my place," answered Jake, thinking about the Ute and Sarah Thurston out at that ranch alone. Something about her caused a feeling he had felt once before when he met Rachel Watkins in Spanish Fork years ago.

"Jake, you and me was deputies together in Platteville back a few years ago. You know the law and I need you. Charlie Barker was part of that bunch I had the shoot-out with when you left to go work for the railroad," said Neel, seriously. "You remember old Nathan Blackburn, don't you?"

"Yeah, the old man we hung for murder?"

"The same. Charlie rode with the son, Joe. I think Joe was the leader of this murdering gang. If he was, he'll be back this way to get me. He's a bad one, Jake. You never met him, did you?"

"No, I was down in Denver when you shot it out with that bunch trying to rob the railroad depot," said Jake, remembering the story of that gunfight. Sam Malone, the town marshall had died in that fight, but old Nathan Blackburn had swung from the gallows for the killing.

"I need you, Jake. You were there for me in Colorado. Now I need you here in Utah," said Neel, almost begging.

"All right Paul, but just till you get back on your feet. I ain't no lawman anymore. Platteville was my last job."

"All right," said Neel smiling.

SIX

Patches watched the faces of his men seated around the fire inside the cave. What words spoken were soft or in a whisper. He noticed all had a serious look on their faces, one of determination, yet in awe of their surroundings. For most, it was the first time to visit the cave. This pleased Patches as he stood and looked hard at the assembled men.

"Brothers...my heart is filled with sincerity at your faith in me and in the powers of the spirits. Too long have the Ute forgotten their sacred ways. Too long have the Ute licked at the hands of the white man. Now...see what that has brought our nation to. The once proud Ute Nation will go to the white man's reservation like a whipped dog with his tail between his legs." Patches waited for those words to sink in before continuing. He noticed that all listened intently, a welcome change from the degrading stares and remarks from Buffalo Hump and his followers.

"The Thunder Moon has spoken to me as I sought guidance as to our future as a nation. Clearly the spirit of the Thunder Moon whispered to me on the wings of the night wind, sealed by the voice of the thunder, followed by the anger of our Sky Spirits in the form of a terrible storm, their eyes flashing their anger for us to see in the night sky. Many saw this, yet fools like Buffalo Hump would deny the sign."

"This is true, my brothers," said Lame Deer, looking at the others for their approval. Many nodded their heads.

Patches smiled as he continued. "Now, the duty of obeying the Thunder Moon falls upon us, the few who are faithful. In the past, many would have joined us, but now, only you have answered the sacred call. I have faith that others will see that we are right and will join us later, but I fear the Sky People will kindle their anger against those who do not obey, and terrible things will befall our people. We must be strong, keep the faith, and never waiver from what we know is right."

"Have you seen these terrible events in a vision, my brother?" asked One Bear, worried.

"No...but I feel them strongly," replied Patches, looking at One Bear. He knew he needed this experienced warrior to keep this group together. "We gather here to all sacrifice and pray for answers from the spirits that guide our lives. Within this cave lies our answers. A return to the old ways is the only way to save our people as a nation. Soon, if nothing is done, the white man will sweep the Ute from these lands and we will be no more as a people."

"What do we hope to find in here for answers?" asked Lame Deer, not fully understanding.

"My brothers...this is the cave of the ancient ones. The old shamans of our people recognized the powers that lay within the confines of this cave. It was a holy place, but now, few even know of it, much less have respect for it. That is why the Thunder Moon has spoken. We have neglected our sacred duties, but how we are to return to our old ways is the question. We start this night to sacrifice, fast, and pray so that we may understand what is required of us."

"And the springs at Red Rock Pass must be cleansed first," said Wild Horse, eagerly.

"I know this is a requirement. The simple way would be to ride into the Pass and kill the white man, but the Sky Spirits work in a different way than we do. The simple way is not always the way of the spirits," said Patches, glancing at Wild Horse. "We must be careful not to offend them, especially the cave spirits, if we want their help and guidance."

"Tell us what we must do," said One Bear, standing. "I am ready."

"We must purify ourselves first. Each man must wash, then search within himself, cleanse his thoughts, and be prepared to hear the whisperings of the spirits. I am the shaman of this band, but I alone cannot do everything. Our strength lies in our unity. Together, we are strong, but as individuals, we are weak," said Patches, walking around the fire to the cave wall. The campfire cast shadows against it, but all could see the ancient markings and drawings. "See here, my faithful brothers. The ancient ones left their mark for all who entered here to see. First, let me say that there are more drawings and marks farther within, but these few here will do to show you the power the old ones had."

Many moved to get a better view. Lame Deer took a torch to stand near the wall to give better light to the side of the cave. Patches walked closer to point out several of the markings. "Here we see the sign of the Thunder Spirits. The lightning flashes tell us the Thunder Spirits dwell within. This other one shows plainly the full moon; possibly a Thunder Moon once lived here with the Thunder Spirits."

Patches glanced at Lame Deer, who stood with a reverent stance which soon fell over the others. Patches smiled as he knew he had their full attention now. He continued. "Here we see drawings of the ancient ones in their hunt of the deer, the elk, and the buffalo, but we see no horses. The God Dogs did not come to these people, but farther back in the cave there is a drawing of a horse. There is also more, but in time I will show it to you. The old ones, our forefathers, clearly saw our time. It plainly shows the Ute defeating the white man."

Many glanced up at him, shock showing on their faces. "We must see this," said One Bear, not fully believing.

"In time, my brother. You are not yet cleansed or purified to stand on that sacred ground," replied Patches, pleased that he now had their full attention. "Come, I will show you more just within the entrance to the cavern that holds the sacred drawings."

They filed into the narrow corridor with torches to light the way, then followed Patches to the entrance of the cavern. The young shaman stopped there to hold a torch toward the wall for all to see. "See, my brothers...and never forget what you have seen," said Patches, smiling as the warriors saw the clear painting of the Thunderbird. Some backed away, frightened, while others stood in amazement.

"We are indeed on sacred ground," whispered One Bear, glancing at the others. All nodded in agreement as Patches smiled again, pleased that they now understood as he did. They must obey the Thunder Moon.

Jake reined in his horse, a dapple gray from Newley Parkins that he had borrowed. He knew he would miss the bay as he glanced at the dog who had stayed at Sheriff Neel's dogyard for several days. Cody Wedgeworth rode beside him, a big British-made Enfield .577 caliber rifle that the old man had somehow picked up from a Confederate veteran years ago. Jake knew the infantry rifle carried a powerful punch from a good distance.

"About there, Cody," said Jake, glancing at Wedgeworth, then at the ranch below the trail.

"Kennon said she probably won't leave. There ain't much here a woman can do," said Cody, frowning. "Women can be hardheaded at times. Reason I never got married."

"Never had that kind of trouble with Rachel," said Jake, a little pain rippling through him as he thought of her.

"Rachel was special. She knew how to put up with you," said Cody, heading his horse down the trail.

"Wonder where she's at?" asked Jake as they entered the ranch. "Don't see her anywhere."

Buster saved them from wondering as he trotted to the barn, wagging his tail. Jake frowned as he dismounted and followed. Cody remained on his horse, glancing around the place, seeing changes he hadn't noticed before.

Sarah Thurston came from the barn, a pitchfork in her hands, with Buster close at her heels, his tail still wagging. "I'm glad you're back safely," she said, smiling as she leaned the pitchfork on the side of the barn door. "I just couldn't wait for your return. I had to see the graves, do something around here."

Jake glanced at the graves near the cottonwood tree. He noticed flowers had been planted at the foot of the graves, and two wooden crosses now rested at the head. "Should have waited. Them outlaws may return to clean out the place."

"Then the more reason for me to be here," she responded, looking sternly at him. "Did you catch them?"

"Only one. The others got away with the horses. The sheriff is laid up with a busted leg and a shoulder wound," said Jake, glancing at Cody, who had now dismounted and walked to join them.

"Name's Cody Wedgeworth. Sorry about your brother," said Cody, glancing at the graves.

"Would you like to come to the house? I have biscuits left over from breakfast," she said, smiling at the older man.

"Why yes, I'd like that, Miss Thurston," replied Cody, smiling. "Missed breakfast with Jake wanting to get out here in such an all-fired hurry and all."

"Is that so?" she asked, smiling as she glanced at Jake, who had turned red in the face.

"Just wanted to make sure you was all right. Neel appointed me a deputy, so I was just doing my job, that's all," said Jake, still embarrassed.

She walked beside Jake as they went to the house. "Thank you for coming. I'm all right here. Just needed something to do."

"Ain't safe out here by yourself. Too many outlaws riding the back trails, and now there may be Indian trouble coming," said Jake, glancing at her.

"Indian trouble?" she asked, alarmed. "I thought the Indians were at peace down here."

"Suppose to be, but I had a run in with a Ute named Patches the other day. May be trouble around here," said Jake, glancing at her.

"What kind of trouble?" she asked, still frightened as they continued to the house.

"None really to worry about, but I think you ought to go back to Brewster's Crossing for awhile. Kennon is taking the stage back to Green River tomorrow morning. He's coming out this afternoon to take you back to town," said Jake, seriously.

"What if I don't want to go just yet?" she asked, stopping to look sternly at him.

"Miss Thurston, it ain't a matter of what you want right now," said Cody, coming to Jake's defense. "Jake ain't telling you much about Patches. That one is a mean Indian, and he ordered Jake to leave his place at Red Rock Pass. Claimed it was sacred ground."

She looked at Cody and quickly glanced at Jake, who avoided her eyes. "You think this Patches will try to force you off your place?"

"Yeah, maybe. Just want to see you safe. He might try something with you if he knows you're out here by yourself," said Jake, hoping that she would understand.

She didn't. "He doesn't think this ranch is on sacred ground, does he?"

"Well...don't rightly know, Miss Thurston. Jake don't want to take any chances. Best you go back to town with Kennon this afternoon. At least until we see what Patches is up to," said Cody, seriously.

"I'll think about it," she said, a little defiance in her voice as she turned to continue toward the house.

Jake glanced at Cody, a pleading look in his eyes, then turned to follow Sarah to the house. Cody followed. "At least she said she'd think about it, Jake."

Joe Blackburn leaned back on the chair, downed the whiskey in the glass, laughed, and reached for the bottle on the table. Bob Hanley handed the bottle to him as Joe almost fell out of the chair. "Getting loaded, Bob," said Blackburn, finally getting the bottle to refill his glass. "Where's that Cathy woman that was here a few minutes ago?"

"Rusty and Buck stole her," laughed Gus Deason, who sat beside the outlaw.

"Hell, Rusty and Buck is a stealing everything that ain't tied down," said Joe, laughing again as he took a sip from his whiskey glass. "Reason I have them two ride with me. Best horse thieves I ever ran across."

"And women stealers, too," added Bob, refilling his glass as he glanced at the two young outlaws at a nearby table with the woman called Cathy and two other women.

"Joe, I like that idea of yours about returning to Utah in a few days instead of laying low here in Colorado," said

Deason, grinning. "Ain't no law a gonna be expecting that of you."

"Who else you got that can ride with us?" asked Joe, returning his chair to the floor to stare at the big fat man.

"Well...I got my kid brother, Lenny, and Curley Benson right now. Everyone else done rode south to get in on stealing silver. Ain't got much use for silver myself, though. Would rather steal cattle and horses. Easier to make money," said Deason, thinking hard through his liquor-influenced brain.

"That would make seven. We might be able to handle the jobs with only seven," said Blackburn, frowning.

"Well...there's Bass Wheeler and Rudy Beecher. They're in town somewhere," said Deason, grinning. "Might could use their guns. Bass is mighty slick with his .44, you know."

"Too hard to handle. Bass is an independent cuss, and Rudy is mean when he's a drinking hard," said Blackburn, glancing at Bob Hanley.

"Might could use their guns, Joe," said Hanley, seriously. "Especially going back so soon."

"You expecting trouble this time, Joe?" asked Deason, concerned now. "You said Neel was dead, didn't you?"

"Seen him go down with his horse at the river," said Joe, frowning. "Besides, if he's still alive, he ain't a gonna be expecting us to come back so soon."

"Well...I don't know, Joe. I don't want to cross trails with Paul Neel, that's for sure. You said this would be a horse and cow stealing job and then we'd take the stock down to Granite to sell to the miners," said Deason, still concerned. "Don't mind sticking up a stage every now and then, but I want to avoid gun play. I'm too big a target."

"You're right there, you old fart," said Hanley, laughing.

Deason laughed and downed his whiskey to reach for the bottle again. "Heck, Joe. I'll ride with you to hell and back. Let's take Bass and Rudy with us...just in case old man Neel is still around. They ain't afraid of Sheriff Paul Neel nor anyone else for that matter."

"Where do we find them?" asked Joe, liking the idea better. Bass was fast with the gun, and they might need that if this Whitmore fellow got in the way. Besides, he wanted to even the score with Whitmore for killing Charlie, and Bass would be the man for the job.

"Don't have to look far," said Deason, pointing to the upper deck in the saloon. "There he is right now with Ruby."

Joe turned to stare at the young man who staggered down the stairs with the redhead on his arm. Joe saw that he wore the .44 Smith and Wesson like a gunfighter. The man made the floor and gave the woman a long kiss, then released her to laugh. He staggered to the bar and Ruby followed.

Joe stood and walked to the bar to stand beside the cocky gunfighter. "Hey, Joe. I heard you were back in town. Too bad about Charlie. I liked him."

"Yeah, I'm a gonna ride back to Utah and take care of that back-shooting bastard that killed Charlie," said Joe, frowning. "Paul Neel is dead, too."

"I heard, but Randy Peterson rode in this afternoon from Utah. Said Neel was laid up, and that he appointed someone who used to be a deputy with him in Platteville. Name of Whitmore or Whitmire. You heard of him?" asked Bass, sipping the whiskey while placing an arm around the woman.

"Jake Whitmore. He's the one who shot Charlie," replied Joe, remembering the shot.

"Heard he plugged Charlie with a Sharps from a thousand yards. That's some shooting," said Bass, turning serious.

"More like eight hundred," answered Joe, glancing back to his table. Deason and Hanley watched the conversation closely. "Got a job over in Utah, again. Thought you might like to talk about it."

Bass finished his whiskey then turned to the woman. "Get lost, honey, but not too far," said the young man, frowning. "Me and Joe got business to talk about."

Bass followed him back to the table to take a chair beside the fat Gus Deason, who offered him the bottle of whiskey and a glass. "What you got in mind?"

"Horses and cattle down near Brewster's Crossing," said Joe, glancing at Hanley. "We'll take them to Granite to sell to the miners, then hang around for an easy silver shipment, then ride back here."

"Too many others down around Granite trying to knock over some silver shipment. I been wanting to rob the bank in Green River. I hear they keep a lot of payroll in the bank there for shipping later to Colorado. Comes out of the banks in Salt Lake City," said Bass, serious. "Ain't found anybody brave enough to ride with me on the job."

"How much in that bank?" asked Joe, interested.

"I hear maybe fifty thousand...at times," said Bass, almost whispering as he looked around to make sure he wasn't overheard. "I done been to Green River twice to case the place. Would be a nice haul for six or eight men.

They been keeping it quiet around there about all that money in the bank, but I hung around long enough to know it's true."

"I'd be interested in that much money," said Deason, his greedy eyes glowing with delight.

"Help me with the bank job, and I'll help you with the job in Brewster's Crossing," said Bass, grinning.

"What do you say, Bob?" asked Joe, looking at Hanley.

"Bass, we got a score to settle with Whitmore for killing Charlie. Thought we'd do that while we were stealing his horses," said Hanley, looking closely at the young outlaw.

"Now Joe. You didn't say anything about riding into Utah to do a killing," said Deason, alarmed.

"You don't have to do the killing, Gus. Thought Bass would like to try Whitmore. Some say he's fast with his gun, a .44 just like yours," said Joe, staring at Wheeler.

"Keep talking. You have my interest," said Bass, grinning as he reached for the whiskey glass to refill it.

"We can throw Neel in, too. If he's laid up, he'd be easy pickings and that whole town too, when you gun down Whitmore," said Joe, liking the idea more. "They got a bank there and no law to protect it except Whitmore."

"What kind of money they got in the bank?" asked Bass, leaning forward.

"Ain't no fifty thousand like in Green River, but we could haul off four or five thousand easy, maybe eight to ten," said Joe, grinning. "Easy job with no law around and few people in town. Won't be no ride in and shoot it out like it would be in Green River."

"You have a point there, Joe. We could round up a herd of cattle and horses, then pull off the bank job and ride like hell for Colorado. Gus here could take care of the cows while we do the bank job," said Bass, smiling. "It'd work. Be easier than trying Green River or trying to bust a silver shipment."

"Then we do it," said Joe, smiling. "You in, Gus?"

"Yeah, if I don't have to go up against Whitmore," said the fat man, frowning.

"Bass will handle Whitmore. You just do your part and things will go fine. In a few weeks we'll all be rolling in high money. Might drift over to Leadville or Cripple Creek for awhile," said Joe, reaching for the whiskey bottle. "Let's drink to our new business partnership."

Patches stood, his trim naked body glowing in the firelight inside the cave. The bear grease smeared over his body gave him a shiny look. Only a loincloth covered his lower body parts. His long black hair was loose, hanging freely about his broad bronze shoulders. "Two Ponies has returned from his scout. We will hear his report before we begin our sacrifice."

The young brave stood as Patches sat again beside the fire to listen. All was in place for the sacred rites to begin. Everyone had cleansed their bodies and, hopefully, their minds. "I went to watch as Patches has ordered," said Two Ponies. "I know some must stand guard against our enemies and those who would betray us."

"Continue," said Patches quietly, listening intently.

"The white man Whitmore has returned to Red Rock Pass. He appears to be staying, with no intent to leave. He returned with the old one who has befriended the Ute before," said Two Ponies, glancing at Patches for his approval.

"That would be the one called Wedgeworth," whispered One Bear, alarmed. "Why would he return to the Pass?"

"To help Whitmore," said Patches, angrily. "He must know the spring is holy ground to us, yet he returns."

"I don't understand this," said Lame Deer, worried. "Didn't he see the warning lance we left."

"They both did," replied Two Ponies, concerned. "They left it where we placed it."

"Then they understand, but challenge us to the springs by leaving the lance in place," said Patches, defiantly. "We will see what the Sky Spirits say about this."

"There is more," said Two Ponies, looking around. "Elk Horn still watches. He reports that Buffalo Hump has moved the camp to the east along the river. Running Horse has been sent to find Ouray to report on us."

"Let them go. They will soon see the error of their ways," said Patches, his anger still with him. "We must concentrate on our sacrifice and find the weakness of the white man who challenges us at Red Rock Pass."

"I know their weakness," said Two Ponies, smiling. "The yellow-haired woman remains at the ranch northwest of Red Rock Pass. She is the woman of Whitmore."

"How do you know this?" asked One Bear, glancing at Patches, who remained seated, staring at the fire.

"I saw her today. Whitmore came to her with the old man. She kissed

Whitmore before he left. She is his woman," said Two Ponies, convinced. "Then later another man came, but left by himself. She is there alone."

"What do you make of this, my brother?" asked Lame Deer, looking at Patches.

"I saw Whitmore take her from the stage that the other men robbed. If she is his new woman, then this is our advantage," said Patches, looking up.

"I thought his woman died of the white-man sickness and is buried at the Pass," said Wild Horse, confused.

"That is true. Maybe Whitmore is a Mormon. Some have more than one woman," replied Patches. "We will delay our sacrifice. I must visit this woman. We need to know if she belongs to Whitmore."

"And if she is, what do we do with her?" asked One Bear, looking hard at Patches.

"The woman may be his weakness. I thought it would be the white man's firewater, but maybe the spirits are already speaking to us. We should visit this woman to see for ourselves," said Patches, standing.

"It is night now, my brother," said Lame Deer, worried. "The night spirits may not favor us to visit the woman."

"Then we ride at dawn tomorrow," said Patches, glancing at Lame Deer. "When the sun rises from his sleep, we will be there to see this woman and learn if she belongs to him and is his weakness. For now though, we continue to cleanse our minds and pray. Tomorrow we can thank the Sky Spirits for the sharpness of vision from our young brother, Two Ponies, who may have found one of our answers to our problems."

SEVEN

Jake Whitmore woke with a scream, then kicked the blanket from himself and sat on the side of the bed. The dream had returned for the second time during the night. Cody Wedgeworth came to the door, a concerned look on his face.

"Dreaming again?" he asked, a pistol hanging from his hand at his side.

"Yeah," replied Jake, standing. "What's happening to me, Cody?"

"Heard of such things happening after a person loses someone close to them," he said, frowning. "Same dream?"

"Same, but more this time," replied Jake, walking past the older man, looking for the whiskey bottle in the next room.

"Sure you want that?" asked Cody as he watched Jake uncork the bottle.

Jake glared at him, the bottle halfway to his lips. Slowly he lowered it to replace the cork and set the whiskey bottle on the table. "Cody, this dream is weird. You think it's some kind of sign from God?"

"Don't know, Jake. I ain't a practicing Mormon," replied Cody, frowning. "I was one when I was a kid in Missouri, but ain't done much about my religion since."

"The dream started out with them graves I dug for Karl and Elizabeth, then Rachel's," said Jake, sitting in the rocking chair and holding his head in his hands.

"She return?"

"Yeah, dressed in that white gown from last time," replied Jake, glancing up. "Didn't say anything to me, just stood there. It seemed so real, Cody."

Cody took the whiskey bottle and uncorked it, then had second thoughts and replaced it. "Scares the heck out of me, kid," he said, sitting on a chair beside the young man.

"Then I see Sarah Thurston all happy and smiling until the Indian appears."

"Indian?" asked Cody, seriously. "You didn't say anything about an Indian earlier in your dream."

"Wasn't there the first time," said Jake, leaning back in the chair to rock. "He was all painted up like I've never seen a Ute do before. All kinds of colors. Blue, white, red, green. You ever seen a Ute paint with so many colors?"

"Can't say I have, son," replied Cody, worried now. "You recognize the Ute? Was it Patches?"

"Couldn't tell. He was all naked except for a loincloth, but he was painted all over his body."

"Heard them Apaches get all worked up over painting their bodies in their rituals, but not the Utes," answered Cody glancing at Jake. "Anything else?"

"The weird part was next. I seen this fire burning, but at first I couldn't tell what it was, then I saw it was a cabin," he said, staring at the fireplace where a small fire still burned.

"Was it this place?" asked Cody, standing to start pacing in front of the fire.

"Don't think so, but the frightening part was the fire got put out real quick by water. Then I saw the pool down by the springs. When I looked closely, I saw a bronze hand slowly rise from the water, then I woke."

"Hell's fire, that's really weird," said Cody, stopping long enough to glance at him before starting his pacing again. "Never really believed in this Indian magic, but maybe there's something to it after all."

"I think I ought to ride over to the Thurston place in the morning and get Sarah to come here until I can convince her to go to town," said Jake, standing. "There must be something to this dream, Cody. Why else would I have it?"

"All right then. I'll hang around here to protect the place. No telling what that heathen redskin Patches will do next," said Cody, worried. "We left that warning lance in the front yard to challenge his right to this ground. It's sacred ground to us, now that Rachel is buried here."

"You think he'll challenge us still?"

"Yeah, he'll have to or lose face with his people. We could just pull out, you know."

"Thought of that. Might have if Rachel was still alive, but now she's buried here. I'll stay and take my chances. It was her dream to make this place work," said Jake, determined. "Like you said, it's sacred ground to me, too.

Patches will have to fight me for it."

"He'll do that. That's for sure, son," replied Cody, still worried. "I'm going to take a walk outside. Need some fresh air."

Jake watched the older man pull his coat on and pick up the double-barrel shotgun leaning against the wall by the door. He opened the shotgun to check the loads and glanced at the younger man. "Might be a varmint outside."

Cody left the house, and Jake returned to the rocking chair. He knew the dream had to mean something. Rachel would have said it came from God. He didn't know, maybe it did. He should have paid more attention to her religion. She hadn't forced it on him, but had made him sit and listen to her reading of the Bible and other books.

He glanced at the bottle of whiskey, the desire for the pain-relieving liquor strong. He wanted to reach out for it, but something deep down inside forbade him and he looked away. The desire didn't leave, and he slowly returned his gaze to the bottle.

Standing, he picked up the bottle, but did not open it. He struggled between his desire for the liquor or keeping a clear head. He looked at the bottle once more, then walked to the door and opened it. One last struggle within came, then he stepped upon the porch and uncorked the bottle to pour out the contents upon the ground.

"About time," said Cody Wedgeworth quietly as he watched from the steps of the porch.

Jake stared at the old man in the dim light of the night, not able to see the grinning face. He threw the bottle into the night air, frowned, and returned to the door to stop and turn toward the man. "It ain't easy, you know, but it's what Rachel would have wanted."

Patches watched from the rim of the canyon as Wild Horse and Two Ponies entered the yard of the ranch to see if the white woman remained alone. He watched closely, unable to see clearly in the early dim light of morning.

"Two Ponies signals that the woman is inside the house," said One Bear, pointing.

"So, we will now see if this yellow-haired woman holds the magic of Whitmore in her heart," replied Patches seriously as he turned the paint horse to descend to the floor of the canyon. The others followed.

At the base of the trail from the rim, Wild Horse met them. "The woman still sleeps inside the house. Should we wait for her to come outside?"

"No, we will go to her," said Patches, riding toward the cabin.

Patches dismounted and silently signaled several warriors to take up positions to watch. He then turned to the others and signaled for them to enter the house. He followed Wild Horse inside to stand in amazement at the interior of the white man's dwellings. It wasn't the first time he had been in a house, but each time was different. He could not understand why the white man would want so many things.

Wild Horse pointed to the bedroom door. "She is in there," he whispered, grinning.

Quietly, Patches opened the door to peek inside. The slight noise of the door opening caused her to stir. Patches waited patiently as she settled back into sleep. His keen eyes scanned the room and noticed the shotgun against the wall beside the bed. He had no doubt that the woman could use it. Whitmore would have a strong woman.

He eased closer to the bed as others entered the room. Wild Horse took the shotgun while One Bear and Lame Deer went to the other side of the bed to stare at the woman. She was beautiful for a white woman, Patches knew, but there was more to the face than beauty. He saw strength...and character. Whitmore had picked well.

Sarah woke startled, feeling their presence before opening her eyes. She first saw the scar-faced Patches, then glanced at the others. She reached for the blanket to cover herself as she thought of escape, only to realize there was none. Fear gripped her, but she fought within to contain it and not show that she was terrified.

"You belong to Whitmore?" asked Patches, staring hard at her, watching her eyes for deception.

"What do you want?" she replied, trying to give herself time to sort out this problem that appeared to have no good results for her.

"You woman of the white man at Red Rock Pass?" asked Patches, suspicious of her as she continued to stall. Maybe they had made a mistake in coming here.

"Whitmore?" she asked, not sure how to answer. A no answer might cause them to kill her, and yet a yes answer could bring the same results. Jake had said there was trouble with one called Patches over his place being on land the Indians claimed to be sacred ground.

Patches reached out to touch her long blonde hair, running his fingers through it. She didn't move, too scared to respond. The Indian smiled as he withdrew his hand, glanced at the others, and spoke to them in Ute, which she didn't understand. The Indians laughed.

"You are the woman of Whitmore," said Patches, satisfied that she had to be his woman.

"Yes...I am his woman," she finally replied, hoping that answer was the one the tall Indian wanted to hear. Apparently it was, for he smiled and spoke again in Ute to the others, who nodded their approval.

"Woman of the white man Whitmore. Tell your man to leave sacred ground at Red Rock Pass. His presence angers our Sky People," said Patches seriously as he turned to leave.

"Yes...I will tell him," she whispered, containing her relief as the Indians filed out from her bedroom.

She quickly followed them at a safe distance and watched as they left the house to mount their horses in the front yard. She clutched the night-gown tighter around her neck as she stopped at the doorway wondering what this visit meant to her safety and that of Jake Whitmore. She watched with relief as the Utes rode quickly from the yard and began to disappear down the trail toward the river. As the last of the Indians disappeared, she realized how close she had come to being murdered. Telling the Indian that she was the woman of Jake Whitmore had been the answer the warrior wanted to hear. She thought of that and tried to smile, thinking about really being the woman of the man who defied the Utes over the spring at Red Rock Pass.

She started to close the door, her fear gripping her again as she noticed the war lance in the dirt in front of her house. She knew little about the Indians, but enough to know that lance had been left as a warning to her and to Jake Whitmore. Frightened, she ran to her bed to cover herself and burst into tears at the thought of what had happened. Jake Whitmore had been right. It was too dangerous for a woman to be out here alone.

Kennon Matthews leaned back on the chair and looked at Sheriff Neel, who lay upon his sofa, his broken leg propped up on several pillows. Martha Neel entered the room with a glass of milk and handed it to Matthews.

"What do you think Jake will do about this Ute trying to run him off the springs at Red Rock Pass?" asked Matthews, sipping the milk from the glass.

"Don't know, Kennon. Jake has changed a lot since them Utes killed his parents on the Green River several years ago," replied Neel, frowning. "Was a time in Colorado that the kid would not back down from anything, but now...well I don't know."

"Marrying Rachel softened him," responded Matthews, concerned. "She was good for him in some ways, but he sort of mellowed out, easygoing in everything."

"Until he returned to drinking. He can turn deadly when he's drinking. Seen it once back in Colorado when we was deputies together in Platteville."

"That when he killed the Henderson brothers?" asked Kennon, seriously.

"It was. Jake Whitmore is fast with that .44 of his. Don't let anyone tell you different," replied the sheriff, glancing at him. "Pete and Marvin were good too, but Jake was faster...and his aim true that day. Killed them both with only one shot each after the Hendersons emptied their pistols at him."

"That why he quit being a lawman?" asked Matthews, sipping his milk again.

"Mostly. He was upset that he let his anger get the best of him. He went to work for the railroad and drifted over into Utah where his parents had moved. Later, he quit the railroad and joined them on the Green the same year Stalking Horse went on the warpath," said Neel, frowning. "I liked him better when he married Rachel, but I'm worried now that she's gone. He may turn mean again."

"Heard he has been hitting the bottle hard lately," replied Matthews, nodding in agreement with Neel.

"Cody ride out with him yesterday?" asked the sheriff, glancing up.

"Yeah, he did. Funny though, as old Cody wouldn't drink with us when the posse returned the other day. Claimed he was quitting his drinking for awhile."

"Cody quit drinking?" asked Neel, shocked. "Must be real serious about the Ute thing out at Red Rock Pass. Maybe we all had better pay attention to Patches."

"Some say he's spoiling for a fight," replied Matthews, worried. "Don't think he's too happy about the government making all the Utes stay on their assigned reservations."

"I heard he was mixed up in that Walker War in '68," said Neel, frowning again. "Even heard he might have been with old Stalking Horse a few years back."

"Let's hope not. If he was and Jake finds out, there won't be anything to stop that boy from going after Patches," replied Matthews, finishing off the milk and placing the glass on the floor beside him. "If Jake keeps drinking hard and turns mean like you said, it's gonna be one hell of a fight between him and Patches."

"One reason I asked Jake to be my deputy," said Neel, adjusting his leg on the pillows. "Maybe being a lawman again will get him to think before acting...besides, I need a reliable man for the job."

"Not to mention one who can use the gun," added Matthews, trying to smile, but finding it hard to.

"He can do that," said Neel, nodding in approval. "What about Miss Thurston? She gonna stay out at the ranch?"

"Tried to get her to come back to town yesterday, but she won't come. I told her I'd be pulling out this evening with the stage. Even Jake tried to get her to leave," said Matthews, frowning.

"Too dangerous out there alone with Patches causing trouble so close to the ranch. Anything can happen," said Neel, worried. "You know when Jake is planning to return to town?"

"Said he'd ride in sometime next week to check on you and see if there is anything that needs to be done. If you need him, he said to send him word. He'll be close to this place until he sees what Patches is up to," replied Matthews, standing. "Well, Sheriff, I gotta go and check on the stage. Want to pull out before dark for Green River. I'll see you in a few weeks."

"Take care, Kennon. Glad you dropped by to fill me in on the latest. I ain't a going anywhere with this leg, so I'll be right here when you return," said Neel, smiling. "You got another guard for this run?"

"Got Henry Bellows. He needs the money," said Matthews, walking to the door.

Neel watched the man leave, then leaned back on his pillows under his head and worried. If Jake was drinking, then making him deputy might have been the wrong thing to do, but he needed the man and his gun. Jake was responsible, and that's what he needed right now, plus he was worried about Joe Blackburn returning to try and get even for Charlie Barker's death. Making Jake deputy would give the young man an edge if he had to go up against the outlaw.

Martha entered the room, smiling. "Paul, is there anything you need? I got a Relief Society meeting down at the church."

"No, go on, dear. I'll be all right here," he replied smiling at his wife. "You gonna take the kids?"

"Yes. Mavis York is going to watch the children while we meet," she replied, leaning over to kiss him on the forehead. "I overheard you and Kennon talking about Jake Whitmore turning back to drinking. Rachel gave him good cause to stop several years ago, but now...I'm worried about him, Paul. Maybe Bishop Newman can ride out and talk with him."

"I'll have Cal talk to him when he rides into town in a few days."

Joe Blackburn pulled his black horse to a stop as Bass Wheeler rode up the trail with a grin on his face. "Well...what's up, Bass?" asked Blackburn, frowning. Nothing had gone right since they entered Utah, having lost a packhorse crossing the Dolores River with most of their food, and now Bass wanting to raid the Ute camp they saw this morning.

"Ain't many Indians around, Joe. Just a few squaws and old men. Seems the bucks are out hunting somewhere," said Wheeler, still grinning. "They got food and horses there. Ain't that what we're after?"

"We could use some food, Joe," said Gus Deason, looking hungry.

"So we ride down there and just take what we want, is that it?" asked Joe, a little anger in his voice. "And what happens when their men return to find out we took what little food there is and stole all their sorry horses? Any of you want them Utes dogging our trail for the next couple of weeks while we try to steal more horses and take care of business in Brewster's Crossing?"

"I ain't worried about a bunch of stinking Indians," replied Wheeler, his grin turning to soberness, having doubts now about the wisdom of stirring up the Indians.

"I am," said Deason, frowning at Wheeler and having second thoughts about having the young gunman ride with them.

"Let's pass on this one, Wheeler," suggested Bob Hanley, who seemed to have more influence on Wheeler than anyone else in the party. "We get closer to Brewster's Crossing, we can find a ranch and there should be plenty of food and horses."

"Well...all right, then," said Wheeler, glancing at Rudy Beecher for his approval and getting it.

Joe spurred the black and headed up the trail toward Doan's Ferry, where they had ambushed the sheriff's posse and where Charlie Barker had died. Thinking of Charlie brought his anger back. Jake Whitmore would pay for making that lucky shot, but he wanted to see the man suffer before dying. He knew Bass Wheeler could take him in a gunfight, but somehow he had to find a way for Whitmore to hurt before the final bullet killed him.

Gus Deason rode to his side, worried. "Joe, maybe it wasn't such a good idea to bring Bass and Rudy along. What are we going to do with them?"

"You worry too much, Gus," responded Blackburn, glancing at him. "I need Bass to help me take down Whitmore, then you can have all his horses and cattle, too. I'll handle Bass, you just take care of all the livestock we steal."

"All right, Joe," replied Deason reluctantly as he dropped back to ride beside his younger brother, Lenny, who was just about as fat as he was.

Rounding a bend in the trail, Blackburn surprised the squaw who rode a sorrel horse. The Indian realized that she may be in trouble with these white men and turned to leave the trail. Wheeler saw her and spurred his horse hard to ride to her side before she made her escape.

"Hold on there, honey," said Wheeler, grinning as he reached for the reins of the bridle on her horse. "No need to be unfriendly to us white folks."

The squaw struck out with her quirt in her hand, landing the whip on the arms of Wheeler, who cried out in pain. She turned her horse to leave as Wheeler released his hold on the bridle, but Rudy Beecher and Curley Benson were upon her. Beecher struck out with his fist, knocking the woman from her horse. She fell hard to the ground, rolled over, and stood to run, but Benson was off his horse and upon her before she made good her escape.

She kicked him on the leg, and he cried out in pain as she struggled to get away. Lenny Deason was off his horse now and joined in the struggle, grabbing her arms and pinning them behind her. Wheeler dismounted, still holding his arm, a red whip mark on it. In his anger, he struck out at the woman with his open hand, slapping her hard in the face. She sagged against Lenny from the blow.

"Damn stinking Indian," said Wheeler, stepping back and rubbing his hurt arm.

Bob Hanley caught her sorrel horse and turned to the others. "She's got food here, boys. Let's take it and her horse and be on our way."

"We'll take her food, horse...and her," said Wheeler, grinning at the frightened woman, then glancing at the smiling Rudy Beecher. "She can warm our blankets tonight."

"We don't need this kind of trouble from the Indians, Bass," said Blackburn, sternly, disgusted with Wheeler and the rest of them. "Raping women ain't what we came to Utah for."

"She's just an Indian," said Beecher, protesting. "Besides, this is gonna be a long ride without women, so I say we keep her for awhile, show her a good time."

"Joe, she marked me with that quirt of hers," said Wheeler, angrily. "She's a gonna pay for that first, then we'll let her go."

"We don't need to stir up the Indians by raping their women, Bass," said Gus Deason, almost begging. "Let her go. We got her food and horse, ain't that enough?"

"It ain't, Gus," said Wheeler, holding up his arm to show Deason the red whip mark on his arm. "All we wanted to do was say hello and she does this to me. No, Gus, she pays for marking my gun hand."

"Come on, Bass. Let it pass," said Joe, realizing that Wheeler was within his rights to avenge the wrong done to him, but wanting to avoid being sidetracked from his own goal to get even with Jake Whitmore and make sure Paul Neel died this time.

"If you don't want any part of this, Joe, just ride on, but me and the rest of the men are going to have our way with the squaw first, then we'll catch up," said Wheeler, determined.

"We'll meet you at the ferry then," replied Blackburn, glancing at the young woman. Any other time, he would have stayed, but Whitmore and Neel were priority and he wanted nothing to distract him from that goal. He kicked his horse hard in the side and rode off, Bob Hanley and Gus Deason the only ones to follow.

Bass Wheeler stood watching the three men ride off, then turned to the others. "Let's build a fire and eat some of this food first, then we'll take turns with the squaw. Someone get a rope and tie her up good. We don't want this little Indian beauty to get away before we show her a good time."

EIGHT

Jake pulled the big gray to a quick stop in the front yard of the Thurston Ranch and leaped from the horse. He noticed the war lance appeared to be the same type as the one in his yard. He wanted to reach out to it and break it, but he knew the results, and he wanted to find out what had happened to Sarah first, then think this out. Now, he wished that he had taken Cody with him as the old man had suggested.

He entered the house, noticing the front door stood open, fear gripping him as he didn't see her in the room. "Sarah!" he called, panic beginning to take hold. "Where are you?"

He heard the muffled cry of the woman coming from the bedroom, and he went quickly to the door to open it, then drew his .44 and entered to see only her head above the blankets, fear on her tear-stained face. "Oh, Jake," she said, relief showing on her face as she recognized him.

He went to her and she came into his arms, the blankets falling from her. He felt her warm body against his, and she began to cry again, wrapping her arms around his neck and kissing his cheeks. Her golden hair was a mess, but at the moment, Jake wasn't noticing. Feelings rose inside that hadn't been there for some time; at least not since Rachel had aroused them in him before her sickness came.

"What happened?" he finally said, trying to look at her, but she continued to cling to him, shaking uncontrollably.

"The Indian...he came," she whispered, her whole body shivering as she buried her head into his shoulder, feeling the strong muscles and the strength he had. Fear still gripped her, but she knew she was safe now, wanting the closeness that he offered.

He attempted to disengage himself from her, afraid of the feelings that she had stirred in him, feelings that only Rachel had stirred. She still clung to him. "Please don't leave me. It was so frightening. I prayed you would come for me."

"I felt something last night," he finally said, surprised that he really didn't want this moment to pass, but knowing if he didn't do something now, this could get out of hand...and so soon after burying Rachel.

"You knew I was in danger?" she asked, wiping the tears away and allowing him to move her from his shoulder.

"I...I don't know what it was. Just knew I had to be here this morning. Should have come last night when I had the feelings." He noticed the thin nightgown barely covered her rising and falling breast, but he allowed his eyes to linger there for a moment more before turning away. He stood and walked to the window to peek outside.

She reached for a robe, watching the back of this man who had stirred emotions inside her that she had felt only once when Richard Woodrow had kissed her at the dance last year. She felt safe with Jake Whitmore. Really more than safe. She stood and placed the robe around her shoulders, feeling its warmth in the crisp morning air. "You were right, Jake. I should gone went to town when I had the chance. I'm sorry."

"You didn't know. Neither did I," he said, slowly turning to her and noticing that she now had the robe on, for what little good it did. She was beautiful and her hair fell past her shoulders, giving her an angelic look. The emotions within still lingered, and he continued to fight for control. This woman stirred him like none others, not even his Rachel. He felt guilty and walked to the door.

"Have you eaten?" she asked, following him into the next room.

"No," he responded, a little nervous. "I'll check the barn and see if your horse is still there. I'm taking you to my place for now. You shouldn't be alone out here."

She smiled as he left the house. There was no "Do you want to go with me?" It was, "I'm taking you." She liked that even though she thought of herself as independent; the incident this morning had shaken that confidence, and right now she would do as she was told. Jake Whitmore stirred deep emotions, and she wanted to be with him. Right now, she would do anything he asked.

She entered the small kitchen, pulled a skillet out from a drawer, and placed it on the iron stove, then reached for the firewood beside it and started a fire. When he returned, she had the fire going and biscuits made to place inside the oven. "No bacon," she said, glancing at him as he sat at the table to watch her.

"Probably stolen by those outlaws," replied Jake, wishing now that he hadn't mentioned them. It brought up too many recent hurts. "Horse is still in the barn. Guess them Indians wanted only to scare you...or me."

"Jake, one had a deep scar on his face. He seemed to be the leader. I woke and there was a room full of Indians. It scared me to death."

"What happened then?" he asked, still watching her as she moved about the kitchen.

She slowly turned to face him. "The scar-faced one asked me if I was your woman."

Now he understood their visit this morning. "Sarah, forget the breakfast and let's go now. It ain't safe here."

She saw the alarm on his face and knew he was serious. She quickly put the fire out and went into the bedroom, gathering up a few things. When she returned to the room he was gone, but she saw that he had her horse saddled now and was leading him from the barn. She went to the porch to wait and saw that the war lance remained in its place in the yard.

Jake reached the porch and helped her mount, then turned to the lance in the ground. He hesitated only a moment, then seized it, broke it in two with his knee, and threw it to the ground. He scanned the rims of the canyon before mounting and drew his Winchester model 73 carbine from the saddle gun boot, resting the rifle across the front of the saddle. "Let's go. They're probably watching us right now."

They rode out of the ranch quickly and headed south toward Red Rock Pass. The young Ute stood from his hiding place behind the cedar tree halfway up the canyon wall and grinned, then turned toward his horse hidden farther up the canyon. Patches would want to know that the white man had broken the warning lance. It would be interesting to see what Patches would do now that Whitmore had accepted the challenge.

Patches stood as the morning sun climbed above the rim of the mountain that overlooked the entrance to the cave. He wore nothing except a white loincloth; the crisp morning air chilled him, but he endured the cold knowing that his sufferings would be seen by the Sky People, and that would help him in his pleadings.

Lame Deer sat behind him beating a drum slowly, watching the sun rise also. Others sat around the small fire, all naked except for the loincloths they wore. They watched as Patches began their sacrifice by wailing a singsong chant as he raised his arms and hands toward the sun.

"Oh Great Spirit, father of all, I Patches, stand before your child, the sun, to give him honor this day as we begin our fasting and prayers for your guidance in the matter of the white men and the one who pollutes Red Rock Pass." Lame Deer continued to beat the drum with the slow rhythm that he had started at the beginning of the sacrifice. "We heed your call from the Thunder Moon. We seek your guidance."

Lame Deer increased the beat of the drum and all stood except the drummer. "Oh, Great Sun Spirit, child of the Great Spirit, we call upon you for guidance. Have pity on your servants, the Uncompahgre Ute. A few of your faithful gather together to plead for guidance and understanding from the sign of the Thunder Moon. What would you have us do?" asked Patches, still standing with his hands and arms outstretched toward the sun.

Patches then fell to the ground and stretched out his arms and hands on the cold ground toward the sun. The others followed, except Lame Deer, who increased the beat of the drum, then suddenly stopped, and he, too, fell to the earth and waited. They lay in that position for some time, then Patches stood and the others followed.

Lame Deer returned to his drum and started a slow beat again, the same as he had done at the beginning of the sacrifice. Patches led the group around the fire in a slow shuffle four times, stopping once to face the east, chanting the low singsong chant that he had started before. Four more times the group circled the fire, stopping this time to face the west with Patches to utter the same chant. Another four times around the fire and the group stopped to face the north. The same chant came from Patches, and a final four times around the fire brought the group to face the south. Finished with the final chant, Patches led the group into the cave.

Lame Deer continued to beat the drum until all had entered the holy cave of the Utes, then quickly threw dirt over the fire. Satisfied that it was completely covered, he stood and took the drum with him to enter the cave.

Inside, Patches gathered the warriors around another fire, this one larger than the one outside. Their shadows danced off the red walls of the cave as they found places around the fire. Lame Deer found a place behind them near the mouth of the cave, adjusted the drum in front of him, and waited for Patches to begin.

"Oh, Great Spirit, we have honored the Sun Spirits this day, and later tonight we honor the Moon Spirits, but now we show respect for the Cave Spirits and the other children you have created," said Patches, raising his arms toward the ceiling of the cave.

Lame Deer began to beat the drum slowly as he had done outside the cave. The others waited and watched Patches as he began another dance around the fire. This time he danced alone, circling the fire to stop after one circle to face the east, chant, then resume the dance. He slowly circled the fire to stop once more and face the west, chant again and continue until he had stopped to face the north and south to utter the same chant. It was different from the one he had performed outside the cave.

Lame Deer continued the same slow beating rhythm of the drum as Patches danced again around the fire, repeating the same dance and chant as before, stopping first to the west then the north and south and finally to the east. Finished, he resumed the dance, to stop first to the north and end at the west and finally completed the dance by stopping first to the south and ending at the north.

Lame Deer increased the beat of the drum now, and all the other men stood to follow Patches around the fire in a slow shuffle as they had done outside the cave earlier. Patches stopped after making the circle around the fire each time to one point of the compass to chant the singsong wail. Finished, the warriors returned to their places around the fire, but Patches continued the shuffle.

Lame Deer stopped his beating of the drum, and Patches stood facing the corridor of the cave tunnel that lead to the sacred drawings at the rear of the cave. "Oh, Great Cave Spirits, home of the Thunder Spirits, we seek your guidance," wailed Patches, stretching his hands and arms toward the dark opening.

Patches danced around the fire once more then went toward the corridor entrance in the slow shuffle while chanting. The others stood and circled the fire, then followed Patches to the entrance. They chanted and wailed their singsong chants until Patches stopped. One Bear exited the entrance dressed in a bonnet of eagle feathers, flapping his arms, where feathers were attached also.

They stood aside for One Bear to enter the main cavern and dance around the fire. Patches followed, mimicking the big bird that One Bear represented. The others followed in the shuffle and Lame Deer increased the tempo of the drum. All found their places around the fire again except for Patches and One Bear.

As the drum beat faster, Patches followed close behind the big bird, a medicine staff now in his hands, chanting another singsong chant. One Bear danced and swooped in and out of the group and the fire with Patches following, shaking the staff at him, his chants more of a plea than a chant now. One Bear finally stopped, and Patches touched him on the head with the medicine staff, and One Bear kneeled before Patches.

The assembled warriors stood as a group, picked up the chant of Patches, and closed in on One Bear, each to touch the staff as it rested upon the head of the man who represented the Thunderbird. When all had completed their touching, Lame Deer stopped the drum; all, including Lame Deer, fell to the floor of the cavern and waited. They lay there for some time before Patches finally stood and walked to the containers holding the water from the springs at Red Rock Pass. He took a deep drink, and as the others stood, each took a long drink of the water then returned to the fire to take their places again. When all had finished, Patches returned the container to the floor and walked slowly to the gathered warriors, smiling.

"The spirits are pleased with our sacrifice thus far. We now will rest, each man to reflect upon our pleadings and continue to cleanse his thoughts and purify himself for the next stage of our pleadings," said Patches, sitting beside the fire. "We eat no food, but drink only water from the sacred springs of Red Rock Pass. When the moon is up tonight, we pray to her for the gifts that the night might bring us."

Jake woke startled and looked around to see that it was dawn now, the early morning sunlight creeping through the window. Something had woke him and he sat up from the bedding he had on the floor in front of the fireplace. He looked at the bedroll of Cody Wedgeworth and saw that the old man was gone. He stood, reaching for his jacket and the Winchester lying beside him. He reached the table and took up his hat, then went to the door to open it carefully and make as little noise as possible, knowing any noise would wake Sarah Thurston, who slept in his bed in the next room.

Once on the porch, he looked around in the dim light, but saw nothing except the outline of his barn. He stepped off the porch to be met by the yellow dog. Buster's ears were alert as he glanced toward the cliffs along the pass. Jake heard the noise again, like drums in the distance. He buttoned the jacket, the cool crisp morning air causing him to shiver.

A slight noise behind him caused him to pivot quickly, the carbine leveled. He lowered it as he recognized Cody in the dim light of morning. "You scared me, old man," said Jake, relieved.

"A little jumpy this morning, ain't ya?" asked Cody, smiling as he cradled the double-barrel shotgun in his arms. "You hear the drums, too?"

"Sounds like drums. What do you make of it?" asked Jake, glancing back down the canyon toward the noise of the drum beats.

"Our friend, Patches, probably making big medicine to his Indian Gods," said Cody, frowning. "He's taking this sacred ground thing seriously. You sure you want to stay?"

“If we leave, then what?” asked Jake, looking at the older man, a worried look on his face.

“Probably just the beginning of things to come,” said Cody, frowning again. “Clearing the springs is the first step. Raids on isolated ranches comes next, then maybe an attack on the town. The Indian has got hisself worked up pretty good over this sacred ground thing. If he succeeds here, he’ll get braver and declare everything around here holy ground, especially if he can get more warriors to believe in him.”

“We stay and finish it,” said Jake, determined, but concerned. “I’d rather die here than give it up.”

“You might just do that, son,” said Cody, turning as Sarah came from the house to stand on the porch, a robe wrapped around her, but doing little good in keeping out the cold of the morning.

“I hear drums,” she said, frightened. “What does it mean, Jake?”

“Means Patches isn’t going to let this pass. He’ll be coming soon as he believes his spirits are on his side,” replied Jake, glancing at her. “Nothing we can do, but wait.”

“I’m frightened, Jake. Will he try to kill us and burn the place?” she asked, her face turning a faint shade of blue from the cold. “What about Karl’s place? Will they burn it down, too?”

“They may try to kill us if we don’t leave. Depends on what magic they can conjure up from their Indian spirits,” answered Cody, walking to the porch. “We had best start getting this place ready to defend properly.”

“What about that Indian war lance in the yard? Are you going to leave it there?” she asked, pointing to the lance still in the ground.

“You don’t know about them Indian warning lances do you?” asked Cody, looking at her.

“No, not really. They left one in my yard, and Jake broke it in two before we left,” she replied, frowning. “What do they mean?”

Cody glanced at Jake, a serious look on his face. “You didn’t tell me about a warning lance at the Thurston Ranch, Jake,” said Cody, not pleased.

“It was for Sarah, not the springs,” answered Jake, turning to walk toward the barn. “I’m going to check on the horses.”

“Cody, what did Jake mean about the warning lance was for me and not the springs?” asked Sarah, frightened more as she watched Jake walk away.

“Them warning lances is a challenge thing,” replied Cody, avoiding her eyes as she turned to stare at him. “They put one here to challenge us for the rights of the springs and warn us away. Since we ain’t picked it up or broke it, we ain’t disputing their rights to the springs nor giving up our rights neither. It's one of them things where the Indian spirits gotta work it out without a big fight if possible."

"And if you break it or throw it away, then what?" she asked, looking hard at him for a truthful answer.

"Then it means we're a gonna fight for the springs. We accept the challenge of a duel for the rights of this land, winner takes all," replied Cody, noticing Jake had entered the barn now.

"Why the lance at Karl's place?"

"It was a challenge for you. A warning that Patches claims a right to you," said Cody, turning to enter the house. "You said Jake broke the lance?"

"Yes, what does that mean, Cody?" she asked, following him inside.

"Trouble, my dear. A lot of trouble."

Joe Blackburn rolled from his sleeping blankets to reach for his pistol at his side and glance at Bob Hanley, who was already awake in the dim light of the morning. "What the hell is that?" asked Joe, grabbing for the blanket to cover his shoulders in the cool of the morning. "Sounds like drums off in them hills near Red Rock Pass."

"Indian drums," replied Hanley, a worried look on his face. "Knew Bass and them others should have left that Indian woman alone."

"You think they're after us?" asked Joe, casting a hard look at Bass Wheeler, who slowly rose from the several blankets he had stacked on the ground to sleep on.

"Who else would they be beating them drums for?" asked Hanley, glancing at Rudy Beecher, who crawled to his side, his pistol out, looking around.

"Was that little Indian gal worth it, Rudy?" asked Blackburn, disgusted. "Now, you boys got them Utes hot on us. We'll have to ride for a town somewhere or back to Colorado until this blows over."

"We didn't do nothing but have a good time with her," answered Beecher, still frightened as he searched the dim morning light for Indians. "She liked it after awhile."

"Sure she did," said Blackburn, reaching for his boots. "Let's get the hell out of here. I don't like the spot we're in if they try and jump us."

Gus Deason was up now, a worried look on his face. "See, I told you so, Lenny," he said, turning to his brother who lay beside him. "You just had to get some of that Indian gal and now see what it got us."

"Everybody else did too," said Lenny, trying to defend himself. "How'd we know them bucks would get all upset over us taking a little tumble with one of their women. Like Rudy said, she liked it. What's the big deal?"

"We didn't kill her," said Rawlins, looking at Mullens for support. "No reason for them to get all worked up."

"What's the plan, Joe?" said Wheeler, dragging his saddle behind him as he approached.

"Think we ought to get on with why we're here and drift over to Red Rock Pass and check out Whitmore's place. If he's around, we'll make a try at him, if not, we'll ride in and take what we want, then steal all his cattle we can find," said Joe, standing and pulling his blankets together. "Then we hightail it out of here until these Indians settle down. The squaw wasn't worth all the trouble she's a bringing us."

"Maybe, but I enjoyed myself and so did she," said Wheeler, grinning. "Should have stayed, Joe. She was good...for an Indian."

Joe didn't answer, but reached for his saddle and headed for the picket line and the big black. The others quickly followed to saddle their horses and follow Joe Blackburn out of the camp without breakfast, leaving the small fire still smoking.

"Something is eating on Joe," said Deason, leaning over to speak to Bob Hanley. "He ain't like the old Joe I used to know."

"I've noticed. Any other time, Joe would have been the leader in taking that squaw," replied Hanley, looking at the back of their leader as he led the men up the trail toward Red Rock Pass. "I guess Charlie getting killed sort of snapped something in him. He won't be the same until this Whitmore fellow is dead."

"Ain't a gonna be easy killing the man," said Deason, worried. "I hear that Whitmore is good with his pistol, and he must be a crack shot if he killed old Charlie from eight hundred yards out with that Sharps."

"Whatever, we gotta back Joe, especially the way he's been acting lately. I've rode with him for years and never seen him act this way," said Hanley, glancing at the fat man.

"I suppose you're right, Bob. Joe has always been fair with me and the boys. I owe him a lot. Reason I rode with him on this crazy job anyway," replied Deason, frowning.

"Things will look better once we get some of Whitmore's cattle rounded up, and we get away from them Indian drums. There's eight of us. We can handle them Indians if they want to cause us trouble," said Hanley, neither fully convinced that things were going to look better with the mood Joe Blackburn was in, nor that eight of them could handle a bunch of Indians bent on revenge for the rape of their woman.

Once Jake Whitmore was dead, maybe Joe would turn back to the old

Joe they all liked. This one was in a killing mood, and when he was that way, he was dangerous not only to the person or persons he was after, but to everyone around him. Hanley settled into his saddle, resigned to see this job through. There really wasn't much he could do about it right now anyway.

NINE

Lame Deer saw Patches turn to him as he sat beside the fire with his drum, ready to begin at the signal of the shaman. He glanced up to see that the moon climbed above the rim in its fullness and knew it was late into the night. They should have begun by now, but he also knew that Patches wanted everything to be just right.

Even the announcements from Two Ponies that Morning Star had been raped by white men and that the main camp had moved across the Dolores River hadn't brought any sign of concern from their leader. Lame Deer knew that it had to be on his mind, but was glad that Patches didn't show it for the sake of the young warriors in their band. If they were to gain the favor of the spirits, all would have to put aside personal things, even at the cost of loved ones.

Two Ponies had also announced that Whitmore had broken the warning lance placed to challenge the rights to the white woman with the golden hair. That would be interesting to watch, as Patches would have to deal with that, but thus far Whitmore hadn't taken the challenge for the springs. Two Ponies said the lance still remained where they had placed it. The white man was a smart one to wait.

Patches nodded to him, and he knew it was time to begin the sacrifice to the moon and night spirits. He began to beat the drum slowly as Patches turned to gaze at the moon and lift his hands and arms toward the bright object in the night sky. They all wore nothing except the loincloths, and Lame Deer was glad he was near the small fire for what little warmth it gave in the cold night air.

Patches began by starting a slow shuffle in a circle near the fire, chanting a different chant than the one he had uttered during the day inside the cave. The circle expanded as he circled the fire and Lame Deer, then returned to the spot where he had begun. "Oh, Great Moon Spirit, night child of the

Great Spirit, a few of your servants gather to ask for your guidance concerning the matters of the sacred springs where a white man lives and has polluted the springs with his presence. We also ask what must be done about the invasion of the whites into our lands and the abuse they inflict upon us. We sacrifice for answers."

Lame Deer increased the beat of the drum, and Patches began another dance, wailing as he circled the others and increasing the wail to a near scream to be in time with the increased beat of the drum. With a final loud beat, Lame Deer stopped and so did Patches. He fell to the ground, lying prone, facing the moon with outstretched hands. The others followed, and the group lay stretched out before the moon for some time.

Patches slowly stood, and the others followed to regain their former positions around the fire. Patches faced the moon and stretched forth his hands again. Lame Deer started beating the drum ever so slowly. "Oh, Great One, we paint our bodies in honor of you," said Patches, reaching for a bowl of paint that One Bear offered him. Patches smeared a strip of white paint across his naked chest, then his nose.

"I, Patches, mark my body in white to show my purity and cleansed body to the spirits that they may know that I am one with you this night." The others followed, but said nothing as Lame Deer continued the very slow beat of the drum.

Patches reached for another bowl of paint offered him by One Bear. This time he marked his chest with a single line across it just below the white one, then marked his face just below the white line. "Oh, Great One, I mark my body with red to show the spirits the courage I have and the blood I will give to accomplish the goal the Thunder Moon has set for us."

The young shaman reached for a third bowl of paint offered by One Bear. This time he painted a yellow stripe on his body and one on his face, each below the red stripe, and then glanced at the moon. "Great One, I mark my body with the yellow paint to show my power from my cleansing that I may accept the wisdom and guidance that you will show us." The others followed in marking their bodies as they had done before.

Lame Deer continued to beat the drum slowly as Patches continued. This time, Patches took brown paint and marked his body and face below the line of yellow and stood before the moon. "Great One in the night sky, I mark my body with the brown paint of the earth, our mother, who gives us life and keeps us safe. In her honor, I seek your guidance."

A fifth bowl was offered him by One Bear; this time he took green paint and drew the line across his bronze chest just below the brown line, then marked his face and stood before the full moon. "Great One that watches over us at night, I mark my body with green paint in honor of the spirits that give life to the trees, the grass, and the water, that we, the children of the Sky People may live. Through them, we seek guidance in our mission and wisdom that we may all understand what must be done and how it is to be accomplished."

A final bowl was offered, and Patches slowly entered his fingers into this bowl and brought forth a blue paint that he first showed to the moon; then he marked his body above the white one, then with care made sure he drew the line of blue just above the white one on his face. Finished, he glanced back to see that the others had done the same. He turned slowly to face the moon.

"Oh Great One, as you can see, we finish with the blue paint to show our understanding of the sacred mission that we must perform for the Thunder Moon. With this holy mark, we will now enter into the cave of the Thunder Spirits to ask for their guidance. We ask that you hear our pleadings and grant us understanding of all that we must do."

Lame Deer increased the tempo of the drumbeat as Patches began a slow shuffle dance around the fire, chanting another singsong chant, having picked up an eagle feather to hold in one hand as he danced. Others joined him as they felt the mood to join, and when all had finally entered the dance, Patches led them to the cave and entered.

Lame Deer continued to beat the drum slowly until Patches reappeared, this time carrying the medicine staff to be followed by the others dressed in head bonnets of eagle feathers, some with feathers flowing down their backs, others, the young ones, with lesser feathers in their bonnets. They all danced around the fire as Lame Deer increased the tempo, and with a final effort, the drum roared loudly in its beats with the Indians dancing quickly, their wailing chants growing louder as they danced around the fire.

With a final blast of the drum, Patches stopped, stretched forth his hands and arms toward the moon, then fell to the earth to lie still. The others followed his example, and Lame Deer placed the now silent drum beside him and joined his fellow warriors on the ground. They would lie there in the cold of night till morning to face the rising sun and perform the sun ceremony of the previous day, making sure not to miss anything that had been done before.

Jake knew it was late at night, but he fought back the sleep his body demanded and continued to work. The place wasn't nearly completed for the defense that he knew would come sooner or later. That afternoon, he had caught a glimpse of a Ute in the cedars near the springs, watching and waiting. Thus far, that was all they had done since scaring Sarah half to death. He couldn't figure out why Patches would want to challenge the right to her unless he had seen him at the stage with her and at the ranch to conclude that she was his woman.

Now that Sarah had told the Ute she was indeed Jake's woman, the challenge was thrust upon him. He still didn't understand why he had broken the lance in her yard, but he had and now he would have to face the Ute if the Indian pushed the issue. He turned as Cody walked to him, several boards in his hands.

"This ought to do for this window, Jake. The place is looking better to withstand an attack."

"If they get close to the house, they can rip these planks off the window with ease," said Jake, worried as he took one of the boards to nail in place.

"True, but they'll make a lot of noise doing it, and that should give us a chance to be ready for them," replied Cody, frowning. "Ain't got much choice in the matter with just the two of us."

"Why would Patches want Sarah?" asked Jake, still thinking about her and the Indian.

"Probably cause you got her, and he wants to sidetrack you on the real purpose of this conflict...the springs," answered the old man. "Still think you ought to take her to town. I can handle things till you get back. As long as them Utes are still working on building up their medicine, they ain't a gonna attack."

"If I do, they may ambush me on the trail. Don't think we ought to separate just yet," said Jake, still worried. "We got them water barrels filled?"

"Sarah did that right after dark," replied Cody, glancing at the porch where she sat on the rocking chair watching them, the yellow dog at her feet. "She's a good woman, Jake. Is there some other reason you want her here?"

Jake's face reddened with embarrassment, but was glad it was dark outside to cover it from the old man. Cody Wedgeworth was a lot smarter than people gave him credit for. Jake searched for that answer as he continued to work. Was there another reason for keeping her here? With all honesty, he concluded that there was. She had stirred that emotion only Rachel had given him, and he didn't want to let go of it with Sarah. That was the real truth and he knew it, but felt guilty for even thinking such things with Rachel not dead a month. He quickly suppressed the feeling and continued the work.

Cody grinned to himself, having a good idea as to why the woman remained. He even saw that same look in Sarah's eyes when she looked at Jake. It was good for both of them if they lived to do anything about it later.

Finished with the window, the two men returned to the porch. "Sarah, you really ought to get some sleep. It's late," said Jake, smiling at her as he sat on the edge of the porch beside her. "Me and Cody got some work to do on the barn, then cut a few extra loopholes in the window shutters and we'll be about as ready as we'll get to defend this place."

"I'd rather remain close to you," she said, glancing at him as she continued to rock, a blanket wrapped around her shoulders to keep warm. "Why don't we all get some rest and finish up in the morning?"

"Best to do this at night when the Utes can't see what we're doing," said Cody, settling down beside the yellow dog. "Don't want them to know what we have done, besides there is something else I want to show you two...just in case things don't go right when them Utes come. Want to show you now before the moon rises."

"What's that, Cody," asked Jake, surprised, yet really knowing Cody Wedgeworth was full of surprises.

"Something I built when I first put the place up years ago. Just for this very reason," he said, standing and walking to the front door.

They followed him as he went into the bedroom of the house, moved the bed, and pulled back the rug that lay under it. With a lantern held by Jake, the old man took his big knife and pried on a plank on the floor to loosen it, then pulled it up to reveal a false floor. Several more planks were removed to expose a tunnel.

"You never told me about this, Cody," said Jake, a little put out with the old man.

"You never asked, besides, didn't ever see any need for it," replied the man, taking the lantern from him to show the way to the tunnel. "It's just wide enough for one person at a time to crawl. It leads out to the hill behind the house. Ain't got no entrance out there. The last two or three feet, I never finished. There should be an old shovel at the end. Think I might ought to finish it."

"We can do that tomorrow and leave the last foot so as not to give it away," said Jake, grinning. Old Cody was full of surprises, and he now believed the old man had known this pass was sacred ground to the Utes. Why else would he have dug this escape tunnel?

Cody replaced the planks and looked at Jake, then avoided his staring eyes. Jake didn't want to push the issue about the springs. What was done was done, and now was the time to finish the defenses to this place. He took the lantern and returned to the front room.

When they got to the porch, the sound of the drums could be heard loud and clear. Sarah clung to Jake as Cody walked to the edge of the porch to listen. Buster had stirred too, alert as the noise of the drum increased. "Them Utes are now a working themselves up day and night," said Cody, frowning. "Never heard of them taking this long to build themselves into a good fight."

"What do you make of it then," asked Sarah, still clinging to Jake and liking it.

"Must be some religious thing concerning the springs. Never could understand much about their religion," said the old man, turning nervously to glance at the couple behind him. "They can get really worked up over some religious thing. Might take them awhile."

"We had better finish at the barn then," replied Jake, worried again as he slipped his arm around the thin waist of the woman. "Sarah, you should really get some rest. Me and Cody will be at the barn."

"I think I'll just wait on the porch for you and look at the moon. It's still full, the same as the night we rode into Brewster's Crossing," she said, glancing up at him, liking the closeness they shared then...and now.

He nodded his approval, hugged her tight, then followed Cody off the porch and headed for the barn, a warm feeling still inside for the woman he had just left. Maybe Rachel would understand. Maybe that was why she had returned to him in the dream to tell him that it was all right.

Patches stood in front of the entrance to the corridor that lead to the depths of the cave. His painted body glowed in the firelight as he turned to face the others who carried torches in their hands. "Brothers, we now enter the sacred home of the Thunder Spirits. If you feel that you are not yet ready to enter, then remain, but feel no shame. When you are prepared, then enter, but not before. We can ill afford to anger the Thunder Spirits in their home," said Patches, staring hard at the warriors.

He turned and entered, chanting as he passed the sign of the Thunder Gods in the image of a Thunderbird. Most followed, but a few, knowing they were not ready, stayed. They watched the others as they walked slowly down the corridor to the main entrance of the deep cavern.

There, Patches stopped, and Lame Deer stepped forward with his drum to begin beating it slowly. Patches began a singsong chant that often raised in pitch as he entered. A few went no farther, their fear gripping them as the others entered. Lame Deer followed, still beating his drum slowly.

Inside the cavern, the floor dropped and Patches had to climb down the fallen rocks to the next level. He turned, holding the medicine staff in one hand and a torch in another for the others to follow safely. At the foot of the downward climb, Patches pointed with the torch to several drawings. "See, my brothers, our forefathers hunted the deer, the elk, the buffalo, and antelope in this land. See their drawings and remember these animals and the strong spirits they have. They are our brothers too, and will help us."

The shaman turned and led the group forward to stop along the wide corridor walls to point to another drawing. Many drew back, frightened as they saw the sign of the Thunderbird, a symbol of the Thunder Spirits. Men dressed in feathers of eagles worshipped before the Thunderbird, each with a medicine staff. "Our forefathers worshipped the Thunder Spirits. We have fallen short in our duties in this matter. We must return to the old ways and place the Thunder Spirits in their proper place in our religion," said Patches, pleased that none had thus far withdrawn to join the weak ones who waited in the corridor or in the main part of the cave.

Farther down the descending path, Patches stopped again to show the men a battle scene. Bronze warriors battled others in a fight to the death, with many drawings showing the feathered warriors killing or enslaving the lesser-dressed warriors. Patches said nothing, letting the meanings of these drawing remain unknown to his followers. He too, really didn't understand them. It would be best not to let the others know he didn't know either.

Again the path widened and led downward. Patches heard the drip of water and knew he was close to the drawings that would really test the faith of his men. Reaching the point where the floor of the path they followed turned damp, he stopped and put his torch closer to the wall for all to see. "This, my brothers is the power the Thunder Spirits have. See, our people defeat the white man."

Many stepped closer to get a better look at the drawings, not sure if what they saw was real. Depicted were bronze warriors killing white warriors or enslaving them. Other drawings showed the white warriors as slaves doing the tasks of women. One drawing showed a horse. Patches smiled as he saw many look on in amazement and glance toward him with the nod of approval.

"Come, my brothers, there is more, but only the pure in heart may enter in the final resting place of the Thunder Spirits. We must whisper from now on. The spirits may be resting within," said Patches, lowering his voice.

They entered a small cavern, and Patches placed his torch in a notch that had been made in the rock wall many centuries ago. He walked to the center of the room and started a small fire of wood that he had previously brought to the spot for the final ceremony. He glanced around as the light of the fire revealed several drawings which he didn't understand; but the markings or sign symbols of the Thunderbird and the lightning across the full moon he did understand, and as the others looked on, he saw in their faces that they too understood that they were standing on holy ground.

"Brothers, I will now sacrifice to the Thunder Spirits and the Thunder Moon that lives here," he whispered, glancing at the others who now took places around the small fire. He noticed that several others, feeling unworthy, had made their way back up the path to the others who waited. He was disappointed in them, but understood fully and was pleased that they took this as serious as he did. With their strength and faith, they would have their visions and would then know what was required of them.

Patches began by dancing around the fire to the beat of the drum, the medicine staff raised above his head. He chanted as he made the shuffle dance around the fire several times, then stopped as the tempo of the drum increased. He took yellow paint and made the sign of the moon on his lower chest just under the stripes of paint made earlier, then with blue paint he made the sign of a lightning blot across the moon. This finished, he danced around the fire several more times and stopped to face the men.

"I have marked myself in the sign of a Thunder Moon, and thus I pray to him for a vision and will not eat or drink until he has granted me one," said Patches, looking at them seriously. He then went to the side of the fire, and in a prone position on the floor of the cave, he waited, facing the drawings of the Thunder Moon.

One Bear stood, took the medicine staff of Patches and began a slow shuffle dance around the fire several times, then stopped and looked at the others as he painted a red bird in the form of a Thunderbird on his chest. Finished, he danced around the fire and stopped to face the men once more. "I have marked myself in the sign of a Thunder Spirit, and thus I pray to them for a vision and will not eat or drink until they have granted me one." He too, fell to the floor of the cave in a prone position facing the drawings of the Thunder Spirits and waited.

Lame Deer followed, dancing around the fire as another warrior took the drum. He marked himself with the sign of an eagle in white and faced the others. "I have marked myself in white in the sign of the eagle and pray to him for a vision. I will not eat or drink until he has granted me a vision." With that, he fell to the floor to lie beside One Bear.

Wild Horse followed to dance the same dance with the medicine staff and mark his body in brown with the sign of the snake. "I have marked myself in brown in the sign of the brown snake and pray to him for a vision. I will not eat or drink until he has granted me one." Wild Horse joined the others on the floor, the drum still beating slowly.

No others stood, but all remained silent, deep in their own thoughts as the drum continued to beat slowly. They all waited for the visions that they knew would come to these four faithful men. They knew that the old ways had been returned to as Patches had preached. Now, they waited patiently for the confirmations of his preaching.

Joe Blackburn reined in his black at the barn of the Thurston Ranch and dismounted. "Looks like someone has been working on the place," he said, glancing around. "Bob, check out the house."

"This the place you gunned down the Mormon woman, Joe?" asked Bass Wheeler, grinning as he dismounted. "Hear it was a real quick draw on your part."

Blackburn cast him a hard stare and didn't answer the jab from the young gunfighter, a little anger building inside at the insult. He led the black inside, noticing work had been done on the place, confirming that someone may be living here so soon after they had killed the couple and stole their horses. He walked to the stalls and noticed one had fresh horse droppings and then turned to the others. "Someone has been here. Buck, you and Rusty go help Bob."

The two young thieves quickly left the barn and headed for the house. "Why you so worried about someone being here, Joe? We can handle them," responded Wheeler, glancing to Rudy Beecher for support and getting it.

"Cause we killed two people here, that's why," answered Blackburn harshly as he turned on Wheeler. "You had best watch your tongue, Bass."

"No cause to get all bent out of shape," said Wheeler, realizing that now wasn't the time for poking fun at Blackburn.

"Maybe we had best ride on and find another place for the night," suggested Gus Deason, worried. "Don't want to bring down trouble on us if we don't have to."

"You worry too much, Gus. I'm a gonna sleep with a roof over my head tonight," replied Blackburn, turning as Bob Hanley entered the barn, followed by Buck and Rusty.

"Nobody here, Joe," said Hanley, frowning. "Looks like there was just a woman here for awhile. Found this broken Indian lance in the front yard.

What do you think?"

Joe walked to Hanley, taking the broken lance to examine it, frowning as he turned it over. "Don't know much about them Utes, but it looks like they may have rode in here and took whoever was a staying at the ranch."

"Maybe we might ought to ride on," said Wheeler, getting worried now. "Them Utes may be looking for us."

"I wonder why?" responded Blackburn, angry now as he threw the lance down.

"You still mad at us about taking that squaw?" asked Wheeler, his own anger building. "Was a time you would have been a leading us in raping that Ute woman."

Blackburn turned on Wheeler, his anger showing. "Well, Bass, this ain't the time, nor the place. We got other things more important to be a doing."

"Ain't nothing more important than women and money," said Beecher, grinning. "Or maybe a good bottle of whiskey."

"Shut up, Rudy," said Blackburn, turning his anger upon the other man. "We'll get the money and women later, but right now, we got a back-shooting lawman to kill and another old broken-down badge carrier to kill later."

"You're really serious about killing this Whitmore fellow, aren't you?" asked Wheeler, realizing now that killing the man was the sole purpose of this ride into Utah as far as Blackburn was concerned.

"Yeah, I'm serious about it. First thing in the morning, I'm riding over to Red Rock Pass and taking a crack at him," answered Blackburn, trying to control his hate and anger, but failing. "You riding with me?"

"One of the reasons I came with you, isn't it?" responded Wheeler, grinning.

"Good, we'll let Gus and the others start rounding up the cattle around here while we take care of business. We'll take Bob and Rudy with us. That ought to be enough to smoke the polecat out and kill him."

"When do we kill Neel?" asked Beecher, smiling. "I owe him one anyway from back in Colorado."

"When we finish off Whitmore there won't be no law in Brewster's Crossing. Gus can round up the cattle from Whitmore's range, and we'll just ride into that little town, kill Neel, and rob their little bank," said Blackburn, pleased with the plan. "Then we sell the stock in Granite and live high on the hog for awhile. Been thinking about riding over to Cripple Creek or Leadville, too."

"What about these Utes that are hanging around here?" asked Deason, worried. "They'll be looking for us."

"Ain't worried about no stinking Indians," said Blackburn, glancing at the fat man. "They're probably already moving their camp into Colorado."

"Yeah, you're probably right," replied Deason, satisfied that everything was going to be all right.

The men unsaddled their horses and headed for the house as the sun slowly sank behind the rims of the mountains in the canyon. They failed to notice the lone Ute hidden behind the cedar trees on the side of the canyon. The warrior frowned, his painted face blending in with his surroundings of green, brown, yellow, red, and white. Only the blue stood out, but that made no difference as the men entered the house, content to be sleeping under a roof. The warrior turned slowly and made his way to his horse, then mounted and rode toward the sacred cave.

TEN

Jake Whitmore opened his eyes quickly, a feeling of danger inside disturbed him. Something wasn't right. He glanced across the room to where Cody should have been, but the old man wasn't there. He turned to see the fire in the fireplace as it burned slowly, giving off little light. Jake turned over to glance about the room, but didn't see the old man anywhere.

Removing the blanket, he stood and moved his bedroll away from the fireplace, then reached for his .44 caliber Smith and Wesson pistol on the table. He went to the front door, then noticed Cody at the kitchen window, a Winchester in his hands. The old man glanced at him, frowned, and returned his attention to the outside.

"Didn't want to wake you," he said, looking back through the loophole in the window. "Ain't seen nothing yet."

"I got a feeling, Cody," said Jake, glancing through the loophole in the door. "Think I'll take a walk outside. It's getting light, but the sun ain't up yet."

"I'll cover you," said Cody, walking to him. "Ain't seen the dog this morning neither."

Jake opened the door slowly, peeking out into the dim light of the morning before leaving the house. He didn't see the yellow dog, which was unusual, as Buster was at the house this time of the morning, but he knew the dog roamed the area at times. This could be one of them.

He walked to the steps on the porch, looking hard into the morning light, the uneasy feeling still lingering. Just what it was he couldn't put a finger on, but he had learned long ago to trust his feelings. Jake stepped off the porch and heard the dog under the steps. Buster growled. He knew something was wrong then and turned to climb the steps back to the porch as the report of a rifle broke the morning silence.

A hot lead round whisked past his head by only inches to slam into the wall beside the door. He went down and crawled toward the open door as Cody Wedgeworth stepped into the opening to fire his carbine. Several more shots rang out in return, lead slamming into the door frame. Cody quickly stepped back into the house as more rounds hit the door and walls.

Jake made it inside and lay against the wall as Cody kicked the door closed while several more rounds slammed into the house and wooden frame.

"That was close," said Cody, frowning. "Did you get a look at who it was?"

"No, but I think there are three or four of them," replied Jake, glancing at the older man. "You think it's Patches?"

"Don't know," answered Cody, turning as Sarah ran from the bedroom, still in her nightgown to fling herself into the lap of Jake, who remained on the floor.

"What's happening?" she asked, fear showing on her face. "Is it the Indians?"

"Don't know, yet," responded Jake, placing his arm around her thin waist. "We're safe inside the house."

"I got movement near the barn," said Cody, firing his carbine through the loophole at the door where he still stood. "Ain't no Indians."

Jake reluctantly released Sarah from his lap and stood to glance through the loophole by the door. "Where?"

"I saw a man crawl into the corral. They may be after our horses," said Cody, walking to a window as another round slammed hard into the house, causing the man to jump.

Jake moved to another window and looked toward the springs. He saw a man there and fired through the window loophole with his pistol, but knew he had missed as the man's hat went sailing into the air along with rock chips and dust.

Jake turned to face Sarah, who still was frightened and sat near the door. "Check the back for us."

He followed her and reached for his rifle that lay on the table. In the room, he glanced through a window loophole toward the barn as she looked through another.

"Nothing," she said, turning to him, her fear still showing on her face. "Jake, what's happening?"

"Outlaws, probably after our horses," he responded, noticing the gown she wore barely covered her ample body. He glanced away and went to look through the loophole at the window she had just used. "This place is built like a fort so they'll not get in here. I'm going out this window to circle around behind them at the barn. Can't let them take our horses."

"Jake, it's too dangerous out there," she said, coming to him as he placed an arm around her shoulders for reassurance.

He heard firing from the front of the house and headed there, Sarah close behind. He saw Cody fire again, then heard the sound of the lead as it struck the house near the window when the outlaws returned fire. "They gonna rush the house, Cody?"

"Naw, they're after the horses it appears," answered Cody, concerned. "Saw two more enter the barn."

"I'm going out the back window to circle behind them that are at the barn," said Jake, reaching for a box of ammo on the table. "We'll have them in a cross fire."

"What can I do?" asked Sarah, the fear still lingering within her.

"Can you use a rifle?" asked Jake, glancing up.

"Yes, but I'm not a good shot," she replied, frowning.

"It'll do," he answered, handing her the Winchester model 73. "Just point it in the direction you want to shoot and pull the trigger. Maybe it'll keep their heads down."

"All right," she said trying to smile but failing miserably to make it.

"Come close and lock the back window when I go out," he said, returning to the bedroom.

She followed, carrying the carbine. He opened the shutters and waited, then glanced at her. "I'll be back. You be careful."

She didn't reply, but watched as he crawled through the window to drop to the ground, then quickly ran to the cover of the rocks behind the house. She closed the shutters, then locked them and glanced through the loophole to see him slowly make his way toward the trees.

Jake neared the barn. He gripped the pistol tight, tension building as he heard firing coming from the barn and the house. He scanned the area, worried about more men around than the ones inside the structure.

Seeing none, he approached the back doors and tried them, but they were locked from the inside. He remembered that he and Cody had locked them from inside last night. He walked to the corner of the barn and peeked around to notice a man kneeling behind the corral fence and firing his rifle at the house.

The man turned as Jake rounded the corner. Startled, the man twisted and fired, the hot lead just missing Jake to strike the corner of the building. "Joe, behind the barn!" the man yelled, chambering another round into the carbine as Jake ducked back behind the corner.

The man ran and Jake fired off a quick shot at him, missing. Then the back door opened and two men came out shooting. Jake jumped to the ground, seeking cover behind the barn's corner as the men emptied their carbines at him and disappeared into the rocks.

The third man climbed over the corral fence, fired twice and ran. One round nicked Jake in the left arm, and hot metal burned into the flesh through his shirt. He managed to give the man a parting shot, but missed again.

Jake lay back against the barn wall, clutching his wound, enduring the pain that swept over him. He heard no more firing, but remained alert. Soon he heard footsteps inside the barn, then the low voice of Cody Wedgeworth. "Jake?"

"Out back, Cody. I think they're gone for now," said Jake, starting to get up. He glanced at his arm and saw blood on it, then settled back against the barn, a wave of faintness sweeping over him. He remembered seeing the concern on the face of Cody just before he passed out.

Patches glanced up at the ceiling of the cavern, his mind wandering as he listened to the beat of the drum. He had no idea what time it was, but he knew of the hunger and even the thirst that gripped him. No vision had yet come, but he was determined to remain until one came. Already, Wild Horse had given up, weakened from hunger and thirst. He had to be carried from the cavern back to the main room where the others waited.

A few had joined the small group deep inside the cave, but a few others had left, their faith or fears either failing them or the awesome weight of the seriousness of what was taking place getting the better of them.

Patches didn't worry about them. It was good to have the few who remained strong to be with him. Lame Deer appeared weak in his search for a vision. He glanced at the faithful warrior, realizing that he would soon be forced to join Wild Horse. One Bear remained, his strength appeared to be strong still; but was his heart pure enough for the Great Spirit to grant him a vision? Patches didn't know, he only knew he must remain to hear the spirits when they spoke. He couldn't fail. He must not fail or all would be lost.

Patches lay back, his mind slowly swirling as he concentrated upon the image of the great Thunder Spirit depicted in the form of a Thunderbird on the cave wall. The great Thunderbird had the power to grant the vision. He had to know the right answers. Hadn't the Thunder Moon spoken in behalf of the Great Spirit of the Thunder Spirits?

Something must be wrong. Maybe he had missed something, thought Patches as he relaxed, but still concerned that nothing had occurred. Slowly he closed his eyes and drifted off to sleep, forcing his mind to relax and apply faith that an answer would come.

The dream came slowly to him. Half awake, but weak from hunger and thirst, Patches looked into a clear blue sky, then a cloud came, followed by others which turned darker. Finally a heavy, dark thundercloud appeared. Lightning flashed and the blue sky turned dark, almost as dark as night. Patches saw the animals take notice. The bear stopped his search for food, the elk formed into a massive herd, the deer sought shelter in the forest, while the buffalo turned their heads away from the coming storm.

Patches looked again and was surprised to see a huge snowstorm burst upon the spring grass, the tender shoots, and leaves from the trees. He saw the animals seeking shelter from the storm, and as he watched, he saw darkness fall across the land with the moon full at night. The lightning flashed across the night sky, and the moon began to disappear slowly.

Little by little, more of the moon became dark until only a small, noticeable ring formed around the darkened night object. Then a giant bird flew across the night sky, and as he passed, the darkness turned to day and the moon turned to be the sun. Patches saw that the big bird was a Thunderbird, and as he flew, he turned his head to stare at him.

When Patches tried to see what the Thunderbird said, water poured from its mouth. The Indian watched as the water descended to the earth. It appeared to him that the water was coming straight toward him. He tried to get out of its way, but the water hit him full in the face.

That's when he woke, startled to realize that someone had poured water upon him. "My brother, Lame Deer has given up, too weak to continue, and One Bear has awakened, preparing to leave also. We were concerned about you," said the man, frowning as he looked into the eyes of Patches and noticed the strange look.

Patches wiped the water from his face, smearing the paint there and sat up to glance around. Lame Deer stood, supported by others, but One Bear sat alone. Patches looked around to see fewer men than before.

"What is it, my brother?" asked One Bear, noticing the silent and strange look upon the face of Patches.

"The Thunder Spirits have spoken to me in a vision," replied Patches, trying to stand, only to fall back.

Two men helped him to his feet. "You received a dream?" asked Lame Deer, trying to smile.

"Yes," answered Patches, glancing around. "Continue the drums. We must continue to sacrifice. The spirits have spoken, but I must have time to sort out this vision."

"Let's not anger the spirits by leaving," said Lame Deer, glancing at the man on the drums. "Let our brother ponder in silence the things which the spirits have shown him. Send word to the others that Patches has seen a vision and that we will return soon for him to tell us what the spirits would have us do."

Patches sat again near the fire. One Bear came to sit beside him and smiled, but said nothing. Lame Deer refused to leave, taking a sip of water, which seemed to restore him. He, too, sat beside Patches and stared into the fire. Another warrior came to drop a blanket around the shoulders of Patches, who nodded his approval.

Others gathered around to wait for Patches to speak. It would be some time as they all knew, but signs of relief shown on their hardened faces, thankful that the spirits had finally spoken. All that remained would be Patches words as to what must be done.

Joe Blackburn turned toward Bass Wheeler, his anger building. "Damn, we almost had him," he said, turning the black horse down the trail that lead to the Thurston Ranch. "Someone should have covered the back of the house. The bastard slipped up on us and almost had us trapped in the barn."

"I think I may have winged him," said Bob Hanley, frowning. "He rounded the corner so fast, I just managed to get off a shot."

"Makes no difference, we didn't kill him," answered Blackburn, still angry. "We'll have to think of something else. He'll be on guard for us from now on."

"What you got in mind?" asked Wheeler, glancing at Blackburn. "We'll never smoke him out of that house. It's built like a fort. Besides, he had some help this morning. I counted at least two rifles besides his."

"Yeah, I noticed," replied Blackburn, worried. "I can't let this pass. Charlie was my partner for years."

"Maybe we ought to continue on with our original plans. If he's a deputy under Neel, then we can lure him into town. Maybe we can get a better shot at him there," said Hanley, frowning. "Or better yet, just drop killing Whitmore this trip and get on with stealing his cattle."

"I ain't dropping it, Bob," responded Blackburn, twisting in his saddle to look hard at Hanley. "Charlie was your partner, too."

"All right, Joe. I said I'd ride with you, just don't do something stupid and get us all killed," answered Hanley, looking away.

"Ain't a gonna do that, Bob," said Blackburn trying to calm down, realizing it was just a trick of fate that they had failed to cover the back of the house. Whitmore was smarter than he had given him credit. Next time, he'd make damn sure none of them took Whitmore for granted again...and there would be a next time. That Joe Blackburn promised himself.

Jake felt the cold, wet cloth on his face and slowly opened his eyes to see the tear-stained face of Sarah Thurston just above his. Her nearness and smell stirred his emotions inside again, yet this time he laid back to enjoy the moment, his head resting on her lap. He closed his eyes to wait as she continued to work over him.

"Jake?" she asked, almost in a whisper. "Do you hear me?"

Even her voice was like that of an angel: soft, sweet, full of concern and love. God forgive him, but she stirred feelings even Rachel hadn't touched. He opened his eyes again to see the worry and concern on her face. "Sarah?" he asked, clearing his mind of the passion that had begun to build.

"Cody, he's awake," she said, glancing at the older man, relieved. "You had us worried." Her blue eyes flashed with concern for him and she finally managed a smile.

"I'll be all right. Don't know why I passed out," he said, feeling the pain associated with the wound in his left arm. "Just a crease in the arm."

"Yes, just a crease that has been bleeding," she responded, sternly. "It's been hard to stop. You should go to bed and get some rest. I've hot soup almost ready. You need it for your strength."

Jake noticed that he lay on the floor near the fireplace, his bedroll under him and Sarah. Cody walked to him, frowning. "You look all right, son," he said, still a little worried. "Lost a lot of blood for just a flesh wound. Might ought to do what the little lady suggested. I'll take care of things."

"They get the horses?" asked Jake, concerned.

"Naw, but it's funny. Don't seem they were after the horses," responded Cody, frowning again. "You recognize any of them bushwhackers?"

"No, didn't recognize any, but you said they weren't after the horses?" asked Jake, trying to understand what had happened.

"Appears they were after us, not the animals. They had plenty of time to take our horses from the barn or the ones in the corral, but they didn't," said Cody, glancing at Sarah. "You think they're the ones who were here a few weeks ago?"

"Why would they return to Utah so soon after committing three murders?" asked Jake, still not sure why they were attacked.

"Wouldn't know unless they thought they killed Paul and there ain't no law around here to keep them from taking what they want," replied Cody, walking back to the door to look outside through the loophole.

"What about the ranch?" asked Sarah, worried. "You think they went there?"

"They rode off in that direction," responded Cody, turning to watch her. "Nothing we can do about it right now. When things calm down, we'll ride over and check on the place."

"Cody, I want to pick up their trail while it's fresh. The Utes haven't been around for several days now, so it ought to be all right," said Jake looking at the older man.

"You ain't in much shape to ride today, boy," he responded gruffly. "Best you go to bed and let me look after things till your arm is better. You may need it later."

"Yeah, but I'll ride out in the morning to check on the Thurston Ranch and see if I can pick up the trail of those outlaws," said Jake, looking at Cody. "I'm a deputy sheriff now, and if those men who attacked us this morning are the same ones that killed Karl and Elizabeth and robbed the stage, I'll go after them."

"Alone?" asked Sarah, worried as she finished dressing his arm with a bandage.

"If it's them, I'll ride into Brewster's Crossing and get a posse. Besides, I need to check on Sheriff Neel and the town," replied Jake, standing. "Think I'll get some shut eye while it's quiet."

Sarah followed him into the bedroom, making sure he was all right. "I guess I worry too much about you," she finally said as she watched him unbuckle his gun belt and lay it on a chair beside the bed, then remove his boots.

"I'm glad someone is fussing over me," he said, glancing at her. "Been awhile since Rachel passed away."

"I'm sorry," she said, turning away. "I didn't mean to bring up something that hurts."

"It's all right," he answered, noticing that she too, had trouble accepting the death of a loved one. "Rachel was Mormon like you and Karl. She believed at death she would be in a paradise, so I guess she's all right now."

"Do you believe that?" she asked, sitting beside him on the bed.

"I guess," he replied, avoiding her stare. "Rachel was teaching me some from the Bible and her Mormon book. Saw no reason not to believe it."

The hurt stabbed deep again, bringing a throb to his injured arm as he remembered the quiet, gentle time he and Rachel had spent together reading.

God, how he missed her.

Sarah saw the pain in his face. "Your arm again?" she inquired softly, concerned for him.

"Yeah, some," he finally replied, looking at her. "We both have a loss to get used to, don't we?"

"Knowing they're at peace now helps," she agreed, standing, having trouble with the memory of the deaths of her brother and sister-in-law. "I'll get you some soup."

He watched her leave the room. Her presence had stirred him again, but he didn't feel as guilty as before. Maybe his head was clearing from all the booze. Maybe her words of comfort had helped. He knew her concern was genuine and sincere. Whatever it was, he knew he couldn't deny the feeling he had for this woman.

Jake lay back on the bed thinking of her. The smell of the woman lingered in the room, causing him to remember Rachel again. Less than a month had gone by since she had lain in this very bed, and now another woman slept here. Would Rachel know? He believed she would, but would she approve? That brought on the guilt and a desire for a stiff drink of whiskey to wash away that feeling.

He started to get up, knowing an almost-full bottle lay in the dresser near the bed. In fact, two full bottles lay beside each other. Enough whiskey to help him forget and to block out the pain within the heart. He sat on the side of the bed, unable to force himself any farther. He knew that he had to forget the whiskey and bear the pain. In time the memory of Rachel would turn pleasant, but she wouldn't approve of him right now.

Sarah returned, a hot bowl of soup in her hands. "You all right?" she asked as she noticed him sitting.

"Yeah, just thinking," he said, avoiding eye contact with her.

She placed the bowl beside him on the dresser, then left the room, only to return with water and bread. He lay back, allowing her to place a cloth over his chest and set the bowl on the cloth. "It's still hot," she said, smiling.

He ate slowly, glancing up often as she sat beside him on the chair, her long blonde hair falling loose about her shoulders. "You have family back in Salt Lake?" he asked.

"My parents are there. I live with them," she said, smiling. "Karl was my only brother, but I have two married sisters living in Salt Lake Valley. They're going to be devastated when my letter arrives about the murders of Karl and Elizabeth."

"I'm sorry about your brother," he said between mouthfuls of soup and bread. "This really is good soup."

"Thanks. It's one of my mother's favorite quick meals," she said, pleased. "You have family?"

"Spanish Fork," he replied, remembering he hadn't written yet to let his brother and sister know about the death of Rachel. "A younger brother and sister. Rachel has family there, too."

Cody entered the room. "Gonna take a walk around the place, then feed the stock," he said, a carbine in his hand. "Sarah, lock the door behind me."

Jake watched her rise and follow Cody from the room. He missed her for the few moments she was gone, then grinned as she returned. Her smile was infectious to him, and he had to admit to himself that he was pleased with it. Maybe Sarah was what Rachel had been trying to tell him about in his dreams. Maybe she really did know and approved of her.

She sat on the side of the bed this time, looking straight at him. "Jake, thanks for being there for me when the stage was robbed and for coming for me at the ranch."

"That's all right. Glad I could be there for you," he replied, his eyes locking on to hers.

"I...want to stay...for awhile, if it's all right with you," she said, glancing down to fold her hands in front of her. "At least until Dad arrives to look after Karl's place and dispose of the property."

He placed the now empty bowl on the dresser, then looked at her. "I would like that very much," he said, lifting her face up with his hand on her chin. "Stay as long as you like. The place seems a lot nicer with a woman back inside."

Her heart pounded with the touch from this man. She wanted to stay, really needed to stay. In fact, she knew she had to stay...at least until she knew for sure what her heart was telling her. This man stirred her from their first meeting. That first touch when he lifted her up onto the horse, still lingered.

Even the ride from the stage to Brewster's Crossing lingered. His strong arms and his words of comfort as he told her about the murder of her brother had helped soften the blow of that disastrous news. Now, just his presence and his touch helped heal, even when his own heart broke from the loss of his wife.

She reached up to hold his hand and look into his soft eyes. There she knew she would find the answer she longed for. What she saw didn't disappoint her.

ELEVEN

Patches waited patiently as the warriors assembled around the fire in the cave. He folded his arms across his painted chest as he sat and glanced at Lame Deer beside him, then to One Bear, who sat across the fire from him. A day had passed since the vision, and he had pondered the meaning, praying to the Great Spirit that he might understand it.

Satisfied that he now understood most of the dream, he had called a council of the warriors that they might hear his vision and the meaning of it. He glanced around the fire and noticed the warriors whispering among themselves, waiting for the council to begin. Patches waited a little longer to give them time to quiet down, then nodded to One Bear for the council to begin.

One Bear stood to gaze upon the assembled Indians. Silence fell upon the group. Tension mounted as One Bear stretched forth his arms toward Patches, an eagle feather in the outstretched hand. "My brothers," he began, a serious look upon his painted face. "Patches, our shaman, has had a vision after pleasing the Great Spirit and the spirits of the thunder, the sun, and the moon. The Great Spirit has whispered to our brother through the voice of the Thunder Spirits in the sign of the Thunderbird, approved by a Thunder Moon, and now we will hear his words so that we too may understand the will of the Great Spirit concerning the white men who have come to our lands in numbers like unto the buffalo of old. Hear the words of my brother, Patches."

Patches stood as One Bear sat. He looked at each man, judging his sincerity, his loyalty, and his faith. Satisfied that all were with him, he began his story of his vision: "My brothers, long has been the suffering of the Ute at the hands of the invader, the white man. Long has the Ute been patient with the wrongs inflicted upon him by the white man whose greed for land and the yellow stones knows no bounds. Long have we suffered, but now the Great Spirit has spoken to me that our time has come to throw off this burden. This life of hanging our heads in defeat before the white man is no more. The Great Spirit has shown me the way we must go and the things we must do to be free from the pollutions the white man brings to the Ute Nation."

Patches paused to let his words sink deep into their minds and hearts. He wanted them to feel the frustrations and anger he felt for all the wrongs done the Ute by the white man. Satisfied that his pause had worked in his favor, he continued: "My brothers, we can be free. I have seen the way. Many have purified themselves before the Great Spirit. He has seen our sincerity and our sacrifice to him for the answers. He is pleased with us and has granted me a vision of our past and the future course we must take. Hear my vision and believe."

Lame Deer stood as a warrior began to beat the drum slowly. "Brothers, I went with Patches and with others deep inside the sacred cave to fast and seek a vision. Though the Great Spirit saw my sincerity and sacrifice, he chose to bless Patches with the vision. I was there and I saw Patches suffer, then purify himself before the Great Spirit. I was there when the Great Spirit granted Patches the vision."

One Bear stood as Lame Deer sat. "My brothers, what Lame Deer says is true. I too, was there. I too, purified myself and went with Patches deep into this sacred cave and saw the signs and the drawings of the old ones. I now know the Thunder Spirits dwell within. Through them, the Great Spirit has granted our shaman, Patches, a vision. I would now hear the words of Patches."

One Bear sat while Wild Horse stood, silent at first, then, after glancing at Patches, he spoke: "My brothers, I went with Patches and the others to seek the vision. My weakness prevented me from being there when the Great Spirit granted Patches the vision, but I saw the drawings and the signs on the sacred cave walls. I know Patches speaks the truth. I know this is the home of the Thunder Spirit of our people. I would even say that the spirit of a Thunder Moon may also live here. I will now hear the words of my brother, Patches."

Patches stood again, pleased that the three warriors had confirmed his vision to the assembled council. He only wished Buffalo Hump could be here to hear these witnesses and experience the power of the Great Spirit within this sacred cave, but he knew the old warrior was too self-centered and hardheaded to believe just witnesses. He would have to be shown and made to feel the power before he would believe.

He put Buffalo Hump from his mind. Now was the time to tell his vision to the ones who had put their faith in him. Buffalo Hump and the other cowards would soon learn that he, Patches, had been right. With an eagle feather in one hand and the medicine staff in the other, he began his story.

"Brothers, I saw the blue sky. It was a peaceful day, then a small white cloud appeared. First it slowly drifted in the peaceful sky, but soon darker clouds came to replace the small one. Finally, a Thunder Spirit cloud came, lightning flashed, and the rains came. The animals of the land took notice. The bear stopped his search for food, the elk formed into a massive herd, and the deer sought shelter in the forest, while the mighty buffalo turned their backs away from the thundercloud."

He paused for just a moment to let his words sink in, then continued. "When the animals did this, the Thunder Spirit cast a huge snowstorm upon the land in his anger. This was a storm of such fearlessness not seen before. The white snow covered everything, including all the land and the animals. The green grass froze, the tender limbs of the spring trees fell and broke under the weight of the snow, and the animals fought the weather to find their own shelters from the effects of the massive storm. Darkness came with the storm and then it was night. I could see because a full moon shown brightly across the night sky."

He paused again, a serious look upon his face, hoping the effect of his appearance would impress them. He glanced around and saw that they needed no impressing as they all sat alert, waiting for more. He continued: "Then a Thunder Moon Spirit flashed across the sky, and the moon slowly began to disappear. Little by little the moon faded until all that remained was a bright circle of light where the moon once stood. That is when I saw the giant bird fly across the sky from the east toward the west. As he flew the darkness changed to day. The circle of light changed to become the sun, and then I could see that the giant bird was a Thunderbird, the sign of the Thunder Spirits."

He stopped again to see several of the warriors glance at him with fear on their faces. He had their full attention as he continued: "The Thunderbird stared at me and opened his mouth to speak. I could not understand his words as water poured from his mouth to fall to the earth. Then the vision ended."

Finished, Patches stood for a few moments to allow the men to ponder his words, then he sat beside the fire, folded his arms, and bowed his head. One Bear stood as the drum continued to beat slowly, and after glancing at all the warriors, pointed to Patches.

"Our brother, our shaman has spoken. It is now for each man to decide if the words of Patches are true. Let each man search his heart for the truth, then let him speak," said One Bear, sternly. "I have heard my brother, Patches. I was there when the vision came. I believe his words."

One Bear sat and Lame Deer stood after a few moments of silence, realizing that the others wanted to hear from him before they spoke. He glanced at Patches who still had his head bowed, and listened to the steady beat of the drum. The rhythm of the beat put him in the mood as it did the others to receive the words of their shaman.

"My brothers, I have listened to the words of Patches. From the beginning I have listened and believed that the Thunder Moon spoke to our shaman. Today, I still believe. Patches has spoken the truth."

He sat and Wild Horse quickly stood. "Patches has spoken for the spirits from the beginning. He still speaks for them. All he has said is true. He has seen the vision of our future."

Others followed quickly until all had stood and voiced their approval of the vision of their shaman. When the last man sat, One Bear stood. "We will rest, my brothers, then we will hear the meaning of this vision from Patches."

Jake rode the gray horse from the yard and twisted in the saddle to wave to Cody and Sarah, who stood on the porch. The dog remained beside the woman. It surprised him some that Buster would stay with Sarah, but since her arrival the dog had remained close to her for some reason.

A full day and two nights of rest had worked wonders for his wound, and the healing had already began. He rubbed the wound, feeling a little stiffness, but it wasn't sore. He stopped at the trail path that led to the Thurston Ranch and glanced back toward the house. Sarah still remained on the porch, but Cody had gone back inside.

He turned the gray and started down the trail, noticing the two-day-old horse tracks of the men who had attacked them. A quick glance along the rims of the pass didn't reveal any Utes. He doubted they would show themselves, but instinct caused him to look anyway. They had neither seen nor heard anything of the Utes for several days now, but he suspected they were still around. The warning lance remained in his front yard just as the Utes had left it. Cody had suggested they were still trying to conjure up some magic, but Jake now believed they had either gone home or were waiting to catch him alone and away from the house. Now was the time if he was correct.

He rode on, glancing often to the rims of the mountains or along the lower edges of the hills. As he continued, he had the uneasy feeling that eyes watched from hiding, and the farther he continued toward the Thurston Ranch, the more eerie that feeling became.

He arrived at the ranch an hour later, having withdrawn his Winchester from the saddle boot as he approached. He saw the horse tracks and the day-old horse droppings in the corral and yard, but saw nothing else. He noticed as he dismounted that the graves of the Thurstons remained undisturbed. He stared at them, then turned and walked to the barn.

Inside, he found evidence that the place had been used recently. He left the barn and slowly walked to the house, alert for signs of danger.

Reaching the house, he opened the door and entered quickly, the carbine ready for action, but found nothing except a ransacked house. They had been here for several days, and he began to worry, but was thankful that he had taken Sarah to his place in time. Anger began to build inside as he thought of these men who were so bold as to return to the scene of their crimes and even attempt to kill him.

He returned to his horse and mounted. Maybe that uneasy feeling of being watched was the outlaws waiting for a second chance. They could be lying in the rocks at the pass, waiting for him to leave to take out Cody. Concern began to build as he reined the horse around and headed for the trail toward his place.

Halfway home, the feeling of prying eyes from hiding bore deep into him. He still carried the carbine across the front of the saddle, ready for trouble. His anger remained unchecked as he continued. He rounded a bend in the trail and decided he had to know who was following him. A stand of cedars grew near the trail where he stopped. After dismounting and hiding the gray the best he could, he climbed into the rocks to wait.

His wait was short. Movement just above him near the rim alerted him. He didn't move, knowing his position could be compromised if he did. The person moved again, apparently searching for him or the horse. He eased back the hammer to the carbine as the man stepped from the cover of a cedar near the horse.

The clicking sound of the hammer alerted the man, and Jake rose from behind the rock to level the weapon at the chest of the man. Surprise showed as Jake saw the young Ute stare at him, surprised also that he had allowed himself to be caught so easily. The Springfield carbine he held in his hands wavered as the Indian struggled with the desire to raise it and fire or give up.

He finally chose the later and lowered the barrel of the gun to look at Jake in defeat and shame for being caught. "Why do you follow, Ute?" asked Jake in Ute, a language he had some command of.

The Indian answered in English. "You Whitmore, man who live at sacred springs."

"Yes, I'm Whitmore, but why is the spring holy, and why should I go?"

"All white man must go. Thunder Spirits speak to Patches. Say white man must go."

Those words hit Jake hard. The Utes believed their gods had spoken, and that meant they wouldn't be leaving until he was gone or dead. "And if I go, will the Ute live in peace with the white man?"

The Ute didn't answer, but Jake saw in his face the determination and hate. Jake knew he had to try and defuse this growing problem. An Indian war could result. "What are you called?"

"Two Ponies of the Uncompaghre Ute."

"Then Two Ponies, go tell Patches I would speak with him about the springs. I have no desire to fight the Ute, but Red Rock Pass is my home. If Patches and his people are hungry, then take a few of my cattle to eat. I have lived in peace with the Ute for some time."

The Indian laughed. "Your cattle are gone. The white ones who attacked you have driven off your cattle and hidden them at the canyon of the wild horses south of here."

Jake looked hard at the Indian, surprised that he should know, but grateful that the information had slipped out. Maybe the attack on his place was just a diversion so the outlaws could successfully steal his cattle. Jake avoided showing the Ute he didn't know of the cattle being stolen.

"Go in peace. I have no fight with the Ute. Tell Patches I would talk with him on the matter of the springs," said Jake, worried.

"I will go white man, but there will be no talk. The Thunder Spirits have spoken, and we will obey."

"Why won't Patches speak with me? I'm willing to talk."

"No more talk, white man. I go," said Two Ponies, turning to leave. "You go too, be no trouble at sacred springs."

"If I don't, then what?" asked Jake, watching the Indian closely for fear he may turn to fire on him.

"Then you die."

Jake watched the young Indian leave, still concerned that he might try to fight, but he had no desire to kill this man. It was either pack up and run or stay and fight at Red Rock Pass. He knew if he left now the Utes would let him go, and Sarah and Cody wouldn't be in danger, but if he stayed he knew now someone would die. He really didn't fear death, but the Pass now had special meaning to him since he had buried Rachel there. It was sacred ground to him also, but was it worth killing for? That he didn't know as he walked to the gray and mounted. He would have to decide soon because time had just run out.

Patches waited a little longer as the warriors gathered around the fire inside the cave. Many were disturbed from the report that Two Ponies had given about facing the white man, Whitmore. He would have withheld that information from them until he had told the meaning of the vision, but Two Ponies had already told Wild Horse, who had told others; thus, he had been forced to allow Two Ponies to tell everyone.

Patches stood and the men quieted, ready to hear their leader. "My brothers, we have heard the report from Two Ponies about this white man, Whitmore, who wishes to talk to us about the springs. This is something we must discuss after we have completed our sacrifice to the Thunder Spirits and understand their will in this matter of Whitmore."

He sat and One Bear stood, gazing at the warriors before speaking: "We will continue our sacrifice by hearing the meaning of this vision that has been granted to our shaman. Each man has pondered and agrees that the vision did occur. It has been several days now. We hear from Patches."

Patches stood again, the fire light dancing off his bronze, painted chest. "My faithful brothers, when I saw the blue sky in my vision this means that long ago, before the white man came, our nation lived in peace as one people. Then dark clouds came. Our people divided into two groups and we, the Utes, left our homeland to the north and came to live here. The Shoshone now live to the north, but as time went by, our own people divided again after leaving this land to live on the plains to our east across the great mountain. There, the anger of the Thunder Spirits was made known to our forefathers. The Thunder Spirits wanted to go back home to these mountains. The Ute returned as the Thunder Spirits desired, but some went south, disobeying the spirits to roam the south plains. The spirits didn't go with them and now the Comanche live on the white man's reservation, no more a mighty nation."

He paused to walk around the fire and stand beside the drawings within the cave. "See, our forefathers drew the animals that I saw in my vision. They understood and listened to the spirits that protected them, and when the storm came they survived, except the buffalo, who turned their backs to the storm," said Patches, returning to the fire to stand before the warriors. "This white snowstorm I saw in my vision was the storm of the white man who came to invade our lands. The white man has come to take everything from our mother, the earth. They are everywhere in numbers like unto the buffalo of old. They control everything and break this land and its people just as I saw in the vision where the snow broke the tender limbs of the trees with its weight."

Patches paused to let his words sink in, then continued: "The animals listened to the spirits and sought shelter from this white storm, but the Ute did not listen. The darkness I saw was this blinding of our true ways. We, as a people, have failed to listen. Now, the Thunder Spirits are angry with us."

Patches moved once more to the wall of the cave. "Here, the moon grows dim, covered by darkness, and the Thunder Spirits show their anger in the form of a Thunder Moon. This I saw in the vision. Then all that was left of our people was a small group. In the vision only a bright band of light circled where the moon had been. The moon is our people. They are gone, but for a few. That few is us, the small bright band that is called upon by the Thunder Spirit to redeem our people."

Patches waited for those words to sink in. It was important that they fully understood, as he had learned deep inside the sacred cave that they had been chosen by the Thunder Spirits to once again save the Ute Nation.

"My brothers, when the giant Thunderbird flew across the dark sky, it turned the darkness to light. We can once again become a mighty and bright people like unto the sun I saw in the vision. The Thunder Spirits have given us the sign of the Thunderbird and the strength of a Thunder Moon to do this. We have been chosen to change this darkness, this defeat of our people, into victory and into the glory of the Utes of old," said Patches, walking back to the fire. "The Thunderbird spoke, though his words were not understood, his meaning is. When the water poured from his mouth, the sacred water fell to the earth at Red Rock Pass. I know this because at the close of my vision it was confirmed with water from the sacred springs upon my head. Now, I know the Thunder Spirits require us to cleanse the sacred springs at Red Rock Pass. This must be done before the bright ring can turn into the sun. We must do this to honor the Thunderbird. There will be no talking to the white man, Whitmore. There is nothing more to say. The Thunder Spirits have spoken. We must obey."

Patches remained standing for a few moments, then nodded to One Bear to signal that he had finished, then sat. One Bear stood and faced the assembled warriors, a stern look on his weathered face. "We have heard the meaning of this vision. It is now time for each man to ponder this meaning and to accept it or reject it. Now also is the time for anyone to question Patches as to the meanings of the vision."

Lame Deer stood and faced Patches. "My honored brother, will the giant Thunderbird ride before us to aid us in cleansing the sacred springs?"

Patches stood, glanced at Lame Deer, then spoke. "Yes, he will send a great storm before him to aid us in our fight. We must be ready to act when the Thunderbird chooses to act."

Patches sat again, satisfied that his answer was correct. Surely the Thunderbird would send the storm. It was what the giant bird had whispered when the water slipped from his mouth. Lame Deer glanced at Patches, then spoke to the rest of the men: "I have no other questions."

No others stood to speak. Minutes passed in silence as each man pondered the words they had heard. Finally, One Bear stood again. "Let each man go and refresh himself, eat now and rest, then we shall assemble again to plan our next actions in order to obey the desires of the Thunder Spirits."

The warriors filed out of the cave and into the cool air of the morning. Patches remained seated by the fire. Two Ponies came to sit beside him. "There is more isn't there?" asked Patches, seeing the concerned look upon the face of Two Ponies.

"Yes, my brother," answered the young warrior, hanging his head in shame. "The white man, Whitmore, tricked me yesterday while I followed. I am ashamed that he caught me."

"Be not troubled, my friend. Whitmore has grown strong by living on sacred ground. We must remember that the Great Spirit who created this earth and the Ute also created the white man," said Patches, placing a reassuring hand upon the shoulder of the young man. "The Thunder Spirits will prepare the way for us to handle Whitmore."

"I believe you, my brother," replied the young man, "but there is more that troubles my heart. The words I bring to my friend, Patches, are terrible for his ears to hear."

Patches stiffened at the words from Two Ponies, but his worry and fear didn't show; only the tightness of his face revealed any concern. "What troubles you, my young brother?"

"Words come to me from those who have chosen to be the guardians and spies for our sacrifice," he said, stalling. "Yellow Feather brings word that the camp of Buffalo Hump has moved into the mountains east of the big river."

"That is all right. Let the coward run and hide," responded Patches, frowning as he sensed Two Ponies had more than this to tell.

"It is not easy for me to tell you this, my brother," Two Ponies finally said, glancing up into the face of Patches. "It is Morning Star."

"What has happened?"

"She...was taken by the white men who stole Whitmore's cattle and also tried to kill him," answered Two Ponies dropping his head again to avoid the fierce eyes of the shaman. "They used her, but she lives as you know. She asks for you to give up this quest or never come back."

Patches said nothing, but remained motionless for some time. Two Ponies could bear the pressure no longer and finally stood, glanced at the haunted face of his leader, and left the cave.

Joe Blackburn followed the small herd of cattle into the narrow canyon past Lenny Deason, who stood guard just above the floor of the canyon in a group of cedar trees, a model 73 Winchester in his hands. He waved as they passed, a wide grin on his pockmarked face.

Bob Hanley followed him along with Rusty Mullens. Joe twisted in the saddle to grin at the two men. "Nice haul this time, I'd say."

"Twenty more head to add to our growing herd," responded Hanley, smiling. "We got a good hundred and fifty head now. I say we light out for Colorado with them and turn some money our way."

Joe's grin turned sour. "We ain't a leaving until we get at least another crack at the bastard who shot Charlie. Besides, Bass and Rudy rode into Brewster's Crossing to check on Neel and their little bank they got there. They ought to be back by now."

Gus Deason met them near the small fire as they rode up to dismount. "Bass and Rudy are back. They say the bank is an easy job. Neel is still laid up, and there ain't no law around except Whitmore, and nobody has seen him in town since the sheriff appointed him deputy."

"Where are they?" asked Joe, handing the reins of the black horse to Mullens as he looked around.

"Over there," pointed the fat man toward the two men sleeping near a lean-to of cedar brush.

Blackburn walked to them, kicking their feet to wake them. "Wake up, Bass," he said, squatting beside the man as he came awake. "Gus says the bank is an easy job. What about Neel?"

Bass Wheeler rubbed his eyes then glanced at Joe Blackburn. "Stayed up late last night with a woman at the saloon. Got a lot out of her," he said, glancing at Rudy Beecher, who had rolled over and gone back to sleep. "Neel got a busted leg when the horse fell on him, and you put a slug into his shoulder which ain't healed yet, so he ain't no problem. The bank ain't much, but it's an easy job. Ought to be worth it if we're riding in to kill Neel. Ain't many men in town during the weekday."

"What about Whitmore?"

"She didn't know too much about him. He ain't been to town since Neel appointed him deputy. Rumor is that he's got Indian trouble out where he lives. Been hanging around out there watching out for his place," said Wheeler, reaching for his boots to pull on. "Probably why we had such a hard time nailing him the other day."

"Damn all the luck. I sure wanted to settle the score with that jasper on this trip," said Blackburn, frowning. "Any chance of getting him to leave the place?"

"Don't know," replied Wheeler, reaching for his gun belt to buckle on. "The gal didn't know, but if stealing his cattle hasn't got him out of the place, don't think much else will. He's got to know he has cattle missing if he's any kind of rancher at all."

"Must be them stinking Utes we heard about in Jacktown. Your little raping of the squaw probably didn't help neither, Bass," said Blackburn, standing.

"But it sure was good, though," said the young gunman, standing also. "I say we forget this Whitmore bastard and ride into Brewster's Crossing and kill Neel, then rob the bank and hightail it to Granite with these cows. We got more than we can handle as it is."

"I agree," added Bob Hanley, nodding his approval. "If these Utes are all stirred up around here, it ain't healthy to hang around trying to kill Whitmore. Let the Indians do it for us."

"Probably right," responded Blackburn, frowning. "We leave Lenny here to watch the cattle, and the rest of us will ride into Brewster's Crossing and take care of business. If the Utes don't kill Whitmore, then we ride back here after selling the cattle and finish him off."

"Sounds good to me," replied Wheeler, smiling. "I'll ride back with you for Whitmore."

"We all will," said Hanley, pleased that Joe had decided to forget Whitmore for now, but knowing the outlaw well enough to know it wouldn't last long.

"Get Rudy up," said Blackburn, walking to the fire to reach for the coffee pot. "We ride tonight and get set up for business in the morning."

TWELVE

Patches tried to control his anger, but found little success, and it showed. His scarred face twisted in hate at the white men, especially Whitmore, as he glanced at the assembled warriors. He turned to face Yellow Feather and spoke harshly, responding to the young warrior's inquiry. "Yes, I was with Stalking Horse when we killed Whitmore's people on the Green River. I received this to my face," he said, pointing to the deep scar and feeling the hatred he had for the man who had put it there with a well-aimed shot that early morning on the Green River six years ago. "But that is not the reason we go after Whitmore. The spirits have said we must cleanse the springs and we must kill Whitmore in order to do that."

"If he leaves, then we will not have to kill him," responded Yellow Feather, looking at the others for support and not getting it. "I have been to our camp in the mountains to the east. Morning Star needs you, and Ouray has sent word that we must not attack the white men. Ouray is our chief. We must listen to him."

"The Thunder Spirits have spoken to Patches," said Lame Deer, standing to face Yellow Feather. "You were not present when the vision came nor at the sacrifice when our shaman told us of the vision and the meaning. The time for talking is over. It is time to act."

"I believe in Patches, otherwise I would not have ridden with him and would not this day be here to report on what I have seen and heard," said Yellow Feather, defending himself. "Even now Buffalo Hump and others ride to find us and make us return with them to the mountains to the east as Ouray has ordered. I am just saying it is impossible to fight the white men and our own brothers at the same time. If Whitmore leaves the sacred springs, that should be acceptable to the spirits, shouldn't it?" asked Yellow Feather, seeing that he wasn't getting very far with his argument.

"The Thunder Spirits will defend us from the eyes of Buffalo Hump and the other fools until our mission is completed. You will soon see that my words are correct. I, of all people, realize that my woman needs me now, but I have a greater mission to perform. The Thunder Spirits have called and I will answer," said Patches, determined as he looked at Yellow Feather. "I know your heart is true, my young brother, but I have put aside my hate for Whitmore and act only at the requirement of the Thunder Spirits. Whitmore doesn't even know that I rode with Stalking Horse to kill his people. It is a matter that should not be talked about. The Thunder Spirits will deliver Whitmore to us when the time comes, and we will kill him; then the Thunder Spirits will be satisfied."

"Are we to kill him on sacred ground?" asked One Bear, worried. "The springs are holy. Is it right to kill him there?"

"His blood running red at the springs will show the Thunderbird that we do the will of the Thunder Spirits as required. It is the only place that he should be killed," responded Patches, looking at the others, then back to One Bear. "We will raid for now and hunt the ones who violated my woman and kill them, then we will return to the springs and destroy Whitmore."

"If he is not there, then what will we do?" asked Yellow Feather, still worried.

"His weakness is his woman with the yellow hair. We will use that weakness to our advantage when the time comes. Have no fear, my brothers, the Thunderbird goes before us," said Patches, seeing that his men were beginning to accept his words. He turned to Yellow Feather. "Go back to the camp of Buffalo Hump and see that he is mislead as to where we are and what we plan. Tell him that we fast and pray only and have no plans to attack the white men. See that he does not find us."

"Yes, my brother, I will go," said Yellow Feather, not really sure what he would do when he returned to the main camp of his people in the mountains to the east. True, he hadn't been present at the vision sacrifice, but still, he believed Patches spoke the truth, but to act upon that would bring untold hardship upon the Ute Nation. Would he do as Patches had said? He didn't know, but he had plenty of time to think about it as he turned to leave.

Patches watched him mount his bay horse and ride off with Two Ponies and the other scouts. He turned to Lame Deer, who stood beside him. "Can we trust Yellow Feather?"

"He is my cousin. He may not believe everything we have told him, but he would not betray me...or you," answered Lame Deer, hoping more than believing. "We should act soon just in case he doesn't."

"Then we will prepare ourselves for battle," said Patches, frowning. "By the time Yellow Feather arrives back at the camp of Buffalo Hump, we will have already struck at the white man, and then there is nothing the great Buffalo Hump can do but run and hide...or join us."

"Where do we strike first, my brother?" asked Lame Deer, glancing at Yellow Feather and the others who were now only specks on the landscape in the distance. "Whitmore or the white men who raped Morning Star?"

"Two Ponies reports that the stinking white men who violated Morning Star hide from Whitmore in the canyon of the wild horses to our south," said Patches, bitterly. "We will visit them first and bloody our knives into their cold hearts for what they have done to my woman."

Jake pulled the gray horse to a stop, dismounted, and worked at the leather strap to the saddle while glancing out of the corner of his eye. The Indian still followed. That worried him, but as of yet the warrior had made no move toward him or given any sign that he would attack. He mounted and rode on, still worried.

It had to be the same one he jumped the other day. What kind of game were they playing with him? The Utes had said he was on sacred ground and to leave or die, yet no effort on their part had been made to force him off the springs at Red Rock Pass. He was confused, and even old Cody Wedgeworth was stumped about their behavior. In all his years of living with them, he was still left with no reasonable answer as to what they were up to.

Jake glanced back along the canyon ridges for the Ute, but he wasn't there now. He gripped the Winchester a little tighter to reassure himself and readjusted it on the saddle in front of him. Maybe he had made a mistake in leaving Cody and Sarah at the ranch, but he had to go on with life. He had a ranch to run, and now he was sure the Ute had been right about the outlaws taking his cattle. He hadn't seen one cow of his all day. A few of the Thurston cattle had been seen, but that was all. The Indian had said the stock was in Wild Horse Canyon to the south. Jake wanted to ride out there now, but knew he needed to get some men from town for a posse first. If they were the same ones who killed five people in Utah recently, then he would need the men.

He had also neglected his duties as deputy and felt guilty, but he had told Sheriff Neel his place came first. He would make Brewster's Crossing before dark, form a posse, and ride out tomorrow morning for Wild Horse Canyon. It would give him the time to talk with Neel and take care of any business, paperwork, or whatever else Neel had for him to do in Brewster's Crossing.

He left the canyon, headed across the mesa toward the town, and glanced to his right at the canyon where the mighty Colorado flowed southwest. This was beautiful country, and he had no desire to leave it. Fighting for the ranch at Red Rock Pass had to be done. The place was too important to him now.

He glanced back again, but saw no Indian following. He doubted the Ute would follow him across the mesa. There was only one place a man headed southwest could go and that was to Brewster's Crossing. The warrior would know that and probably return to Patches and report.

What would happen then? He didn't know what the Indians were up to, but Cody could defend the place if he wasn't caught outside. Sarah worried him the most. She had refused to return to town with him, pleading to stay. What could he have done anyway? Her soft tear-stained eyes begged to remain, his own feelings told him that was what he really wanted, but common sense told him she would be safer in town. His heart had won out, yet he still worried about her safety.

Patches had challenged him for Sarah. Was the Ute serious in his threat, or was it another game the Indians were playing with him? It was hard to judge what an Indian would do. Six years ago, Stalking Horse had showed his family friendship one day and the next had killed his parents. Who could have predicted that?

He felt that he should return to the ranch; instead, he reasoned that he needed to check on the town and Paul Neel. He was a deputy sheriff, and he owed some responsibility to the county and its citizens. Besides, he needed a posse to recover his stolen cattle. His worry about what the Indians would do would have to wait. So far, they had only watched.

It didn't take him long to catch a glimpse of the town below the mesa. He could easily see the river and ferry and a few of the taller buildings, especially the two-story hotel. It would be dark by the time he reached Brewster's Crossing, and knew he still had work to do forming a posse, talking with Sheriff Neel, and catching up on the paperwork that had surely piled up since the sheriff was laid up.

Jake rode into town as the sun began to set behind the mountains to the west. The first man he saw was Kennon Matthews coming from the saloon. "Hey, Jake," said Matthews, shouting happily as he stepped down from the sidewalk onto the street. "What brings you to town?"

"Rustlers," replied Jake, pulling the gray to a stop. "Need a posse in the morning. You free?"

"Naw, gotta take the stage out tomorrow for Green River. Got two passengers," replied Matthews, frowning. "Wish I could go, though."

"How is Sheriff Neel?" asked Jake, dismounting to tie the horse to the hitching rail.

"Like a caged mountain lion," answered Matthews, grinning. "Shoulder is healing fine, but he can't get around much with that busted leg. He's been wondering when you was a gonna show up."

"Anything happen that needs my attention?"

"Nothing of importance," responded Matthews. "Got a few wanted posters in from Salt Lake City and a few papers from the court to serve, but that's all Paul said he had. Going over to visit now?"

"Yeah, guess I ought to see the sheriff first, then see if I can get a posse together. A bunch of rustlers got my cattle and some from the Thurston Ranch hid out over in Wild Horse Canyon."

"I'll get your posse started," said Matthews, turning to re-enter the saloon. "I'll meet you back here for a few drinks."

"Ain't a drinking no more," answered Jake, glancing away, "but I'll meet you here in awhile."

"How is old Cody doing? He still off the bottle?" asked Matthews, looking seriously at the young man.

"Ain't touched a drop yet, if that's what you mean," answered Jake, looking up. "Been a little worried about them Utes and them rustlers who shot up our place, too."

"The Indians cause any trouble yet?" asked Matthews, worried.

"Done nothing but watch me and my place. Been up in the hills beating on their drums for the past week. Don't know what they're up to."

"Sarah doing all right out at the Thurston Ranch?"

"Can't get her to come to town, but I did manage to get her to my place. She's with Cody now," responded Jake, concern showing on his face.

"Figures," responded Matthews, turning again to enter the saloon.

"What do you mean by that?" asked Jake, confused as he looked at the man.

"Simple, Jake. Can't you see the woman is in love with you," answered Matthews, stopping to turn and grin at him. "Seen it the other day that I tried to get her to return to town with me. Yes, sir, the little woman has her mind made up and you ain't got much of a chance...now."

Jake could only stare at him, lost for words. Was it really true? Was he ready to receive her love so soon after burying Rachel? Deep down inside he knew he wanted it to be true, but something held him back, lingering dark inside, refusing to allow him to express his feeling for Sarah. He finally turned and walked toward Sheriff Neel's house, no business, outlaws, or

Indians on his mind. Only a blue-eyed, blonde lady occupied his thoughts for the moment.

Jake finished his breakfast and looked up at Paul Neel, who sat across the table from him. "Thanks for the breakfast and a bed to sleep in," he said, placing the empty glass on the table. "As soon as Jed King and his two boys get here, we'll ride out to Wild Horse Canyon and see if we can round up some rustlers."

"Where's your posse?" asked Neel, glancing up.

"Most of them are down by the stables or over at the hotel eating breakfast," said Jake, frowning. "Wanted to leave early this morning, but I needed King. He knows those canyons out near Wild Horse Mesa like the back of his hand. He couldn't get into town until ten."

"Jed King is a good man to have along in a posse. So is those two grown boys of his. He won't quit on you like some I know who are riding with you," responded Neel, frowning also. "You still taking Wallace Granger?"

"Yeah, as far as Wild Horse Canyon. If the outlaws are gone, I'll send him back with a message for you," answered Jake, his frown turning into a wide grin.

"Letting him save face, is it?" responded Neel, grinning also.

"Naw, just being smart. Don't want to listen to his griping all day," said Jake, standing. "Think I'll go over to the hotel and check on my posse. Don't want some to get cold feet on me and change their minds."

"Good idea," replied Neel, nodding his approval. "Wish I could go, but I guess I'll have to be satisfied to wait for your report or Wallace Granger to return. Watch out for Joe Blackburn if he's the one leading this bunch. He's as deadly as a diamondback rattler."

"I will," said Jake, taking his hat from the rack beside the door and walking out to the porch.

He saw Jed King and his two sons riding into town from the southwest and waved to them as he stepped off the porch. He was halfway across the street to the hotel when he noticed the eight riders enter the town from the southeast, all eight hard-looking, lean, and up to no good as far as Jake could tell.

Jake glanced around and noticed the streets were clear of anyone except himself and the Kings, who continued to ride into town. The eight riders rode quickly to the bank, three dismounting while the others spread out, still mounted. Jake watched in disbelief, his hand close to the .44 caliber pistol at his hip.

Something wasn't right, and his suspicious were confirmed when one of the riders pointed to him, yelled, and drew his carbine from the saddle boot. Jake realized then that he wore the deputy badge in plain sight on his chest. He moved then, heading for the hotel steps, but was too late as the rider fired at him with the carbine. Jake felt the round zip past him by inches and drew his .44 to answer the shot by popping off three quick shots at the riders. None hit, but they scattered the five remaining outlaws, which allowed him to seek cover behind a wagon beside the hotel.

The firing also brought the posse into action. Baker Stevenson with Ben Westman following were the first out the door of the hotel, their weapons drawn. Several rounds from the riders forced them to seek cover. Others came from the hotel firing. Herman Hielmann dropped down beside Jake at the wagon.

"Looks like our outlaws found us first," said Hielmann, grinning as he fired off two shots at the riders.

"They're after the bank," said Jake, glancing at the man, then turning to empty his pistol at the outlaws.

Jake saw three men run from the bank, one carrying a canvas bag. The three mounted their horses only to be met by a volley of fire from the stables. One outlaw slipped from his horse to lie still in the dusty street. The others joined their gang and headed out of town at a dead run, firing as they went.

As the robbers rode from the town, Jake ran forward, reloading his pistol. "Come on boys. They're getting away."

Men ran from the hotel as others charged from the stables firing. Another outlaw fell from his horse, rolled over, and tried to stand, only to be hit several times again and fall backward to lie still in the street. Jake emptied his pistol at the fleeing riders and glanced at the barn as several posse members rode out to follow the outlaws. Jed King and his two boys pounded past him on their horses to join the group and take up the chase.

Jake reached the stables and broke down the .44 to watch the six cartridges pop out. He reloaded quickly as Amos Dryden led the gray to him. "Them outlaws sure picked the wrong time to try and rob the bank," said Dryden, grinning.

"They sure did, and we're lucky they hit it while we were still here," he responded, taking the reins of the bridle and mounting. He didn't wait for the others from the hotel to reach the stables as he spurred the horse hard and left to follow King and the rest of his posse.

He rode past Herman Hielmann, who squatted beside one of the outlaws, working quickly to save his life. It was a waste of time, because if he lived, they'd hang him. Baker Stevenson ran past him. "We're right behind you," he yelled, the big Sharps in his hands.

Jake spurred the gray hard again and rode out of town to follow the dust clouds ahead. He heard a shot fired and pushed the gray faster to catch up with his men. Jake caught up with Wallace Granger, who had been at the stables when the fighting began. He pulled his laboring horse to a halt beside the man.

"There was eight of them," said Granger, excited. "Jed and the others are hot on them. My horse came up winded. I'm sorry."

"Head back to town and take charge there. See about the bank and the two outlaws we shot, and round up anyone else and send them our way. We'll need all the help we can get if they scatter," said Jake, jerking the gray around and riding off.

He glanced back to see Westman and Stevenson and the men from the hotel riding hard to catch up. He slowed the gray to give him another breather. This could turn out to be a long chase. He would wait up for his men, then ride on to catch up with King and the others. By now, they ought to be about run out. Maybe they had caught up with some, but he doubted it, as he heard no firing.

Bishop Newman was the first to reach him. "Where you think they're headed for?"

"Probably try to give us the slip, then sneak back to Wild Horse Canyon and the stolen cattle," replied Jake, frowning. "We had best save our horses. This could turn out to be a long chase."

"Just what I was a thinking, too. Jed and the others will run their horses till they're winded. We can take up the chase then. Might catch some of them before they make it to Colorado," said the bishop, frowning. "They got away with a sack full of our money. Gonna be hard times for some folks if we don't get it back."

"You're right. If they split up, we could have a long chase, and we gotta get the money back," replied Jake, seriously. Some of that money was his, and he'd need it bad if he lost his cattle. Already he had noticed the outlaws had split into two groups. "Say a prayer for us, Bishop. We'll need it."

"Already did," replied Newman, grinning. "The Lord has done his part, now it's up to us to finish it."

Joe Blackburn lowered the Winchester when he recognized Bass Wheeler and Bob Hanley as they rode through the stand of cedars into the draw where they hid from the posse. Wheeler pulled his lathered horse to a stop, dismounted, and glanced around. Joe approached him, concern on his face.

"You lose that posse?"

"Hell, no, they're no more than half an hour behind us and coming fast," replied Wheeler, worried.

"What happened back in town? They was a waiting for us, Bass," said Blackburn angrily.

"Hell if I know. Benson went down and they dropped Rudy when we left town. Where's the others?" asked Wheeler looking around.

"Rusty and Buck are back in the canyon along with Bull. We found Lenny full of arrows, and Bull insisted on burying his kid brother," said Blackburn, disgusted. "Everything is falling apart. We'll be lucky to get out of here with our hides."

"It was Whitmore," said Hanley, adjusting his saddle on his horse. "I seen him."

"How did he know we were going to hit the bank?" asked Blackburn, glancing at Hanley. "This whole trip has been bad from the beginning."

"You're telling me," responded Wheeler, turning as Mullens, Rawlins, and Bull Deason returned from the canyon. "I'm for cutting our losses and heading for Colorado now."

"Ain't got no choice now with that posse hot on our heels," said Hanley, worried. "Don't even have time to take these cows with us."

"We got what little pickings there was in that bank," said Wheeler, looking at Joe Blackburn. "You still got the money bag?"

"Yeah, I got it, but ain't had time to count it. Don't look like much," replied Blackburn, frowning. "We need to make tracks fast. That posse has horses that won't quit."

"There was two groups. One ran us hard while the other one took it slow," said Hanley, stepping into the saddle stirrups to mount. "We can make the crossing on the Dolores River, then there ain't nothing a gonna stop us from reaching Colorado."

"Except maybe those Utes," said Bull Deason, looking at Hanley. "They killed Lenny. Shot him sixteen times with arrows. He never had a chance."

"Didn't think them Utes would get all worked up over that squaw," said Wheeler, mounting.

"Should have thought of that first, Bass," said Blackburn, mounting his big black. "Now we got Indians on our trail along with a posse."

"There's more to it than us taking that squaw," said Wheeler, turning his bay horse to follow Blackburn. "Something else has got them worked up."

"Whatever it is, we're heading for Colorado fast and that posse can worry about the Utes," said Blackburn, glancing back as they climbed out of the draw. "I see the dust from the posse. Let's get out of here."

"Didn't get to bury Lenny deep," said Deason, complaining. "The wolves will get to him for sure."

"Be glad you're alive, Bull," said Hanley, riding beside him. "We ain't out of this yet. That posse is awful close."

That didn't cheer Bull Deason up, but he didn't complain anymore. Hanley was right. They'd all be real lucky to beat this posse to the Colorado border. Bull worried if his horse would make it. Already, the sorrel was breathing hard. Another long run and the horse would be finished. Deason was concerned and thinking of Lenny full of Ute arrows and the top of his head scalped sent cold shivers down his spine. Added to that was the feel of a hemp rope around his fat neck if the posse caught up with them. The urge to urinate was strong as his fear gripped him. He wanted to stop and relieve himself, but that fear of the rope or a Ute arrow in his back was too much. He spurred the sorrel hard and caught up with the others.

THIRTEEN

Kennon Matthews glanced at his new guard, Henry Bellows, who gripped the heavy ten-gauge shotgun loosely. Matthews cracked the whip over the rumps of the two lead horses of the stage coach, then leaned over to Bellows. "Ought to make Newton's Station within the hour. Harvey will change out the team, and we'll make the night run on into Green River."

"Sounds all right with me. Mrs. Newton serves up a fine supper," replied Bellows, hungry. "Them two drummers aboard is in for a treat."

"Sure is," replied Matthews, shaking out the long, black snakelike whip to crack it again over the rumps of the lead horses. "Know one of them drummers, but didn't get the name of the other man."

"Sam Poritier," answered Bellows, glancing at him. "Frenchman from down New Orleans way. Came west a couple of years ago. Right nice fellow."

"So is Calvin Dobbs," responded Matthews, smiling. "Especially when he's giving away free samples of his whiskey."

"Don't see how he makes much selling whiskey in Mormon country," replied Bellows, frowning.

"Plenty of non-Mormons around and a few Jack Mormons like old Cody Wedgeworth," said Matthews, wondering if Jake Whitmore was really telling him the truth about the old man giving up his drinking. That Indian trouble over the springs at Red Rock Pass must be real serious to cause Cody to stop his drinking.

"You worried about them Utes stirring up trouble?" asked Bellows, glancing into the rocks with suspicion.

"Don't know what to think," replied Matthews, worried now. "You ever hear of a Thunder Moon, Henry?"

"It's one of them Indian superstitions, isn't it?" responded Bellows, gripping the shotgun tighter now. "Suppose to be some hard times a coming to someone according to the Indians."

"Yeah, suppose to be someone is a gonna get killed, either an Indian or their enemies," said Matthews, showing concern on his face. "Saw one a few weeks ago when that big storm came through. Been Indian trouble ever since."

"You really believe in all that Indian superstition?" asked Bellows, glancing at him.

"Might be some truth to it," replied Matthews, popping the whip over the horses again as they neared an outcropping of rocks beside the road. "The sooner we get to Newton's Station the better I'll feel."

"Me too," said Bellows, turning at the sound of running horses coming from the rock outcropping.

"Indians!" shouted Matthews, cracking the whip hard over the lead horses. His second crack landed on the rumps of the two horses, which put the team into a hard run. "They're all painted up for the warpath."

Bellows fired off both barrels of the shotgun, then broke down the weapon to reload. "Why are they after us?" he asked, closing the shotgun, fully loaded now.

"Don't worry about why right now, just keep them away from the stage. They kill one of our horses, we're done for," said Matthews, shouting as he popped the whip repeatedly upon the rumps of the team to force them to move faster.

Matthews heard firing coming from inside the stage. The sharp crack of the pistols told him Calvin Dobbs and the Frenchman were doing their best to beat off the Indians.

He glanced back, but saw only a few Indians in the trailing dust. He knew there had to be more. He turned in time to see several mounted savages up ahead, waiting, one carrying a medicine staff and riding a paint horse. "Up ahead, Henry. We got more trouble."

Bellows turned as the stage charged into the waiting Indians. The ten-gauge discharged twice, but Matthews failed to see any Indians go down. All he saw was the warriors scatter, firing their rifles and arrows as they passed.

Bellows fell back, an arrow in his chest. He dropped the empty shotgun, clutched at the arrow shaft deep into his chest, moaned, then rolled to the side of the stage and fell off.

Matthews tried to reach him before he fell, but trying to hold the man and drive six hard running horses was too much. He glanced back, but saw nothing except the dust. As he turned back to the front, he saw a young Ute ride in close to the team, an arrow notched in his bow, ready to sink the shaft deep into the side of one of the lead horses. Matthews drew his Colt .44, fired several times, and grinned in delight as he saw the young warrior fall from his horse, the arrow falling with him.

He heard firing coming from inside the coach again and knew at least one person was alive inside to help. Newton's Station wasn't far away. He returned the big pistol to the leather holster at his hip and picked up the black whip to pop it again upon the rumps of the horses as he glanced around for more Indians. They were close behind, but none wanted to ride in close for a shot at the stage horses now. Maybe with luck they'd make it to the station.

Matthews saw the station ahead and popped the black whip once more over the horses for the final run to what he hoped would be safety. He saw Harvey Newton step from the front door, level his big Sharps, and fire. At least they were safe there. He hauled the stage to a stop near the front door, reached for his Henry rifle beside him, and bounded off the stage as the Utes rode past the stage firing. Calvin Dobbs made it to the door at the same time Matthews did.

"They got the Frenchman," said Dobbs, a .36 caliber Smith and Wesson in his hand.

Harvey Newton's big Sharps thundered again. "Git your tails inside. These Utes mean business."

Matthews slammed the front door shut behind Newton as an arrow embedded itself into the door. Two lead rounds hammered into the door also, and Matthews moved away from it to lean against the log wall. "Henry got it a ways back, and the Frenchman is dead inside the stage," he said looking at Newton reload the Sharps.

"Nothing we can do for them now. They jumped us a few hours ago. Wounded one of my boys," said Newton, going to a shuttered window loophole to fire off the Sharps, then reload.

"They got the stage, paw," said Newton's son as he fired through a window loophole.

Newton returned to his window. "Damn, they're leading off the stage horses. Already got all the ones at the barn. We're afoot now, that's for sure."

"How are we for water and ammunition?" asked Matthews, concerned as he glanced at Newton.

"Got plenty of both," replied Newton, frowning. "They have ridden out of gunshot range. Bastards know just how far this Sharps will shoot."

"What set these Indians off, Kennon?" asked Cal Dobbs, reloading a

Winchester carbine.

"Heard old Patches was all worked up over too many settlers moving into the area," he replied, looking up. "Jake Whitmore said they been up in the hills near Red Rock Pass beating on their drums trying to get some strong medicine. They must think they got it now."

"Maybe so, but for a couple of them red devils it didn't work. I killed at least two," said Newton, looking back through the loophole.

"What will they do next?" asked Mrs. Newton, looking at Matthews, a worried expression on her face.

"They may hang around for awhile or might try to burn us out if they're serious about getting to us," responded Matthews, not really sure what they would do. "This place is built like a fort. Gonna be hard to burn us out, but my best guess is they'll ride on for an easier target."

That easier target, Matthews knew, would lie at Red Rock Pass, where old Cody Wedgeworth and Sarah Thurston were by themselves; Jake was out with the posse to round up rustlers on Wild Horse Mesa. Cody and Sarah might already be dead by now. If not, they stood little chance by themselves against this bunch of savages.

Jed King squatted, studied the ground, then stood to remove his hat and wipe the sweat from his forehead. "The two we were trailing met up with the other four here. Don't know what's in the canyon, Jake," he said, glancing at him and the others who remained mounted on their horses.

"All right then. Jed, pick up their trail out of this draw. I'll take some men and search the canyon," said Jake, checking his Winchester before turning the gray toward the entrance of the canyon.

Jake led his men into the canyon, searching the sides for signs of the outlaws. He pulled the gray to a stop near the cedar lean-to, then noticed the shallow grave. "Ben, some of you check the grave—see who's in it."

Several men dismounted. Baker Stevenson rode to his side. "See your cows are here. Them rustlers didn't have time to move them."

"Yeah, we're about an hour behind them. Their horses can't last much longer. We'll catch up to them before dark," replied Jake, watching Westman and the others uncover the shallow grave.

"Don't recognize him, Jake," said Westman, looking up. "We didn't kill this one. Got a dozen or more arrow shafts in him."

"Indians?" asked Jake, turning.

"Yeah, scalped, too. Big man like the one that was with the gang who robbed the bank, but younger. Say he's been dead since early morning," answered Westman, beginning to cover the body again. "Want us to rebury him deeper? The wolves will get to him if we don't."

"Yeah, a couple of you who got horses that won't last the day stay and bury him good, then head my cows back toward my range. The rest of us will go on after the outlaws," said Jake, turning his horse to ride out of the canyon.

He was worried now, not about the outlaws, but Cody and Sarah. The Utes had finally acted, and he was sure his place at Red Rock Pass was on top of their hit list. His desire to let King take over the posse was strong. He knew he must return to his place as soon as possible, but his duty to catch these murdering outlaws was his and his alone. They were close, real close. A little more pressure on them and their horses would soon start falling out. Then the showdown he had long awaited would come, and these killers would pay for murdering five people in Utah.

Jake caught up with Jed King. King twisted in his saddle to face him. "Ain't a gonna be long, Jake. A couple of them horses is about give out."

"How long, Jed?" asked Jake, hoping it would be soon.

"Another half hour for the fat man on his horse. Maybe another hour for the others," replied King, grinning. "We may catch them before they reach the river."

"What we got left in our horses?" asked Jake, knowing his gray was in a lot better shape than most of the other horses of his posse.

"About the same as theirs, except mine and my boys' will last a lot longer. So will your gray," replied King, glancing at him. "What you got in mind?"

"You, me, and your boys push them hard," said Jake, seriously. "Baker can bring up the rest of the posse slower. We run their horses to the ground then pin them down until the rest of the posse arrives."

"Sounds good to me. The sooner we get up to them, the sooner we can go home. Besides, if they beat us to the river, they got a chance of getting away," said King, worried.

Jake turned to Baker Stevenson who rode up to the two men. "Me, Jed and his boys are going to push these outlaws hard until their horses give out. You bring the rest of the men along at a steady pace, but save your horses. I hope to run them into the ground before they get to the river."

"Sounds good to me, but just save some of them for me and my Sharps. I owe them for killing Henley at Doan's Crossing," replied Stevenson, angrily.

"We'll pin them down until you can arrive with the rest of the posse," said Jake, nodding as he turned the gray toward the east and set him at a hard pace to be followed by Jed King and his two boys.

After almost an hour of hard riding, Jake realized the gray was just about at the end of his endurance and would need a long rest or he would go down. He glanced at Jed King and saw that his horse was about in the same shape as his gray. King's boys' horses looked in better shape, but they wouldn't last another half hour at this pace.

"Ought to be seeing something soon, Jake," said Jed, looking at the trail they were following. "The fat man's horse should have gave out over a mile ago, but he's pushing the horse to death. Better we spread out and keep our eyes peeled."

Jake nodded his approval and watched the three riders fan out from him, their Winchester carbines resting on their hips as they all scanned the trail ahead. Jake saw the big sorrel first. The horse was down and kicking, which meant the horse had just given out. He pointed forward for the others to see as he pulled the gray back to allow him to slow down.

Nate King pointed to the fat man crawling into the sagebrush, raised in his saddle, and fired. Dust kicked up near the man, who rolled over and disappeared into the sage for cover. Jed King and his other son had ridden around to the right to circle the outlaw as Nate continued to fire his carbine in the general direction of where the man had disappeared.

Jake spurred the gray for one final push of the horse's strength, his own carbine ready. The gray responded and Jake flew across the short distance to where the man had disappeared but did not see him. He circled the area and saw the man jump up to his right, his carbine at his shoulder. Jake snapped off a shot, but missed. The fat man fired and didn't. The big gray horse screamed in pain, kicked, and went down, but Jake jumped from him in time to miss the kicking heels of the dying horse. He hit the ground hard and rolled away from the animal, still maintaining control of his Winchester.

The outlaw fired again at him, but missed by several feet. Jake rolled to his left and came to his knees to level his carbine at the man and fire. The slug caught the fat man in the right shoulder, spun him around, and knocked the rifle from his hands. A second shot knocked the man down, and Jake approached with caution as Jed King rode up to dismount.

"Winged him good, Jake," said King, grinning. "We got one here we can hang later."

Jake reached the downed outlaw to see that his second shot had hit almost in the same spot as the first, but higher up on the shoulder. The fat outlaw lay moaning in pain, fear written all over his face as he glanced at him.

"Where are the others?" asked Jake, squatting beside the outlaw.

"Up ahead," whispered the outlaw, disgust on his face. "The bastards left me to shift for myself."

"Who are you?" asked King, poking him in the gut with the end of the barrel of his carbine.

"Deason," he replied, frowning. "I had no part in killing them people. I was in Colorado and only came along this time to steal cattle, not kill or rob anyone. I swear."

"Who are the others?" asked Jake, staring hard at the outlaw, not yet ready to believe him.

"Joe Blackburn, the bastard who left me on my own. He's the leader, and he's the one who killed that Mormon couple," said Deason, his hatred for Blackburn showing. "Then there's Bass Wheeler, Bob Hanley, and two kids named Mullens and Rawlins. I'll testify against them, just believe me that I didn't have any part in those killings."

"The dead man back in the canyon, who was he?" asked Jake, glancing toward the east where the other outlaws had gone.

"My kid brother, Lenny. Them damn Indians killed him. Lenny didn't do nothing wrong, except he was in on raping that squaw," said Deason, glancing from Jake to King, then back to Jake.

"You bastards raped an Indian woman?" asked King, poking the man hard into this gut again.

"I didn't do it. Bass Wheeler and Rudy Beecher were the ones who started it. Lenny just got carried away, that's all," responded the outlaw, lying back on the ground to moan in pain.

"Jed, loan me your horse. I'm going to try and catch up with them. Send Baker and the others fast when they get here and tie this one up good. We'll sort out the truth later," said Jake, frowning.

"Take Nate and Randall with you. I'll be all right with this no account outlaw," said King, poking the man again with the rifle barrel. "He ain't a going nowhere but to jail and a hangman's party."

Jake took Jed's horse, mounted and rode off toward the east, the carbine still in his hands. King's two boys joined him, a determined look on their hard faces. Jake was pleased that they had caught at least one of the bank robbers and that he had learned who had killed Karl and Elizabeth. Joe Blackburn would pay for his crime even if he had to chase him into Colorado...and to hell if necessary.

Patches watched the five white men pull their horses to a stop near the arroyo before entering. The two young men rode ahead, their carbines resting on their hips, their eyes scanning both sides of the gully. The black-bearded white man on the black horse waited to glance back along the trail they had just traveled.

Patches knew the white man Whitmore followed with others to kill these bad men, the ones who had raped his woman. He glanced to his left and watched Lame Deer, who also waited patiently, a bow with a notched arrow ready for his signal. Others lay along the arroyo ready to kill these men. One Bear waited on the other side to trap them in a cross fire.

Two Ponies had suggested they let Whitmore take care of these men and go on to the sacred springs and cleanse it while Whitmore was away, but Patches had overruled this suggestion. The burning desire for revenge flamed hot inside him for these men. He would take care of them for the white man Whitmore, then Whitmore wouldn't have anything else to do but return to the sacred springs where he would die according to the whisperings of the giant Thunderbird. All would see that the Thunder Spirits delivered the white man into his hands for the revenge needed to satisfy the spirits.

As the two young men rode from the gulch, Patches signaled Lame Deer, who stood, pulled the bow string back, aimed, and let the arrow go to sink deep into the chest of the first white man. The man tumbled from his horse, crying out as he fell. The other jerked his horse around and attempted to flee, but a volley of rifle fire knocked him from his horse. He fell hard to the ground and didn't move.

The third white man fired his carbine, turned his horse, and rode from the arroyo as the other two men fired from the top of the gully. Patches leveled his Springfield carbine and lined up the sights upon the back of the fleeing man and fired. The impact of the weapon slammed into this shoulder, but he smiled with satisfaction as the man toppled from his horse, the heavy .45 caliber slug passing through his body, driving the life from the man.

The other two men turned their horses and fled. Lame Deer, One Bear, and the others swarmed after them. Patches mounted his paint horse and rode into the gulch as Two Ponies and several others scalped the two young men. "The other one is yours, my brother. He is your kill," said Two Ponies, looking up and holding the scalp of one of the dead men.

Indeed the scalp was his, but he didn't want it. He only wanted the other two white men dead, then Whitmore. He would gladly take Whitmore's scalp to show the Thunder Spirits that he had obeyed. As he rode from the arroyo, he saw more white men coming from the west, riding hard. That would be Whitmore and his men. They were closer to catching these bad men than he had thought.

Patches signaled Two Ponies and pointed to the advancing white men, then turned the paint to chase after Lame Deer and One Bear. He glanced back to see Two Ponies and his men mounted and advancing toward Whitmore and his men. Two Ponies would give him time to retreat with Lame Deer and the others. Whitmore had too many men to have a stand-up fight; besides, the sacred springs remained open to attack with Whitmore gone. Only the old man and the woman remained there. It would be easy to take the house.

With the woman captive, Whitmore would be sure to come and fight him for no other reason than to regain his woman. That Patches knew he could count on, and he had no doubt that in the final battle he would kill the white man, Whitmore, and thus please the Thunder Spirits. Then the Ute would return to being the powerful tribe they once had been. The white man would flee in fear of the Ute, and once again the buffalo would return. The Utes would be a mighty people once more.

Lame Deer and One Bear returned as Patches glanced back at the firing coming from behind him. "Two Ponies will delay the other white men until we escape," said Patches, frowning. "Whitmore came faster than we thought."

"Why not fight him here?" asked One Bear, looking toward the fight where Two Ponies had now engaged the advancing white men.

"The Thunder Spirits want him to die at the sacred springs or at the holy cave. It will be a sign to all, both Buffalo Hump and any whites who may doubt the determination we have in obeying the spirits," said Patches, turning his horse to leave. "The other two escaped?"

"Yes. If we had time, we could catch them. Their horses are about gone," replied Lame Deer, frowning.

"We have avenged Morning Star with four of the white men dead who violated her. Let us get on with what the Thunder Spirits really want us to do," said Patches, glancing at Lame Deer. "Whitmore and the sacred springs are more important."

Jake pulled his horse to a stop beside the arroyo and looked down into the gully. Three men lay dead, each scalped. What he had hoped to do to these men wasn't much different than what the Indians had done. He dismounted and turned to young Nate King. "Nate, you and Randall ride out and see if the other two got away," he said, watching Baker Stevenson and some of the others dismount and climb down into the gulch to check on the dead.

"This one here is Bob Hanley," said Ben Westman, glancing up. "Been riding the outlaw trail for years over in Colorado."

"Anyone know the others?" asked Jake, climbing down into the arroyo to look closer at the dead men.

"Two young ones. Ain't Blackburn or that gunfighter, Wheeler," said Morgan Davis, rubbing his graying beard and squatting beside one of the dead men. "I know Wheeler when I see him. He ain't here."

"Anyone find the bank money bag?" asked Jake, looking around, but not seeing it.

"Ain't here," said Stevenson, frowning. "Gonna be hard on some folks around Brewster's Crossing if we don't get that money back. I'm for riding on into Colorado after those other two and getting the money."

"Me, too," replied Davis, standing. "I ain't a gonna make it through the spring and summer without what little I had in that bank."

"What about those Indians? They're still around and could be causing more trouble," said someone standing behind Jake. "Some of us need to get back to town and warn the others."

"Let's bury these three here and wait for Nate and Randall to return, then we'll decide what to do," responded Jake, worried about his place, Cody, and Sarah. "Those Indians are not wanting to fight us. Probably were after these men for raping that squaw the outlaw we caught told us about."

Jake wasn't sure of that, having more hope than conviction that it was true. Patches could very well have let him catch up to these outlaws; instead, he had killed them. That meant he was out for revenge for what they had done. What would he do now? The Ute had made the threats to remove him from Red Rock Pass. It appeared Patches believed he was ready to do just that.

Jake returned to his horse to wait for Nate and Randall King to return, still thinking about Patches and what was taking place at his ranch. He knew he should return now, but he had two more killers still loose, a town's bank money to try and recover, and one outlaw to return to Brewster's Crossing.

The King boys returned, riding slowly as their horses were about ready to drop. Jake waited impatiently for them. Bishop Cal Newman and Baker Stevenson came to stand beside him. Nate reined his mount to a halt and dismounted.

"Appears they made it to the river. The Utes pulled out when they crossed and headed into the hills to the north," said King, frowning. "You find the money bag?"

"No. Must be with those two," replied Jake, disappointed. "Can we catch them before they make it to Colorado?"

"Not much of a chance now, Jake," answered the young man. "That black horse one of them is a riding is some animal. He ain't quit yet."

"If we want the money back, we'll have to ride into Colorado after them," said Stevenson, worried.

"We ain't got no authority over in Colorado, Baker," replied Bishop Newman, frowning.

"Don't need no authority to get that money back, Bishop," responded Jake, glancing at him. "Too many people are depending on that money to see them through the spring. We don't have much choice but to follow them into Colorado."

"Our horses are give out, Jake. We'll never catch up to them," replied Newman, glancing at Stevenson for his help but not getting it.

"We're gonna have to rest them anyway," said Jake, squatting to draw in the dirt. "Bishop, I need you to take the prisoner back to town and lock him up, then warn the town and the area about the Indians. You'll be needed there to organize that through the church."

"True, best I get back to Brewster's Crossing and get the word out," responded Newman, relieved some.

"What men want to go on with me, can," said Jake, pointing with his finger in the dirt to a spot on the ground he had marked. "We'll cross the river here and cut off several hours getting into Colorado. There is only one town for them to head for and that's Jacktown, here. I'd bet that's were we'll find them and our money."

"Jacktown is a mean place, Jake. A lot of outlaws hang out there. Some may shoot at a Utah lawman on sight," said Newman, concerned.

Jake removed the badge and dropped it into his coat pocket. "This ain't going to do me any good in Colorado," he said, standing. "Someone round up the outlaws' horses. The fat man killed my gray."

"Ben done caught them. We gonna hang the fat one?" asked Stevenson, seriously.

"Ain't up to me, Baker. You know that," replied Jake, glancing at Stevenson. "We'll let Sheriff Neel see that he has a fair trial."

"We'll give him a fair trial...then hang him by his fat neck until he's dead," said Stevenson, angrily.

Jake turned away from Stevenson, seeing the anger building inside the man. The fat man would get his trial, fair or not, then hang regardless if he was guilty of killing the Thurstons, Vern Perkins, or Henley Ferguson. Just being associated with the ones who actually did the murders was enough evidence to convict him. The fat man would swing, but Jake only hoped he could catch two more outlaws so they could hang with him.

FOURTEEN

Joe Blackburn turned in the saddle as Bass Wheeler's big bay horse fell. Wheeler jumped clear from his saddle, but fell to the ground, rolled away from the horse, and stood cussing. "Damn all the luck," he said, brushing the dirt from his clothing. "What are we gonna do now?"

Blackburn dismounted, his own horse breathing hard and about ready to drop. "These horses lasted longer than I thought they would, Bass. Give him a long breather. Maybe he'll recover."

"That posse still on our trail?" asked Wheeler, walking to his horse and trying to get him to stand, but not succeeding.

"I think they gave up for now," replied Blackburn, shading his eyes from the sun with his hand to scan their back trail.

"Probably just long enough to give their horses a good breather, too," responded Wheeler, trying again to get his horse to stand. "Good thing they came along when they did or them damn stinking Indians would have had us for sure with their fresh horses to run us down."

"Only luck we have had all day, I'd say," said Blackburn, leading his black horse to the shade of a cedar tree. "Gonna miss Bob for sure. Me and him been riding together for some time."

"Yeah, old Bob was all right. So was them two young fellows you had riding with you. Gonna miss Rudy, too," answered Wheeler, finally getting the bay to stand. "We got the money from the bank, and we don't have to split it but two ways now."

"Hadn't thought of that," said Blackburn, a wicked grin coming to his worried face. "That damn Whitmore fellow is gonna have to pay for all this. First Charlie, now Bob gone, all on account of him."

"First, we gotta get to Colorado, Joe. Then we can start thinking of getting to this fellow," responded Wheeler, leading the bay to the shade of the tree also. "We're gonna have to lay low for awhile, then sneak back here and pop him from ambush or something."

"If them Indians don't get him first," said Blackburn, frowning.

"You think they killed Bull?" asked Wheeler, taking the saddle off the bay.

"Don't know," answered Blackburn, taking his saddle off the black also and laying it beside Wheeler's. "Bull was alive when we left him. Maybe he got away."

"Yeah, maybe," said Wheeler, taking his Winchester carbine and walking away. "I'm gonna watch our back trail for the posse or them Utes."

"We're going to need a good hour for these horses to rest, or we'll go nowhere but to jail," said Blackburn, squatting beside his saddle to withdraw his carbine.

"I ain't a gonna go to no jail to hang, Joe," said Wheeler, turning to look at him. "They'll have to kill me, cause I ain't ever gonna die from a rope."

Joe didn't answer, but lay beside his saddle, the carbine cradled in his arms. He remembered the day they hung his paw. He had watched from the window of a building nearby. Watched helplessly as Paul Neel pulled the lever that dropped his paw to his death while Jake Whitmore stood beside him to help. They would pay for that. They would also pay for killing Charlie and Bob.

Joe rubbed his neck, an odd feeling coming over him as he pictured a hangman's rope around his neck, then quickly withdrew his hand, angry at himself for allowing his feelings to get to him. No lawman was going to hang him. They had to catch him first and none had ever done that yet. If they did catch up to him, they'd have to shoot it out with him, and Joe planned on never being taken alive. Still the haunting feeling of the rope around his neck lingered, but he soon forgot that and drifted off into an uneasy sleep.

Cody Wedgeworth eased back the hammers on the shotgun, opened the door just enough to slip though, and stood watching the shadows of the early morning light near the barn. He was sure he had seen something, and Buster had confirmed it with his low growl from under the porch.

"You see anything?" asked Sarah, whispering as she stood just inside the door, Cody's Henry rifle in her hands.

"Don't see anything, but the dog knows someone is out there," whispered Wedgeworth, gripping the shotgun tighter. "I'm gonna slip around the house and check things out. Keep an eye on the barn."

Sarah closed and locked the door as Wedgeworth stepped off the porch to stand in the yard. The yellow dog came from the porch to follow. Sarah watched from the loophole in the door as Wedgeworth slowly walked toward the barn, the shotgun in his hands ready for action.

She saw the Indians then, in the dim light of the early morning. They rode from behind the rocks near the spring, painted for war and clothed with nothing but loincloths. Their naked bodies were painted with various symbols and signs, some with lightning bolts, others with animal designs, but the one on the paint horse, the same one who had questioned her in her bedroom at the ranch, had the design of a bird on his chest painted in blue. His war bonnet flowed behind him, and he carried a war lance which he leveled at the old man, who had turned to meet the charge.

Indians ran from the barn also, screaming their fierce war cries. Wedgeworth leveled the shotgun at them and pulled both triggers at the same time, the recoil of the gun forcing him backward. The buckshot from the two barrels slammed into the charging Indians, knocking down several. The man turned to flee toward the house, but the big warrior on the paint horse rode in close and thrust forward with the war lance, impaling the man in the back. He rode past Wedgeworth as the man went down, the shaft of the lance protruding from his back.

Sarah leveled the carbine barrel through the loophole and aimed the best she could, then fired at the warrior as he turned his horse around. The paint horse screamed in pain as the round struck him. He went down to his knees, throwing the Indian over his head, then rolled over to his side kicking. Sarah jacked the empty cartridge from the firing chamber and chambered another round into the barrel and fired at the Indian, kicking up red dust inches from him.

She chambered another round and saw two Indians ride past the downed warrior, one on each side. As they passed, they each grabbed an outstretched arm and pulled the man to safety. Sarah fired a parting shot at the warriors, but missed. In answer to her firing, several rounds and arrows slammed into the door where she stood. The sound of the lead hitting the door frightened her, and she moved to a window and looked out through the loophole.

She saw Wedgeworth struggling to crawl toward the house, the war lance still in his back. The yard was clear of Indians, except for the paint horse, who still kicked in pain and struggled to stand, but kept falling back to the ground. Sarah glanced toward the barn and saw two Indians lying still on the ground and one crawling slowly away toward the corral.

Sarah returned to the front door and looked through the loophole at Wedgeworth, who was making progress toward the house. An Indian ran toward him from the barn, his knife raised to make the kill. Sarah opened the door and rested the barrel alongside the door frame for support and placed the sights on the painted naked chest of the advancing warrior. As he reached the man, she pulled the trigger. The impact of the carbine slammed hard against her shoulder, but she saw the Indian fall backward and roll over, bright red blood covering his design of an eagle on his chest.

She stepped onto the porch, jacked the empty cartridge from the gun, and chambered another, then went to the steps. The dog came from under the steps to stand beside her as she stepped off the porch. She ran to Wedgeworth. "Cody," she said, kneeling beside him, tears beginning to cloud her vision.

"Woman...get back...inside," whispered Wedgeworth, glancing up at her.

"No," she responded, trying to help him with one hand while holding the rifle in the other.

"The Indians," whispered Wedgeworth, moaning in pain.

She heard the war cry again and looked up at the Indians as they charged from behind the rocks and from the barn.

"Cody," she said, screaming in panic as she leveled the Henry and began firing at the Indians on the horses. One horse went down, causing several others to trip over him. A mass of horses and Indians kicked up a huge cloud of dust, blocking the vision of all involved, including Sarah.

She heard the Indian before she saw him and wheeled to meet his attack, firing the carbine, but missing. Before she could chamber another cartridge, the Indian was upon her, grabbing the weapon from her, twisting, and throwing her to the ground. Others were upon her, forcing her back to the ground, shouting their victory cries.

The yellow dog attacked then, biting and mauling the warriors, who quickly released the woman and fought off the dog. Sarah ran toward the house, screaming in terror. One Indian followed, but she made the house first to slam the door shut and bolt it tight. The Indian pounded his body into the door with little success of opening it.

Panic gripped her whole body, and she shook in terror, unable to clearly think or even scream again. She remembered the rifle now and that it was outside, and also remembered Cody's shotgun and the pistol that he wore. She ran to the bedroom, not knowing what to do without a weapon, as she heard the pounding on the door of the screaming Indians trying to get inside. She knew it wouldn't take them long to break down the door.

In her frightened state, she reached for the blanket on the bed to wrap herself with, still shaking with fear. The warmth of the blanket helped clear her mind; she remembered the tunnel under the bed which she quickly crawled under to removed the carpet over the trapdoor. Her fingers clawed at the planks that covered the openings and finally removed them as she heard the Indians using something to batter in the front door.

The hole opened for her, and she slipped into it and stood to replace the planks as best she could, the last one falling into place. With no light and little air, she began to crawl, fear still gripping her, but she stopped several times to readjust the blanket and listen. She heard nothing so continued until her hands touched the shovel handle that Cody said would be at the end of the tunnel.

She felt the dirt at the end of the shaft and began digging at it with the shovel. Cody had said only two to three feet remained. The air was stale and stuffy in the confines of the tunnel, and with the fear of being discovered, or worst yet, trapped here to die a slow death, she forced the work to go faster. A final thrust with the shovel blade broke through the tunnel into the light of the morning sun. She felt the cool morning air slip into the hole, and she sucked in the fresh air and finished the opening to squeeze through, then covered it the best she could.

She heard the Indians still trying to break into the house and silently crawled away into the cedars behind the house to lie still behind one to watch in horror the activities in the front yard. At least twenty Utes swarmed in the yard, some mounted, but most milling around outside as a few continued to batter in the door with a pole from the corral.

With a victory war cry, the door crashed in and the savages swarmed inside. Sarah scanned the yard and saw Cody still on the ground, facedown with the lance shaft protruding from his back. The yellow dog lay beside him and Sarah saw the dog covered in blood. Tears took over the panic and fear, and she watched as the Indians came from the house.

The lead Indian, whose paint horse she had shot out from under him, was now mounted upon another animal, a sorrel this time. He carried a staff and spoke angrily at the others who fanned out and began to search the area. The fear returned as she sank deeper into the cover of the cedar tree for protection, praying that Jake would come for her and rescue her from this horror. He had come once before and she knew he would come again. Fate had brought them together, and she knew with all her heart that they were meant for each other. He had to come. He just had to.

Joe Blackburn dismounted from the big black horse slowly, stretched his arms above his head, and glanced at Bass Wheeler, who had climbed off his bay horse, the animal hanging his head. They had ridden as hard as the horses could stand, which wasn't much, but an all-night ride had finally put them in Jacktown.

Content with their efforts, Blackburn walked to the barn door of the livery stable of Cal Burrell and opened the double doors to lead the black inside. A lantern burned dimly over the doorway, but he could see fairly well inside. Burrell would probably be in the back tack room, drunk as usual.

"Don't see Burrell around," said Wheeler, leading his horse to an empty stall. "Guess we'll have to put our horses up."

Joe started to unsaddle the black, pulling the leather strap from the ring of the girth and releasing the girth and strap to pull the saddle and blanket from the horse. He noticed Wheeler did the same, only to glance around with suspicion.

"Don't worry, Bass. We lost that posse before dark. They'll not likely ride into Colorado after us."

"We gonna divide up the money now?" asked Wheeler, watching Blackburn closely, mistrust and suspicion showing.

"Let's get to the room first. I'm heading for Leadville later," said Blackburn not failing to notice the mistrust. "You don't trust me?"

"About as much as you trust me, Joe," replied Wheeler, grinning.

Blackburn smiled, then laughed. "You want to ride with me over to Leadville?"

"Yeah...I think I will. Ain't too healthy around here. We coming back for Whitmore?"

"Was thinking we ought to try and even the score," replied Blackburn, his laugh turning serious as he thought of Whitmore. "We'll let things die down around here for awhile, then drift back to Utah this fall."

Cal Burrell stumbled from the tack room, a bottle of whiskey in his hand as he tried to pull up his pants and slip the suspender straps over his shoulders. "Hey, Bass, Joe," he mumbled, getting one suspender over a shoulder. "Thought I heard somebody out here. It must be three in the morning. You boys look like you been riding hard for the past couple of days."

"Yeah, Cal, we been riding all night," replied Blackburn, swinging his saddle over the saddle rack beside a stall.

"Things go all right over in Utah?" asked Burrell, taking a sip from his whiskey bottle.

"You ask too many questions, old man," replied Wheeler, his suspicion returning as he locked his bay in a stall.

"You ain't seen us, Cal, you understand?" responded Joe Blackburn, a stern look on his face as he turned to face the old man.

"Yeah, I ain't seen you two," replied Burrell, nodding his head and taking another sip of whiskey from the bottle. "Where's Bull Deason and the others?"

"Cal, like Bass said, you ask too many questions," said Blackburn, taking the heavy saddlebag from the saddle to swing it over his shoulder and turn to leave.

"Just wondering. Bull owes me for some horses," said Burrell, avoiding the harsh eyes of the outlaw.

"Bull and the others don't ride with us anymore. That's all you need to know, Cal," said Blackburn, stopping to turn and face the man.

"You just get our horses fed and rubbed down good," said Wheeler, walking to stand beside Blackburn. "We'll be pulling out later today."

"Sure," said Burrell, puzzled at the actions of the two men. They had never acted like this before. He followed them to the door and watched as they walked toward the Red Bull Saloon that remained open twenty-four hours a day, seven days a week.

He finally closed the doors and took another sip of the whiskey, glanced at the two horses, and decided they could wait till morning to get their grain and rub down. From the looks of those two horses, it appeared things went real bad in Utah, especially for Bull Deason and the others.

He knew it was no real concern of his, but he would have to find another source of cheap horses since Bull was gone, and it appeared that Wheeler and Blackburn would be pulling out soon, too. He took another sip of the whiskey, forgot about the two outlaws, and headed back to his bed.

Jake Whitmore shaded his eyes with his hand and pulled his horse to a stop on the hill overlooking Jacktown, then turned to Jed King, who sat on his horse beside him. "Ain't many people stirring this time of morning."

"To be expected from a town like this. Most are up all night," replied King, frowning. "Think our boys are still here?"

"They're here," answered Jake, quietly. "Finding them is our next problem."

"Should have rode all night," said Baker Stevenson, adjusting the big Sharps rifle across his saddle.

"Our horses needed the rest and so did all of us," responded Jake, glancing at Stevenson, who took his hat off to wipe his balding head. "They're not expecting us so they're probably laid up some place feeling mighty safe right now."

"I think we ought to check all the livery stables first, see if we can locate their horses," said King, looking at Jake, worried. "Might find out where they're bedded down."

"I'd guess they're in one of them all-night saloons drinking up all our money they stole," said Ben Westman, angrily.

"We'll all ride in together, then search the three stables I count from here. Their horses ought to be in one of them if they're still here," said Jake, turning to face the ten men who rode with him. "Remember, we ain't the law here, but we got a right to our money."

"Think the law will help?" asked Morgan Davis, worried.

"Probably not for what we got in mind for those two," replied King, glancing at him. "Don't make no difference anyway. We're gonna take these two with us, dead or alive."

Jake nodded in agreement and headed his horse down the hill toward the nearest livery in town, the Circle B Stables. The sun was well up, but few people were on the streets as they rode in. Jake dismounted in front of the business as did King and several others. Baker Stevenson and Ben Westman remained mounted and rode down the street to take up positions to cover the stable in case of trouble.

Jed King entered the stables first, his .45 Colt in his hand. Jake followed, his own hand close to the .44. An older man stopped near the rear of the barn and placed the bucket of feed he carried on the ground, suspicion showing on his face. "Howdy," he finally managed to say. "Can I help you fellows?"

Jake nodded. "Two fellows ride in here early this morning? One rode a big black horse, the other a bay."

Burrell glanced at Jed King, who had walked to the stalls looking at the horses, then back to Jake, and finally to Morgan Davis, who stood near the front doors. "You fellows the law?"

"If we were, would we get a straight answer from you?" asked Jake, staring hard at the man.

"Makes me no difference," said Burrell, frowning. "Ain't been nobody here last night...nor this morning. If you fellows ain't got business with me, I've got work to do."

Nate King came through the rear doors of the stable. "Paw, the black is out back with the big bay."

"You sure, son?" asked King, glancing toward Burrell, who had picked up his feed bucket.

"Yeah, Paw. Been following them horses all the way from Brewster's Crossing. These are the ones."

Cal Burrell looked like the kid who got caught with his hand in the cookie jar. "I...I don't know how them horses got there. Maybe them fellows rode in and I didn't know," said Burrell defensively.

"What about the other horses? They all belong to you?" asked Nate King, glancing at his father, then back to Burrell.

"What's all these questions? I don't have to answer to you fellows," said Burrell, heading for the tack room to escape any more questions.

The click of the pistol hammer brought him to a quick halt, and he turned to gaze into the barrel of Jed King's big Colt .45 single-action revolver. "Now fella, we ain't got a whole lot of time to jaw with you so we'll cut right through the horse crap and get down to some answers, like where are those two outlaws that rode in on the black and the bay."

"I...don't know," said Burrell, trying to judge the man with the pistol. One had said they had trailed Joe and Bass from Brewster's Crossing, so these men were from Utah.

"Your name?" asked Jake, walking to stand beside King.

"Burrell. Cal Burrell," he replied, a little nervous as the big Colt continued to point at his head.

"Jake, them horses out back has Karl Thurston's brand on them," said Nate King, looking hard at Burrell. "I say we take this fellow back to Utah with us and hang him alongside the fat man."

Jake looked up in surprise, then sternly at Cal Burrell. "Burrell, you got one chance to come clean or we'll hang you in your own barn. Them fellows killed five people over in Utah, one a woman, stirred up the Indians, stole those horses, and robbed our bank in Brewster's Crossing. We mean to have them, so you can tell us where they are, and we'll forget you got stolen horses here...or you can hang with them. What's it going to be?"

Burrell hesitated, glanced at Jake, then Jed King and over to Morgan Davis, who had one of his ropes in his hands. Davis grinned at him and Burrell spoke quickly. "They're over at the Red Bull Saloon. Got a room in the back, but I seen them this morning. They came to check on their horses. Gonna pull out within the hour," replied Burrell, worried now. "Don't know them horses was stolen. You can take them back to Utah. Want no part of stolen horses."

"I'll bet you don't," said Jed King, his pistol still pointed at him. "Be sure we'll take the horses, and if you're lying to us, we'll take you with us, too."

"Nate, you and Morgan stay here with Mister Burrell and see that he gets those stolen horses ready for us to take with us," said Jake, turning to leave. "We'll see if he's telling us the truth."

Jake left the stable and headed across the street toward the Red Bull Saloon, Jed King following. The other six men of the posse saw him and followed, Jake pointing to the rear of the saloon for Ben Westman and Baker Stevenson to cover. Randall King dismounted to follow them.

"Chad, you and Randall watch our back at the front door," said Jake stopping at the doors of the saloon to peek inside.

"They there?" asked Jed King, his hand not far from his pistol at his hip.

"Yeah, both of them at a table near the back," answered Jake, peeking inside again.

"How are we gonna take them?" asked King, worried. "I ain't no gunfighter like I hear this Wheeler fella is."

"I'll take Wheeler. You watch the other," answered Jake, checking his .44 pistol before entering the saloon. "Stevenson and Westman will back our play from the back."

The two men entered through the swinging front doors and walked toward the table where the two outlaws sat. The saloon had few customers: two stood at the bar and two others sat at a table near the front door. The bartender, a thin, tall, aproned man with a mustache nodded to them as they continued to the table where Blackburn and Wheeler sat, still unaware of their presence.

"Joe Blackburn, stand up," said Jake, loud enough for everyone inside the saloon to hear.

Blackburn turned quickly, recognized Whitmore, and spilled his whiskey as he stood, fear on his face. Bass Wheeler stood also, but no fear showed on his young unshaven face.

"I'll handle this, Joe," said Wheeler, seriously. "I'll take Whitmore. You take the other one."

"So...the back shooter comes to us," said Blackburn, his fear fading as he moved to a position that he felt comfortable with for the coming shoot-out.

"One chance," said Jake, watching the eyes of Wheeler as the man moved away from the table, his hand close to his pistol at this hip. "Just one chance to give up. It's more than you gave those five people in Utah."

"They was no-account Mormons," said Blackburn, backing into the bar, his anger getting the best of him as he glanced at Wheeler, who stood ready to draw.

Jake saw the slight gleam in the eye of Wheeler, a signal that the man was going to draw. Jake moved like lightning, filling his hand with the deadly

.44 Smith and Wesson, then bringing it quickly in line with the taut body of Bass Wheeler.

The young gunman was fast, but not quite fast enough as Jake's pistol spoke first, the round slamming hard into the exposed chest of the gunfighter, driving him back against the table. Wheeler's own .44 wavered, and the man fired once, missing Jake by inches. Jake's .44 spoke again, and Wheeler was knocked off his feet and back into the table, tipping it over. He fell into the chair and finally landed on the floor, the pistol still gripped in his hand as he died.

Jake glanced quickly to Joe Blackburn. The man remained frozen, his hand quivering just above his pistol, fear gripping him to the point that he couldn't draw. Jed King had his .45 Colt pointed at the man now, and he walked slowly to him.

"No fight in you, Mister Blackburn?" he asked, mockingly, a wide grin on his face. "You face real men and you can't draw, is that it?"

An older man wearing a star on his vest entered the saloon, a double-barrel shotgun in his hand. "Hold on here," he said, shouting. "Everyone, drop your guns."

Jed King kept his gun on Blackburn and Jake turned to face the man. "We're from Utah, and these men robbed our bank and killed five people, including a woman. We're taking him back with us along with a string of stolen horses."

"Don't think so," said the lawman, the shotgun still pointed at Jake and Jed King. "You two will hang for killing that man. This ain't Utah, fella. You're in my town now."

"This man is a murderer," said Jake, protesting. "So was the other; besides, he drew first."

"Don't make me no difference. Bass Wheeler caused me no trouble around here. You just gunned him down," said the man, grinning. "I'm gonna hang you for it."

"Don't think so, lawman," said Baker Stevenson, stepping through the back door, the big Sharps leveled at the man's gut. Several other men entered also, and Randall King came in behind the man to take his shotgun away.

"You can't do this," said the town marshall, protesting.

"We just did," said Jake, frowning. "You come over and visit us sometime in Utah. Maybe we'll welcome you like you did us, or better yet we can take you back across the line and hang you with this killer."

"No need. You can have Joe Blackburn," said the lawman, thankful to get out of this alive as he saw the determined looks on the faces of the men.

"Saddlebag in the back room is full of our bank money," said Ben Westman, coming from a back room with the bank bag. "We got what we came for. Let's ride."

The men filed out of the saloon, Joe Blackburn now in handcuffs. He turned to the marshall, a pleading look in his eyes, but got no response from the lawman. Jed King pushed him out the door. Jake turned to face the lawman. "No hard feelings, Marshall, but we're gonna take this man back to Utah to hang. You're invited to the hanging...if you want to come."

FIFTEEN

Sarah Thurston watched the last of the Indians mount their horses and leave. Smoke boiled upward from the house as the warriors slowly rode down the canyon toward the trail that led to the river. She had spent the night under the cover of the cedar tree, and now with the sun well above the canyon rims, thirst had finally driven her toward the spring. She crawled slowly, stopping often to listen, her fear gripping her as she recalled how close the Utes had come yesterday to finding her. Thirst for water had caused her to approach the water hole last night, only to discover the Indians waiting to ambush her. She had avoided them, but now they had left and thirst for water was first on her mind.

The Indians had moved Cody Wedgeworth to the springs last night. As far as she knew, he still lived, but for what reason, she didn't understand. The Indians hadn't burned the house until this morning. She walked past the burning building, satisfied that there was no more danger. There was nothing she could do about the fire.

Sarah stopped short of the water hole to glance around. Cody lay near the spring, leaning in a sitting position against a rock. He appeared dead, but she wasn't sure. Slowly she approached, like a wild deer, alert for danger as she stopped several times to look around.

She saw Cody open his eyes as she approached, a flicker of life showing. "Water," he whispered softy.

"Cody, I thought you were dead, "she said, kneeling beside him, worried.

"Not...yet," he managed to whisper. "Don't know...why."

"I'll get you some water," she responded, standing. "They left a few minutes ago, but they set fire to the house."

"Damn..." replied Wedgeworth, moaning in pain. "The...barn?"

"They left it alone," she said, squatting beside the pool of water, not sure how she was going to get water for him.

She scooped up the refreshing liquid with her hands to satisfy her thirst, but failed to notice the reed poking up from the pool or the Indian who lay under the water at the end of the reed. Slowly a hand raised from the pool, a knife in it that shone in the morning light. She saw the knife, then the hand and tried to jump away, but the Ute was too quick. With a war hoop, he was upon her, his knife at her throat.

Sarah struggled to get away, but his powerful arms held her down. She saw in his face victory and hate at the same time. A final attempt to break his hold failed and defeat took over. Frustration came first, then the fear.

The Indian turned her over and pulled her arms behind her back to tie them with the rope he carried. Secured, the warrior stood, laughing. "Now woman of Whitmore, you are mine."

Soon, other Indians appeared, shouting their war cries and patting the warrior on the back who had captured her. The Indian squatted beside her, smiling as he ran his wet hand through her hair. His touch sent cold shivers down her spine, and he saw the fear he had struck in her. He stood and laughed. So did the others.

"We go, white woman. This man we leave alive to tell Whitmore what we have done. I, Patches, now have you. He will have to come to me to reclaim you. When he does, he will die as the Thunder Spirits have said."

A tear formed in her eye as she realized the Indian was right. Jake would return to the ranch to find the house burned, Cody near death, and her a prisoner of these savages. She knew Jake would attempt to come for her and he would die in the Indian ambush.

She stood with the help of two warriors, and as she passed Cody, who watched with sad eyes, she spoke to him. "Cody, don't let Jake come for me. It's a trap. He'll be killed."

"Silence, woman," said Patches, slapping her hard on the face with an open palm. "White man Whitmore will come for his woman, and Patches will kill him on sacred ground as the spirits have said. Nothing you can say or do will change that. You are the bait that will force him to me, then the giant Thunderbird will deliver his life into my hands and the sacred springs will be cleansed."

Jake saw the smoke long before he saw the source. He had little doubt that the source was his place, but was surprised when he topped the rim of the pass to see that only the house had burned. A quick scan of the scene below revealed nothing more than the smoking remains of the house. He turned the big bay horse that had once belonged to Bass Wheeler and rode to the floor of the canyon.

He rested the Winchester easily across the front of the saddle, making sure it was ready for action if necessary. His worries continued for the safety and welfare of old Cody and Sarah, and he blamed himself for not returning sooner. Maybe he could have helped. Guilt continued to build as he rode closer to the house. He saw that most of the wood frame and logs had burned, but some still smoked. The foundation of red rock was now charred black.

In the yard he first noticed the paint horse, swelled now after almost two days in the sun. Cool weather had prevented the horse from issuing the foul smell that would come soon. The yellow dog lay nearby, covered in blood.

Jake remained mounted as he continued to ride around, looking at signs, tracks, and dried blood. Apparently Cody and Sarah had put up a good fight, but where they were at, he could only guess. Had they died in the house, only to be consumed by the fire, or had they escaped?

He finally dismounted and walked to the barn carefully, the Winchester in his hands. Inside, he found the barn undisturbed, only the horses gone, which he had already guessed had happened, but no Cody or Sarah or any sign of them.

Jake returned to his horse, then noticed the grave of Rachel had been desecrated. Anger swelled inside as he walked to the grave of his wife. He glanced around, hoping to see an Indian to take out his anger on, but nothing stirred, not even the wind. Only the noonday sun burned bright.

He squatted beside the grave and ran his fingers through the red dirt, his anger still unchecked. He straightened the wooden cross and did his best to repair the damage, but knew he would need a shovel to do the work properly.

He stood, looked around, and walked to the house to stand and stare at what remained. He would rebuild, that was for sure, but anger, frustration, and guilt continued inside him. He returned to the barn and found the case of unopened whiskey bottles near the feed bin inside the tack room.

His angry feeling and mood didn't allow for reason, and he quickly pulled the cork free and took a deep drink of the booze. It went down burning, stinging his senses, dulling the guilt, but doing nothing for the frustration or anger. He took another long drink and walked outside, then noticed movement near the spring.

The bottle flew high into the air as Jake pitched it away from him to grip the Winchester tight and start toward the pool, his frustration and guilt gone, but the anger increased. He carefully approached the rocks where the spring lay, glancing around for danger. The booze settled with a sour note in his stomach, and now he wished he had left the rotgut liquor alone.

Approaching the clear pool of water, he saw Cody lying against a rock. Jake stopped to scan the area for danger before advancing closer to the man, who stirred at the sound of someone approaching.

"Cody?" inquired Jake, still suspicious of a trap as he glanced around, the Winchester ready for action.

The old man slowly opened his eyes, trying to focus them on the young man who kneeled before him. "Jake," he managed to whisper. "They...jumped us...early...yesterday. They took Sarah."

"Where are you hit, old fella?" he asked, concern for the man replacing his anger.

"Jake...get out...of here. It's...a trap," whispered Wedgeworth, closing his eyes.

"Not without you," said Jake, laying the carbine on the ground to check the man for his wounds.

"I got a...lance in the back," Wedgeworth managed to say as he moaned in pain from being moved.

Jake checked him closely. "The lance blade is still in there and part of the shaft is sticking out," said Jake, trying to make the man comfortable.

"They left...me to warn...you and tell...you they got...Sarah," whispered Cody, almost not getting the words out. "Leave me, I'm...finished, Jake."

"Ain't leaving you nor Sarah," said Jake with determination as he stood. "You know where they took her?"

"No," replied Wedgeworth, moaning. "I'm slowly dying, Jake. You gonna...go after her...then go, but I'll...be dead...before you get...back."

Jake realized Cody was speaking the truth. If he went after Sarah now, Cody would die. If he took Cody to Brewster's Crossing, then Herman Hielmann might be able to save him, but Sarah would be lost. He knew he loved both of them. The choice was his. Cody's life or Sarah's.

Cody's wound wasn't bleeding, but the man had lost a lot of blood and was weak. It surprised him that Cody had lasted this long. The old man was tough as an old boot.

I'll be right back," said Jake, walking back to his horse for his bedroll. What was he to do? He knew he couldn't ride out and leave Cody to die alone, nor could he leave Sarah at the mercy of the Utes.

Jake reached the horse and began to untie the bedroll, then noticed the war lance in the front yard, the same one placed their earlier as a warning and challenge. He walked to it, although it had fallen to the ground. He picked it up and glanced around, scanning the rims of the canyon, then held the lance high above his head to be sure the Indians were watching. He had little doubt that at least one was nearby, watching his every move. He didn't want them to misunderstand.

Quickly, he brought the lance down to break it on his knee, then flung the two pieces to the ground. He scanned the rims once more, then spit upon the two pieces and stomped on them. Finished, he led the horse to the springs and carefully placed the injured man on the saddle and mounted behind Cody to hold him in place.

"Jake...you don't have to do this," whispered Cody, protesting. "Sarah comes first."

"Be quiet, old man and save your strength. We got a long ride ahead of us."

"Jake...Sarah loves you...you know? She...needs you, now," said Cody, protesting again.

"Yeah, I know she loves me, and I love her, too," replied Jake, guiding the horse down the canyon. "She'll be all right for now till I get back."

"Them savages...are real mean," said Cody, his strength almost gone. "They'll kill her...before you get back."

"Don't think so, old man. I accepted Patches' challenge and broke the war lance. She'll be here when I return."

"So...will the...Indians."

"I hope so. I surely do. Time we settled who has the right to Red Rock Pass. Patches...or me."

Sarah leaned against the wall of the cave, her hands hurting from the ropes that held her secure. She pulled her knees to her chin and watched the Indians who slowly danced around the fire. She had long since abandoned all hope of rescue and had replaced her fear with fascination at the actions of these savages. Did they really believe their chants and dances would bring them success? Surely God would not listen to these lost children of the Almighty.

Sarah watched the one called Patches, stripped naked except for a loincloth, lead the dancers around the fire once more, chanting a weird singsong chant that pierced deep into her ears. She glanced around the cavern and saw that the drawings and markings indicated it had to be a very old cave used by the Indians for centuries.

Her fascination turned to caution as the dance and chanting ended and

Patches came to squat beside her. "Woman thirsty?" he asked, a stern look falling across his painted face.

"No," she replied, a little fear creeping into her voice.

"Patches see that Whitmore choose strong woman. Patches have respect for white man Whitmore, but he be warned to leave sacred ground. Now, he must die according to will of Thunder Spirits."

"Why must he die? He believes the land is sacred ground to him now that his wife is buried there," responded Sarah, trying to reason with the Indian.

"No matter now. Thunder Spirits has spoken through the Thunder Moon. Giant Thunderbird flies before us and Whitmore will be destroyed."

"He may not come back to fight you," she said, hoping he wouldn't, but not really believing he would abandon her.

"He will come. The Thunderbird will bring him," replied Patches, feeling secure about that. "You will see. White man Whitmore will come for his woman."

Sarah's face reddened in anger at the Indian who was so sure of himself. "Maybe when he comes he will kill you."

Patches stared at her in disbelief, then stood without speaking and rejoined the others. Sarah watched him closely and thought she had caught a glimpse of doubt on his face and then turned to see that the warriors had began to repaint their naked bodies with signs, symbols, and markings.

The dance began, slowly at first, then increasing in tempo with the beat of the drum. She realized these men really believed that spirits, even unseen spirits of mountains, trees, and this cave, would come to their aid.

Patches glanced once at the white woman and then tried to subdue his feelings of doubt that she had stirred in him. He had allowed only a slight moment to think about Whitmore winning. He now knew he had been foolish to even allow that moment to occur. Surely the Thunder Spirits would allow him to win. He had seen that in his vision. Even the giant Thunderbird had whispered it to him.

Patches continued to lead the warriors in their last dance, thinking more of what he would pray for to the Thunder Spirits after the dance than the dance itself. He continued through the steps, but was relieved when the drum stopped to end the dance. Men settled around the fire, with some sitting against the cavern walls. Patches remained standing, waiting for them to settle down. When he was satisfied that he had their full attention, he began: "Brothers, the Thunderbird has flown before us and has prepared the way for our success. Some of our brothers have given their lives for our cause. The Thunder Spirits have noticed this great sacrifice, and those men now ride the winds in the sky, honored by the Sky People for their deeds, but for us who remain, our mission is not finished."

Patches paused to allow his words to sink in, then glanced at Sarah, who remained against the wall, silent and wide-eyed at these proceedings. He continued: "My brothers, the Thunderbird went before us to cleanse the sacred springs at Red Rock Pass. Some were required to die for our cause, but the way has been opened to us now. The Thunder Spirits gave us victory, and now the white man Whitmore has no house to live in. It still smokes its last breath of life. Whitmore will come to our place at our time of choosing. Two Ponies reports that he took the old man we allowed to live to the white man's town. Some have suggested that he will not return, but I say he will."

Patches pointed toward Sarah and grinned. "He will come because of her. She is his weakness, and the Thunder Spirits have shown us this. She is in our hands, and we bait the final trap with her. We will prepare her before the Thunder Spirits, and if she is truly his woman and his weakness, then the Thunder Spirits will confirm this to us in the sign of another Thunder Moon. When that sign is given, we must strike at that very moment. Whitmore must die at the time the signs are given, and he must die on sacred ground. It is the true sign of our obedience to the will of the Thunder Spirits. Now, my brothers, go, prepare yourselves for the final battle. Pray and ask the Great Spirit to bless your weapons and your heart that it will remain pure. Soon, the land will be cleansed of the white fools who have polluted it. Soon, this land will belong to the Ute again as it should be."

Finished, Patches sat beside the fire as One Bear stood. "Brothers, we have heard from our shaman again. We know he speaks true words. Already, we ride with success. Already, the white man flees before us in terror. The final struggle is near. We will prepare ourselves for it."

Wild Horse stood to speak. "What sign should we look for, my brother?" he asked, looking at Patches.

Patches stood and gazed at the assembled warriors. "I have seen the great sign in my vision. The Thunder Spirits will cause the giant Thunderbird to send a huge storm. When the wings of the Thunderbird flap again this storm will come. Whiteness will cover the land and will be our friend, while Whitmore will see it as his enemy. This storm will pass and as the snow melts, so will the white man disappear with it, but Whitmore must be dead before the snow is gone. It is the sign, and it will be confirmed by the terrible Thunder Moon Spirit."

Patches sat and no others stood to speak. One Bear stood again, glanced at Patches, then nodded to the others that the conference was over. Patches stood and walked to stand before Sarah, who avoided his piercing eyes. He turned to One Bear who stood beside him. "Prepare her for tomorrow. Paint her completely red, a symbol of the sacrifice she will become when the Thunderbird brings the storm. When the Thunder Spirits see her tomorrow, they will surely bring Whitmore to us. Then we will kill him...and she can die with him."

Jake saw the few lights of Brewster's Crossing as he rode down from the mesa toward the town. The big bay was strong and the trip, though slow, had been easier than he had expected. Cody Wedgeworth hung on for his life, dropping in and out of unconsciousness. He grew weaker by the hour, and Jake worried if they would make it. Even if they did, Cody's life would hang in the hands of Herman Hielmann.

Jake had plenty of time to think. Most of his thoughts were upon Sarah Thurston and the terror she was enduring in the hands of Patches. What would the crazed Ute do to her? Why did he want her?

He had questions, and deep down he knew the answers, but didn't want to accept them. His desire for a strong drink of the painkilling whiskey was strong, but he also knew he needed to face this problem with a clear head. Sarah's life now depended upon it.

Cody Wedgeworth moaned and leaned against him. "Take it easy, Cody. We're about there," said Jake, holding the man in the saddle.

His thoughts returned to the woman he knew he now loved. His dream came to his mind, the burning house which he had seen already as his own, the screaming woman who had been Sarah at her ranch when he found her terrorized in her bedroom, and the hand with the knife coming from the water. That hadn't happened to him yet, but everything was falling into place. Rachel had come in his dream, and now he knew she had approved of Sarah, or at least he thought she had.

Jake guided the surefooted bay along the trail that led to the valley below. He knew now he had to face the Ute in battle in order to destroy not only the Indian, but his strong medicine the other Indians believed Patches had. Failure could lead to a long Indian war and a lot of people killed on both sides.

Jake knew he had to return to Red Rock Pass again and face Patches for the sacred ground of the Pass and for Sarah. Jake also knew the fight would be to the death for either him or the Indian. There could be no other way now.

He entered the town and headed for Herman Hielmann's house that sat just behind the hardware store he owned. Jake noticed the moon was out now, the fullness almost gone as it was just about through the cycle. It had to be near one o'clock at night, but the saloon was still in full swing. Most of the other lights in town were out.

A couple of men staggered from the saloon and recognized him and Cody. One yelled something toward the saloon while the other man made his way to them. "What happened, Jake?" asked the man, concerned.

"Utes hit my place. Cody is hurt bad, and they captured the woman," he replied, stopping the horse. "I need Herman here fast. Cody is in bad shape."

"I'll get him," said the other man turning to run toward the hardware store.

"Utes hit a few other places, too. Morgan Davis got it, but lost only horses, but Billy Nevells had some bad luck. They killed his oldest boy and wounded his wife," said the remaining man. "A lot of settlers have already come into town for protection. Most are camped down by the ferry."

"The army been notified yet?" asked Jake, noticing others came from the saloon, Jed King one of them.

"Word went out to Green River yesterday," said King, stepping off the porch. "What's this about the Thurston woman being taken by the savages?"

"Cody said they took her. It's something personal about her, me, and the Ute, Patches," said Jake, allowing men to take Cody from the saddle.

"The springs?" asked King, frowning.

"Yeah. Patches thinks it's holy ground for some reason. I brought all this on. Should have moved," said Jake, dismounting from his horse.

"Naw, wasn't your fault. That crazy Indian has been spoiling for a fight for years. Some say he rode with old Stalking Horse several years ago up on the Green River," said King, watching the men carry Wedgeworth inside the saloon.

"He rode with Stalking Horse?" responded Jake, remembering the terrible raid that Sunday morning six years ago on his parents' home.

"It's what I heard, Jake," replied King, noticing the tightening of the face of Jake Whitmore and the hard, serious look he gave him.

"My parents were killed on the Green River six years ago," said Jake after a short pause. "I scarred one of them Utes on the face in that fight."

"Patches has a scar on his left cheek," said King, worried now. "Sorry I brought up the subject. You going back to the pass after that Ute?"

"I have to. Patches has Sarah Thurston, and she means a lot to me, Jed.

I have to go."

"No man stands alone, Jake. Me and my boys will ride with you," said King, turning to enter the saloon as Herman Hielmann rushed past him to enter.

Jake followed and spoke to King after they entered the saloon. "This is between me and the Ute," said Jake, looking at King seriously. "He has to be killed, otherwise the rest of the Utes will continue to believe in his medicine, and they'll stay on the warpath. We need to end this once and for all."

Herman Hielmann turned to face Jake after examining Cody. "It's gonna be a toss up if I can save him or not. The lance head is deep into him, right against his left lung. Another half inch and he would be dead."

"Do your best, Herman," replied Jake, turning away.

He sat at a table to wait for Hielmann to finish his work on Cody. Jed King and several others sat with him. "Jake, word had already gotten out about the woman. Most everyone wants to ride with you when you leave," said Ben Westman, leaning back on his chair. "There's a lot of people come into town for protection and are camped down by the river. I'm sure most of them will want to ride with us."

"Thanks. We'll ride out tomorrow after I know Cody is gonna be all right. We'll take all who wish to go, but make sure everyone knows this could be a dangerous fight," said Jake, glancing at Westman.

"Kennon Matthews is in town. Staying over at the sheriff's house. His stage got hit by the Indians out near Newton's station. The shotgun guard and one of his passengers are dead," said King, frowning. "I know he'll want to go, and Bishop Newman will, too."

"Remember this men. Patches has got to die. If he lives, this mess will continue, but if he's killed, I think the rest will go home," said Jake, frowning. "If I die in this fight, I want all of you to promise to kill the Ute. Is that clear?"

"Yeah, it's clear, Jake," said King, glancing at the others who nodded they understood. "Patches dies, one way or the other."

SIXTEEN

The night was cold and the sky overcast, but Patches neither wore a shirt nor covered his naked body with a blanket. He sat close to the fire for its warmth just outside the cave. Others sat beside him while a few remained standing as Two Ponies continued his latest report.

"Buffalo Hump continues to hunt for us," said Two Ponies, glancing at the stonefaced Patches, who showed no emotions. "They came to the springs but could not find our trail, so they have returned to their camp at the rock with the big hole to wait out this coming storm."

"The Thunder Spirits are displeased with Buffalo Hump and the other fools for not obeying. The giant Thunderbird will continue to blind them as to where we are," replied Patches, speaking low and not looking at anyone. "The coming storm will be here soon, and then Whitmore will be delivered to us, and we will end this matter quickly with his death. It will be too late for Buffalo Hump and the others to do anything about it."

"We see that the great snowstorm you saw in your vision is coming," said One Bear, glancing at Patches. "Will it bring just Whitmore, or will others come with him to fight us?"

"Others ride with Whitmore now," said Two Ponies, concerned. "They left the white man's town today and camp on the high mesa this very night."

"How many?" asked One Bear, worried.

"Because of our raids, many whites have fled to the town beside the big river. Whitmore has many who come with him. More than we have," said Two Ponies, still concerned.

"It will make little difference," said Patches, showing no outward concern. "Whitmore will die. We may lose some warriors, but in the end he will die because he is the symbol of the pollution the whites have brought to our land. When he is dead the Thunder Spirits will be satisfied, the Thunderbird will flap his great wings, and the land will be cleansed of the white man forever. Then the buffalo will return and the Utes will be a mighty people once more."

"How do we know Whitmore will fight us?" asked Lame Deer, worried. "What if he joins with Buffalo Hump against us?"

"Two Ponies saw him break the war lance. He has now accepted my challenge; thus, he will come. He has grown strong just by living on sacred ground. He must die on sacred ground to please the Thunder Spirits."

"Then we will see that he does," replied Lame Deer. "We have his woman, and she has been prepared to be the bait that will draw him to us."

"It's true," said Patches, standing. "The woman is the bait, but we must be strong to fight and kill him. I will try, but if the Thunder Spirits are not pleased with my efforts, then others must try. He cannot be allowed to live. We must fight our way through the other white men that come with him in order to get to him."

"We will obey," said One Bear, glancing at the others. "We shall prepare ourselves for the coming storm and the battle that will follow. Each man must be ready for tomorrow."

"I will prepare and then perform our final sacrifice ceremony to the Thunder Spirits," said Patches, turning to enter the cave. "Bring the woman and secure her to the stake before the fire and assemble everyone. When I return from the cave, let the drums begin. This is an old ceremony from the ancient days and few know of it, but it has been passed down to each shaman for many generations."

"We wait for this, for I have never seen this sacrifice," said One Bear, seriously. "Does the woman die in the ceremony?"

"No," replied Patches, frowning. "In the ancient days, the blood sacrifice required the spirit of the victim, but she will only stand as a symbol for the death of Whitmore that will come later. Let us begin."

Warriors went to the cave and returned with Sarah. She wore a buckskin dress that had no sleeves and went only to her knees. Her long blonde hair was tied on each side and wrapped in otterskins died red. The dress was red also, and upon the front was the painted emblem of the Thunderbird in black. Below the bird was a yellow moon with a lightning bolt across it.

She wore red moccasins and a feathered bonnet with each eagle feather painted red. Each part of her exposed skin was also painted red, except her face. Even the ropes that secured her had been died red. She was fastened securely at the stake, and the warriors joined the others near the fire.

The drum began to beat slowly, and Patches exited from the cave mouth, an eagle-feathered bonnet on his head and a row of eagle wings on each arm from the shoulder to the hand. His body was naked except for a loincloth and a row of eagle feathers was attached around his waist. Even his legs had circles of eagle feathers, and he came forth flapping his arms and mocking a giant bird.

Upon his bronze chest was painted the emblem of a Thunderbird in red. He danced to the beat of the drum and came straight toward Sarah, still acting as if he were a great bird. When he reached her, he stopped, but the drum continued. He withdrew a knife from the feathered belt at his waist and quickly pricked the left cheek of the woman, who cried out in pain.

A trickle of blood appeared on the cheek, and Patches allowed some to form on the knife blade, then danced away from her to smear the blood upon his hands and face, then his chest, but was careful not to get any on the emblem of the Thunderbird. The tempo of the drum increased and he danced around the fire four times, then around Sarah four times, stopping at the four points of the compass to chant a song.

At the end of this dance the drum slowed, and he approached her again to prick the right side of her cheek and perform the same dance and ritual as before. The drumbeat changed and so did the tempo. Patches, screamed and danced faster toward Sarah, this time to prick his chest at the spot where the emblem of the Thunderbird was painted. With his own blood, he smeared some upon the face of the woman, then her arms and finally upon her breasts and danced away.

With a loud shout, he stopped and all the warriors stood, chanting; they then followed him toward the woman. As Patches passed her, he symbolically killed her with his knife, careful to keep the deadly blade from her skin. The other warriors followed him in the same act, and as the last man passed the terrified woman, the drumbeat stopped; slowly, each man disappeared from the campfire, leaving only Patches.

Even the drummer left. Patches approached Sarah, who was in tears now, too frightened to scream or speak. The Indian stared at her, his eyes flashing with hatred and anger. She felt his hatred, and in his fierce eyes, saw his determination to kill Jake Whitmore. She had no doubt that she would die when Jake and those who rode with him walked into whatever trap they had planned for him. As the Ute turned and left to disappear into the cave, she began to pray for deliverance and the protection of the man she loved.

Jake Whitmore pulled his big coat tighter around his shoulders and neck to keep out the snow and lowered his head so that the brim of his hat kept the blowing storm from his face. Kennon Matthews rode beside him, his gray overcoat pulled tight around his neck also.

"This is one hell of a storm, Jake," said Matthews, leaning over so that the younger man could hear him. "Think we might ought to try to return to Brewster's Crossing?"

"We're almost to my place now," replied Jake, frowning as he guided the big bay down the trail toward Red Rock Pass. "The barn is still standing and it will give the horses shelter in this storm. Probably gonna be a big one from the looks of things."

"Ain't had one of these storms this late in the spring in over twenty years," said Matthews, glancing at Whitmore. "Think Sarah is all right?"

"She'll be fine for now. Patches wants me, and Sarah is his bait to get to me," responded Jake, glancing back at the other men to see how well they were making it in the storm.

"What's our plans when we get to Red Rock Pass?" asked Matthews, a little concerned.

"It's almost daylight, so we'll put the horses in the barn, then start preparing for a fight," said Jake, frowning again. "I'm sure the Utes will be coming as soon as they know we're at the place. This is what this fight is all about, you know? They want us white folks off their sacred springs at the pass. They'll come to us."

"How soon?" asked Matthews, adjusting himself in the saddle for more comfort.

"Soon as it gets good daylight. Reason I wanted to leave early this morning and get to my place before daybreak," replied Jake, noticing the trail was building up with snow and making travel harder. "We'd have had a hard time making it back to town in this storm. Snow is building quick."

"Fork in the trail to your place is just up ahead," said Matthews, pointing, a little relieved. "You gonna try and rebuild after all this is over?"

"Plan on it," responded Jake, getting a halfhearted grin to form on his face. "First, I gotta take care of this Indian problem."

"Most of the men in town rode with us. Didn't think some of them farmers would come," said Matthews, glancing back to see the men struggling with their horses in the snow.

"Everyone realizes we gotta pull together on this thing. The Utes could really cause a lot of trouble around here if they remain on the warpath," said Jake, stopping the bay and holding up his hand to halt the group of riders that followed. "We had best rest the horses for the final push to the ranch. The Utes could be waiting for us there."

Jed King rode to their side. "We gonna ride into your place from different sides?"

"Thought it best to come in from the south with one group and the rest to make a frontal move to the ranch from the west," replied Jake, glancing at King. "Just in case Patches is waiting in ambush for us."

"It was what I was a thinking, Jake. I'll take a bunch to the south," said King, turning his horse around. "Give me a ten minute head start, and we'll be in place when you come up with the rest of the men."

Jake watched as about fifteen men followed Jed King, who made his way through the snow toward the south. Jake knew King and his men would ride into his place from the low rim just above his barn and would be able to give him and his own force good covering fire just in case the Indians were lying in ambush at his place.

Baker Stevenson rode up as the last of King's men disappeared on the south fork of the trail. "Think that stinking Ute will be waiting for us at your place?"

"If you were Patches, where would you ambush us?" asked Jake, glad that Stevenson rode with him.

"If I was the Utes, I'd gone home in this kind of storm. This ain't good fighting weather," said Stevenson, frowning. "Reminds me of the fighting back in the war in Tennessee. Them rebel boys hit us hard in a driving snowstorm just like this. Almost whipped us good, too."

"I figure Patches will try us at the springs. No other good place to ambush us," said Jake, turning the bay to head him down the trail to the Pass. "If I was him, I'd not let an enemy force take root in the Pass beside the springs. Would be harder to force us out into the open to fight."

"I figure the same, Jake," said Stevenson, frowning. "I'll drop back and get the men prepared."

"We'll ride in hard and let Jed and his men cover our move from the rim to the south," said Jake, pulling out his Winchester and checking it to make sure it was ready for the coming fight.

Kennon Matthews pulled his Henry rifle from the saddle boot and laid it across the front of the saddle, then glanced at Jake. "Snow ought to thin out when we hit the bottom of the pass."

"Yeah, it'll be less snow there and a good running field of fire for those Indians who will be waiting for us," said Jake, trying to grin, but finding it hard. "You ready?"

"Ain't been in a horse charge since Virginia in '65, Jake," said Matthews, glancing at him.

"Me either. I was just a kid near the end of the war when I joined up. Rode with Sherman across Georgia. Gonna be my first in a long time, too."

Patches waited impatiently for the white men to approach from the canyon valley. Just what they were up to, he could not quite figure out. They had formed into a battle line and now sat on their horses, waiting. Just what they were waiting for worried him. He signaled to Lame Deer and his men to remain in position near the rocks at the springs as he crawled away toward the remains of the house where One Bear and his men lay hidden behind the rock foundation of the burned house.

One Bear greeted him with a nod. "Is Whitmore with them?"

"He rides the big bay horse," said Patches, frowning. "I do not understand what he's up to. It's some kind of trick."

"The Thunderbird has delivered him to us as you said he would. Now, the rest is up to us," said One Bear, peeking over the low rock foundation. "They still wait."

"What could it be? There is no other way to the springs except from the old trail just above the water hole," said Patches, still worried.

"The storm has lessened some, my brother. Maybe the Thunder Spirits have allowed the storm to quiet for our battle," responded One Bear, concerned also.

"Maybe," replied Patches, glancing over the stone wall to watch the white men. "It is now time to expose the white woman. That should bring Whitmore and his men to us. I had hoped he would have ridden into our ambush, but he is a wise one and a worthy opponent to fight."

"Then let this final battle begin before some lose faith and sneak away," said One Bear, checking his Spencer rifle to be sure it was ready for the fight.

Patches crawled away, heading for the barn where Wild Horse and his men waited on horses to charge into the white men when they got into the yard. Maybe that surprise would still work, but he grew more suspicious that Whitmore had his own trap in place. He reached the barn and crawled into it from a hole made for that purpose on the east side of the barn. Wild Horse greeted him.

"Now is the time to use the woman. Is she ready?" asked Patches, looking around.

"Yes, my brother. She's prepared as you instructed. Whitmore does not ride into our ambush as we had expected," said Wild Horse, frowning.

"He is wise, but the woman should bring him," said Patches, turning to see Sarah, dressed as before in the red dress she wore at the last ceremony.

Patches nodded to Wild Horse, and the warrior grabbed the reins of the horse she rode, her hands still tied behind her back. The horse was painted red with drawings of the Thunderbird and the Thunder Moon. Wild Horse rode from the barn leading the horse and halted in the middle of the yard in plain sight of the waiting white men, then raised his voice into a long, piercing war cry.

The long line of white men started at a walk, and Patches smiled, believing his bait had worked to his advantage. The line of horsemen changed from a walk to a trot as the men advanced, Whitmore in the lead on his bay horse. Patches checked his Springfield single-shot carbine once to make sure all was ready, then mounted a horse and waited.

The barn door had been left open, and he could plainly see that the white men now came at a gallop, the line wavering some, but still the battle line remained intact. Patches realized now that most of those men had fought before, probably in the white man's war twelve years ago. They would not be easily defeated, but if they continued their charge, his ambush would work.

The horsemen rode into the yard at full speed, snow flying from the pounding hoofs of their horses. Wild Horse led the woman toward the rock wall as the first volley of fire came from One Bear and his men from behind the house foundation; another volley followed from Lame Deer and his men firing from the rocks.

Horses and men went down, and Patches led his men from the barn screaming their war cries. He saw the white woman leap from her horse and roll on the ground as Wild Horse turned to see what had happened. Patches saw a white man advancing toward Wild Horse and the woman, then leveled his carbine at the man. Patches fired, but the heavy .45-55 caliber round slammed hard into the neck of the horse, bringing the rider and horse to the ground.

Wild Horse was upon the woman now, his knife raised to plunge it deep into her heart when a volley of fire came from the south rim of the canyon. Patches' horse went down, throwing him over the head of the animal. He rolled away and dropped his carbine to crawl away from the kicking animal as it struggled on the ground. He glanced around and saw that Wild Horse was down, blood coming from his chest and head. Others were down also, and One Bear and his men had abandoned the walls of the house. Several of his men lay dead from the firing that came from the rim.

Patches saw Whitmore dismount from his bay horse and run toward the woman. He picked up his carbine, leveled it at the chest of the hated white man and pulled the trigger. Disappointment washed over him as the hammer slammed on an empty cartridge. In his anger, he rushed the man using the rifle as a club.

Whitmore turned to face him, his pistol in his hand, but before he could fire, Patches was upon him, swinging the carbine by the barrel. It landed on the upper shoulder of the man, knocking him to the ground. Patches was on top of him then, drawing his knife, but Whitmore grabbed his hand and they both rolled over, struggling for control of the deadly weapon.

An older white man entered the fight, slamming into Patches and knocking him from Whitmore. Patches swung with his knife, cutting the man on the shoulder, then turned to see that Two Ponies had grabbed the white woman and had dragged her toward the springs, kicking and screaming. Whitmore was up and reaching for his pistol. Patches attacked and kicked the weapon from the white man's hand, and lunged at him with the knife.

Whitmore sidestepped and tripped him as he passed, then fell upon his back to twist the knife from his hand. More men joined the fight, and Patches was knocked to the ground by one of them. He rolled away from the man's foot and glanced toward Whitmore to see him struggling with One Bear, who had his tomahawk out trying to kill him. Another white man rushed in, and Patches jumped upon him to throw him on the snow-covered ground before he reached One Bear.

The man tried to level his big pistol, but Patches kicked out with his foot and knocked the weapon from the man's hand. He saw that he was outnumbered and turned to flee to the protection of the rocks near the springs, but saw One Bear go down, his own knife turned against him by Whitmore; the blade was buried deep into the chest of his trusted brother.

Anger flared inside him as he made it to the rocks where Lame Deer lay loading his single shot Springfield carbine. "There are too many for us to hold this position," said Lame Deer, shouting. "They have good covering fire coming from the south rim."

"Where is the woman?" asked Patches, taking a carbine offered him by a warrior.

"Two Ponies has her and is taking her to the springs," replied Lame Deer, worried. "We must retreat and regroup. This position is bad for us."

"Then do it, my brother. Withdraw our men and we will regroup above the old trail to the cave," said Patches, looking for Whitmore in the group of white men who had now taken cover behind the rock walls of the burned house. He saw the man he wanted and aimed to fire. The shot went wide and Patches swore. "Go, some of us will cover our retreat."

Patches flipped the lever up to dislodge the spent .45-55 cartridge and reloaded with a fresh round. Locked into place, he glanced back toward the wall and ducked as several rounds slammed into the rock near his head, knocking bits and pieces from the rock and into his face. The pain stung, and he withdrew his hand from his face to reveal blood. He swore again and followed Lame Deer and his men up the trail past the spring. Wild Horse and One Bear were dead. It was a heavy price to pay, but in the end the Thunder Spirits would deliver Whitmore to him. He still had the woman, and that would bring Whitmore once again into his rifle's gun sight. He wouldn't miss next time, that he promised himself.

Jake crawled behind the low rock foundation of his burned house as a heavy slug fired from the rocks near the springs slammed into the foundation inches from where his head remained exposed to the Indian's rifle fire. Baker Stevenson stood and returned fire in the direction of the rocks, the big Sharps' booming discharge echoing down the wide canyon. The big man hunkered down behind the wall to reload the deadly rifle. He extracted the .50 caliber cartridge, grinned at Jake, and threw the spent casing on the ground beside him.

"We got them on the run, Jake," said Stevenson, standing again to fire. "Jed needs to flank them to our left, then we'll have them bastards where we want them."

Jake glanced over the edge of the foundation. Baker was right. A flanking maneuver was in order, but King and his men still remained on the south rim firing irregularly into the rocks where a few Indians remained. "Baker, get a man up to Jed and get him to flank them," said Jake, rolling over to face the bald-headed man as he reloaded the Sharps again.

"I'll go myself and make sure it's done," said Baker Stevenson, crawling away.

Kennon Matthews crawled to his side, a bandage wrapped around his injured head. "Tried to rescue Sarah, Jake. That bastard, Patches, got to her first," he said, rubbing his sore head. "Storm is still with us some. We gonna have to move fast to end this in our favor."

"Baker went to get Jed to flank them on our left," replied Jake, looking at the man. "At least a flanking maneuver will flush them from the springs, then we can look for Sarah."

"It will do that, but what next?" responded the older man, worried. "If the snow continues, we'll pay hell trying to track these redskins down and rescue Sarah."

"I know, but it's the best we can do. Signal the others to charge the rocks on foot when Jed makes his move."

"We're ready," said Matthews, his Henry rifle gripped tightly in his hands. "Just give us the word."

"Here comes Jed now. Let's go," yelled Jake, standing to fire several shots toward the rocks with his Winchester.

His men leaped the stone wall and charged toward the rocks where the spring lay. One man went down, screaming in pain, grabbing his leg, but the rest continued the charge, firing their weapons as they went in an irregular line. Jake followed and saw several Indians fleeing, trying to climb the rocks above the springs. Some never made the rim, but others did; Jed King started up after them with most of the men.

Jake stopped beside the springs to kneel for a scoop of water. He noticed the reed sticking up from the water and within an instant remembered his dream of the Indian hand coming from the water with the knife. He jumped back trying to bring the carbine to bear as Patches leaped from the water, screaming a blood-curdling war cry. Jake fired, but missed as the Indian slammed into him, knocking him backward to the ground.

Patches fell upon him, bringing the knife up to strike a death blow. "You are mine, white eyes," he yelled bringing the knife downward. "I finish what I started on the Green River six years ago."

Jake blocked the blow with the butt of his carbine and then pushed the warrior off him and struggled to stand. Patches regained his balance and charged, but Jake met the advance with a blow to the midsection of the Indian with the barrel of the carbine, then attempted to jack in a fresh cartridge. Patches kicked out with his foot as he fell backward, catching the barrel of the Winchester and knocking it from Jake's hand. Jake reached for his pistol, but discovered it was missing from his holster.

Patches circled, thrusting the knife at him, but missing each time. Jake caught a glimpse of Sarah, dressed in the red Indian dress, lying against a rock, fear showing on her face. That glance cost him as Patches lunged forward, striking Jake across the chest with the blade. He felt his clothing ripped open with the knife, but the thick coat and shirt prevented the blade from reaching his body.

A second lunge by Patches failed as Jake grabbed his arm and pulled him forward to trip him as he went by. The Indian landed in the pool of water and struggled to stand, but Jake was upon him and the two went under the water struggling for control of the deadly knife. The water turned red as the two men surfaced, Jake backing away in the waist-deep water to watch the surprised face of the Ute, the knife blade buried deep in the center of the warrior's chest, red blood seeping from the wound to trickle down the painted Thunderbird design on his body. Patches staggered once then fell backward to sink into the water.

Jake struggled to the shore and crawled out as his men returned. Most stood around the pool in amazement as Jake lay gasping for air beside the water, Sarah now beside him, crying softly as two men entered the water to drag the dead Indian from the springs.

"It's Patches all right," said Kennon Matthews, grinning as he turned to Jake. "Reckon it's over."

Jake glanced up toward the rim of the canyon to see several Utes mounted. One he recognized as Two Ponies, the one who had followed him for several days. The Ute raised his war lance, then threw it to the ground, turning his horse and disappearing. Several others remained for only a few more moments, defeat written on their painted faces, then turned their horses to follow Two Ponies.

"I reckon you're right, Kennon. The others are going home. Patches has paid for what he did to my family six years ago. It's over."

Joe Blackburn cursed once more as Sheriff Paul Neel placed the black hood over his unshaven face, then tightened the hangman's noose around his neck. "I hanged your sorry, no-good paw, Joe Blackburn. You should have swung with him, but now I reckon I'll finish the job I started in Colorado," said Neel, backing away to the lever that controlled the trap door that Blackburn and Gus Deason stood on.

"I'll see you in hell, Neel," shouted Blackburn, his courage beginning to fail him as he knew his death was only moments away.

"Don't count on it, Joe," replied Neel, glancing at the judge, who stood below the gallows, ready to give the order to fulfill the court's judgment upon these two men.

Deason tried to shift his three hundred pounds on the trap door, his legs barely able to support his body now that fear had taken total control of him. "Joe, tell them I didn't have nothing to do with these killings here in Utah. Tell them, Joe."

"Too late, Bull. We're dead men," sobbed Blackburn, finally giving into his fear as he heard the lever flip. It was the last sound he heard as his neck snapped at the end of the rope, ending his life.

Sarah's body jerked at the sight of the two men's lives being snapped from them at the end of the hangman's rope, then turned to bury her head into the chest of the man she loved, a soft cry coming from her. "Justice is done. May Karl and Elizabeth rest in peace."

Jake patted her on the shoulder and turned her away from the gallows to walk toward the waiting buggy nearby. Cody Wedgeworth and Kennon Matthews waited for them. "Ready to go home, Mrs. Whitmore?"

"Yes, dear. I would like to stop by Karl's place and put some fresh flowers on the graves."

"Army says all the Utes are back on the White River Reservation over in Colorado," said Matthews, grinning. "Got a new Indian Agent named Meeker who promises to change all them Indians to farmers within a year. Ain't a gonna be no more Indian trouble around here."

"Yeah, maybe you're right, Kennon," said Wedgeworth, frowning as he leaned on his cane. "Not until the next time some young shaman thinks he's seen another Thunder Moon."